Falling in

MW01088835

Anything can happen in a year! Unemployed, homeless, and left at the altar, Vivia Perpetua Grant could see her future as a flannel pajama wearing spinster—or worse, a bag lady shuffling around Golden Gate Park. But for a girl obsessed with rock music, Chinese take-out, and the color pink, misfortune is another word for opportunity. Vivia has found her niche as an international travel writer and the long-distance lover of Jean-Luc de Caumont, an über-hot French literature professor and competitive cyclist.

Still, even with so much going right, Vivia can't help but wonder if something isn't missing. The long distance thing is taking its toll on a girl who didn't have that many tokens to begin with. And fate seems to be tempting her at every turn, first with a hunky Scottish helicopter pilot, and then with a British celebrity bad boy...Will Vivia continue to keep it real or will she discover some old habits die hard?

Books by Leah Marie Brown

The It Girl Series
Faking It
Finding It

Published by Kensington Publishing Corporation

Finding It

An It Girl Novel

Leah Marie Brown

LYRICAL PRESS
Kensington Publishing Corp.
www.kensingtonbooks.com

Lyrical Press books are published by
Kensington Publishing Corp. 119 West 40th Street New York, NY 10018

All Kensington titles, imprints, and distributed lines are available at special quantity discounts for bulk purchases for sales promotion, premiums, fund-raising, and educational or institutional use.

To the extent that the image or images on the cover of this book depict a person or persons, such person or persons are merely models, and are not intended to portray any character or characters featured in the book.

Special book excerpts or customized printings can also be created to fit specific needs. For details, write or phone the office of the Kensington Special Sales Manager:
Kensington Publishing Corp.
119 West 40th Street
New York, NY 10018
Attn. Special Sales Department. Phone: 1-800-221-2647.

Kensington and the K logo Reg. U.S. Pat. & TM Off.
Lyrical Press and the L logo are trademarks of Kensington Publishing Corp.

First Electronic Edition: September 2015
eISBN-13: 978-1-61650-810-4
eISBN-10: 1-61650-810-8

First Print Edition: MONTH YEAR
ISBN-13:
ISBN-10:

Printed in the United States of America

I would like to dedicate this book to Kevin Douglas Brown, who puts up with my verbal incontinence, chocolate addiction, and impulsive whims. Thank you, Kevin, for supporting my dream to travel the world, remaining calm when I called and told you I was detained by Buckingham Palace Guards, and letting me wear my RAF Search & Rescue woolly cap out in public.

I would also like to dedicate this book to my son, Kevin Connor Brown, for buying me the shiniest Wellies to ever stomp a Scottish bog, and my daughter, Mikayla Faith Brown, for working so hard to keep me "cool" and "current."

Author's Foreword

Although this novel is a work of fiction, I based several of Vivia's outrageous adventures and mishaps on my own outrageous adventures and mishaps. All of the characters in the novel are figments of my overactive imagination. Any similarity to those I have known/loved is merely coincidental.

Acknowledgements

I would like to thank Mister Russell Brand for prodigously sharing his words of wisdom on politics, philosophy, and Pilates. How I delight in listenting to your warbling voice - more Mockney than Cockney - that affected, upper-middle class British accent that one might expect from a cheeky street urchin with posh pretentions.

Thank you André Rodriguez of Countless Goodbyes for providing me with aweome tunes to and for agreeing to become Vivia's lastest "crush."

Thank you to the real Angus and Fiona, for letting me stay in your lovely cottage, traipse around your land, and pepper you with questions about sheep. Thank you for not laughing too hard when I ran down the hill screaming like a mad, bloody American, because I thought your old sheep was having a seizure.

Finally, I would be remiss if I didn't thank Cindy Miles, my cord-twin and travel partner, for dragging me to Schotland. Remember fifteen years ago, when you tried to get me to go to the Highlands with you, but I only wanted to go to France-France-France? Yeah, I was wrong. I dinnae ken i'twould be so bonny, lass!

Chapter 1

Rubbing with Royals

Vivia Perpetua Grant @PerpetuallyViv
Don't believe the hype: Prince Harry is not a regular approachable bloke. #IAmNotAStalker #FreeVivia
   8:22 AM

Vivia Perpetua Grant @PerpetuallyViv
Dear Buckingham Palace Guards: Well done, you! One less tourist with a tripod off the streets. #KeepingLondonSafe
   8:34 AM

Vivia Perpetua Grant @PerpetuallyViv
I keep asking myself, "What would @wizkhalifa do?" #FreeVivia #TooPretty4ThePokey #PrisonCellfie
   8:35

Vivia Perpetua Grant @PerpetuallyViv
If #GetArrested is on your London itinerary, head to the Westminster Borough. The cells in Belgravia Station are really quite comfortable. @MPSWestminster
   10:41

"I am not stalking Prince Harry."

Basil Rathbone ignores me and jots something in a slender notebook.

"I am not a stalker!" I wipe my sweaty palms on my jacket. "This is such…"

He looks up and raises an eyebrow.

Bullshit!

"This is ridiculous."

Basil resumes writing in his notebook.

I cross my legs and wait. I have seen enough crime dramas to know that most perps incriminate themselves during questioning. I'm not bumping gums. I'm not going down like that. Not me, man.

Basil is still writing, his fine-tipped pen scratching against the paper. Scratch. Scratch. Scratch.

He pauses, flicks his cool gaze in my direction, and resumes writing.

It's been several hours since Buckingham Palace Guards and Westminster Police burst into my hotel room, slapped handcuffs on my wrists, and transported me to the Belgravia Station. The initial terror I felt over being arrested on suspicion of stalking a member of the royal family has been replaced with insolent outrage. I was raised to respect the badge, but the whole situation really is…ridiculous bullshit!

Our silent game of chicken continues. I shift positions, slouching in the cold metal chair and crossing my arms like a gangster, hands shoved in my armpits, chin lifted defiantly. You're not gonna break me, Po-po.

The door opens. A uniformed officer pops his head in. "Call for you. Line seven."

Basil stops scratching and closes his notebook. He tosses the notebook on the table between us before striding out of the questioning room.

I maintain my "Get back, muthafucka" pose until the door closes, and then my bravado fails. My arms and legs begin to tremble. Despite my *Boyz in the Hood* demeanor, I am no Ice Cube. I've never popped a cap in someone's ass. I've never been in the pokey. I've never even gotten a speeding ticket!

Who cares if the stalking and harassing charges are totally bogus? I am going to have a record! An international rap sheet. I'll never be able to make a run for the presidency, or get a top secret security clearance, or adopt a rescue poodle.

What will my parents say when they find out my new crib is Shawshank? My poor mum. She always hoped I would spend my life doing charity work, like collecting unused eyeglasses for the blind or doling out mosquito netting to malaria-plagued Africans. She even has a journal wherein she records her "Visions for Vivia." I found the journal one day, in a lockbox, in the back of her closet. In her neat, tight script, she recorded her highest hopes for my future. The list would intimidate Mother Theresa.

1. I named you after Saint Vivia Perpetua, a blessed woman revered for her chastity and charity. Always conduct yourself in

a manner that pays homage to your namesake. (Fail)
    2. Attend Ivy League university, study medicine, graduate summa cum laude, and devote your life to caring for the ill. (Fail)
    3. Never lie. (Fail)
    4. Attend church twice per week. (Fail)

The list went on and on and on. I stopped reading when I reached number 132—"Think before you speak." (Epic Fail). I am pretty sure "Go to prison and become some skanky crack ho's bitch" wasn't on my mum's Visions for Vivia list. Maybe she could start a new journal and title it "Dreams My Daughter Dashed."

    1. Audition for and win the part of the Virgin Mary in our church's annual Nativity Play. Then, humiliate your mother in front of Father Escobar by dropping your woolen robe and marching around the stage in your Wonder Woman bathing suit. (Check)
    2. Let your high school boyfriend feel you up in a movie theater. Get caught by your mother's gossipy nemesis. (Check)
    3. Fall in love with a handsome, wealthy man from an influential family. Tell him you are a virgin (when you are not) and then confess the truth on the eve of your wedding. Lose man of your mother's dreams. (Check)
    4. Get stupid drunk in Cannes, France, and let mega movie star talk you into getting a tattoo of a cartoon sushi roll on your ass. (Check)
    5. End up in the pokey for stalking a member of the British royal family. (Check)

Basil's notebook distracts me from thoughts about my disgraceful past and my bleak poodle-free future. It's still lying on the table in front of me, close enough to touch.

I grab the notebook and flip through the pages until I come to the last page with writing on it.

I am trying to decipher Basil's shockingly illegible script—but can only make out random words like *barking, mad, colonial, media,* and *suspicious activities*—when someone clears their throat. I spin around to find the detective leaning against the door, his eyebrows arched, a thick manila envelope in his hand.

"This is not what it looks like…"

"Really? Because you appear to have nicked my notebook."

Basil's clipped, posh accent is as intimidating as his piercing, accusatory gaze. He is staring at me as if he knows all of my deep, dark secrets, like I am a twisted puzzle he effortlessly solved. I am waiting for him to point his bony finger at me and say, *"It's elementary, my dear Miss Grant, when I eliminate all other factors, the one which remains is the truth, and the truth is, you are barking mad, a stalker of princes, a quibbler of truths, an imposter in a wretched Burberry knock-off."*

As so often happens when I am nervous, I begin blabbering ridiculousness, incriminating myself.

"Look," I say, dropping the notebook on the table. "You got me. I was reading your notebook, but I wasn't stalking Prince Harry."

"Mmm-hmm."

He drops the manila envelope on the table beside his notebook and perches himself on the edge of the desk, crosses his arms, and looks down his beak-like nose at me.

"I am a columnist with *GoGirl! Magazine* on assignment to cover the lifestyles of the rich and royal. I told my editor I could get an interview with a member of the royal family, that I have connections, but…"

"You lied."

"Yes!" I toss my hands in the air. "I lied! I lied!"

I'm squealing like a jailhouse snitch. I draw a deep breath and try to channel 50 Cent, Eminem, and Snoop Dogg, but I think I am projecting more Vanilla Ice than hardcore hood rat.

"Listen Basil—"

"Basil?" The detective looks at me beneath knit brows. A second later, his brow relaxes and a reluctant smile tugs at the corners of his mouth. "Rathbone?"

"It was an obvious comparison," I say, my own lips twitching. "You look a little like the actor."

The detective rolls his eyes. "Why can't Americans make British literary references beyond Sherlock or Shakespeare?"

"You mean like Austen, Dickens, Shelley, Byron. Brontë, Tolkien…" Now he's pissed me off. It's one thing to call me out on my cheap trench coat and my penchant for snooping, but don't insult my knowledge of literature. "You might want to actually consider leaving your little island and crossing the pond. You would be amazed to discover most Americans possess a refinement beyond *Real Housewives* and Honey Boo Boo."

"Have you taken any photographs?"

The abrupt change in conversation throws me off my game.

"Photographs? Yeah, I took a selfie in one of those red phone booths, another beneath the Harrods sign, one with the cab driver who picked me up at the airport..."

Basil releases a sigh "Out the window, madam. Did you take any photographs of the palace out your window?"

"No...but if Prince Harry happens by, I might take a snappie or two." Shit! Why did I say that? "Kidding. I am just kidding. I haven't taken any photographs of the palace, and I won't be taking any of Harry."

Old Basil frowns. If we moved through life with thought bubbles suspended over our heads, his would read: *We are not amused.*

"Right," Basil says, retrieving his notebook. "Again, why did you have a tripod in your hotel window aimed at the palace?"

Although I explained the situation to the Buckingham Palace Guards who busted through my hotel room door *and* the uniformed officers who escorted me to the Westminster Borough Precinct, I take a deep breath and begin again.

"My editor texted me last week to ask if I would like to write a piece on rubbing elbows with royals. You know, an article detailing all the places the royals like to romp: über-swank restaurants, shops, clubs. Well, who wouldn't want to rub elbows with Prince Hottie Harry, right?"

Basil's stoic expression remains frozen in place.

"Did I mention I am a magazine columnist?"

"*Go, Girl.*"

"That's right! You are paying attention."

"Yes, well"—Basil sniffs—"attention to detail is rather a prerequisite of my occupation."

I fiddle with my trench coat belt and try to remember Basil's original question. The unflappable British detective has rattled my nerves like a coffee can filled with coins.

"The tripod?"

"Yes! The tripod," I say, warming. "I might have exaggerated my connections to the royal family just a little."

Basil smirks.

"Okay, a lot. I exaggerated a lot. But my mother has a cousin who shares a hair stylist with Fergie..."

Basil looks at me blankly.

"The Duchess of York, not the Black Eyed Peas singer."

"I trust this pointless but scintillating information is but a prelude to the story of how you ended up stalking His Royal Highness, Prince Henry of Wales?"

"I am not a stalker!"

"I beg to differ, madam." Basil flips through the pages of his notebook. "'Suspect detained after Buckingham Palace Guards observed questionable movements in a hotel room window facing the palace. WMB officers questioning hotel staff learned suspect made numerous inquiries as to the movements of members of the royal family and possible 'hidden' access points into the palace.'"

"I was only joking."

"Joking?"

"Yes."

"About stealing into the palace?"

"I'm an American. I have a sense of humor. I realize it's a foreign concept to the British, but humor is a common conversation starter in America."

"Let us assume you are telling the truth, that your ill-conceived comments about 'hunting down Hot Harry' and sneaking into the palace 'like a thirteen-year-old Belieber at a Justin Bieber concert' were woeful attempts at humor..."

I knew I shouldn't have made the Belieber comment.

"That still doesn't explain what you were doing at the Rubens?"

"I was in the hotel because I am a paying guest."

"Naturally," says Basil in his easy good-cop voice. "And what made you choose that particular hotel?"

"Duh!" Though I try, I can't keep the sarcasm from staining my tone. "It's called Rubens at the Palace for a reason. It's the closest hotel to Buckingham Palace. Proximity is everything in reporting. I thought staying close to the palace would increase my chances of running into a royal. Besides, I am writing a piece about London's poshest places, and the Rubens is pretty posh."

"How do you explain the tripod in the window?"

"I was hot."

Basil frowns.

"The air conditioner at the Rubens is crap. I used the tripod to prop the window open so I could get a breeze. That's it."

"And your questionable movements?"

"Questionable movements? What questionable movements? I came back to my room, took off my clothes, jumped in the shower, and—" A horrifying thought suddenly occurs to me. "Hang on! How long were the palace guards watching me? Did they see me naked?"

Basil's cheeks flush crimson, and he studies his notebook with a new intensity.

"Oh, yeah, and I'm the sick one! Does the queen know her palace is crawling with pervos?

Basil clears his throat. "According to the report, the guards witnessed suspicious movements."

"Brilliant!" I clap my hands, humiliation fueling my petulant sarcasm. "They foiled my diabolical plot to dance naked in my room. Did they check to make sure my iPod wasn't ticking? I would love to see their end of shift report. *'Watched naked woman dance in her hotel room. That is all. God save the Queen.'"*

"Yes, well…"

"Naked! I was naked in my hotel room! What kind of threat does a dancing naked woman pose to Prince Harry? Give me a freaking break! I have seen the photos of him partying naked at a Vegas rager, surrounded by naked girls. Where were your guards then, huh?" My boiling anger tempered only by my complete and utter mortification. "I was alone…in my hotel room…NAKED!"

Basil clears his throat. "We've established you were starkers. Now then, if we could-"

My cheeks grow hot. The word starkers paints a far more vivid picture than the word naked. Stark naked. Totally exposed.

Basil seizes the initiative. "And I suppose your appearance at the hospital was merely coincidental?"

"I was following Prince Harry."

"Right." Basil leans forward, his narrow nostrils flaring as if scenting prey. "Now we are getting somewhere."

Chapter 2

Poking a Mangina

"I think I have it now. First, you lied to your editor about your connection to the royal family because you thought your press credentials would get you close enough to rub elbows with 'Prince Hottie Harry.' Then, you followed the prince around London, hoping to get close enough to ask him which 'über-swank' club he prefers?" Basil shakes his head. "Brilliant! Crack reporting, Miss Grant."

To hear the detective describe my farfetched plan makes me sound like a crap reporter. It doesn't help that he speaks with a British accent. A British accent makes a person sound more intelligent.

"You must have been away with the fairies to believe you could approach Prince Harry as if he were P. Diddy," Basil says. "Did you think you could just slip the Prince's bodyguard a twenty and suddenly find yourself whisked through the palace gates? You made a right royal cock-up, Miss Grant. Next time, contact the appropriate channels, or you'll find yourself living at Her Majesty's pleasure."

I don't need Benedict Cumberbatch to translate the phrases "right royal cock-up" and "away with the fairies." The detective is implying I am a lousy reporter with a tenuous grasp on reality, but I am having a little difficulty working out the phrase "living at Her Majesty's pleasure." The Queen lives in a blooming palace. She probably has Google Fiber, three thousand thread count Egyptian cotton sheets, and a small army of domestics to scrub her golden commodes and serve her raspberry crumpets in bed. If old Basil meant to frighten me, throwing down the phrase "living at Her Majesty's pleasure" wasn't the way to go.

"No, Miss Grant, living at Her Majesty's pleasure does not mean invited to stay in the palace," Basil says, correctly reading my confused expression. "Living at Her Majesty's pleasure means thrown in prison."

"Listen Basil—"

"Mangina."

"I beg your pardon?"

"I am Detective Inspector Harold Mangina, not Basil Rathbone."

I can't keep a bubble of laughter from rising up my throat. "Mangina? Are you serious?"

The detective presses his lips together.

"Mangina? Harold Mangina?" My laughter ricochets around the questioning room. I should show the detective the respect he deserves, but my pent-up fear and humiliation is spilling out in near-hysterical mirth. "Harry Mangina! Your name isn't really Harry Mangina, is it?"

The detective reaches into his pocket, pulls out a business card, and hands it to me. I look at the words printed beside an embossed police badge.

> *DI Harold Mangina*
> *Westminster Metropolitan Police*
> *Special Branch*
> *Belgravia Station*
> *202-206 Buckingham Palace Road*
> *Belgravia SW1W 9SX*

I am laughing so hard now tears are spilling down my cheeks and my stomach feels like I've just completed Jillian Michaels's ab-shredding Six-Pack Ab Workout. I keep hearing the name in my head—Mangina. Harold Mangina. Harry Mangina. The detective continues to stare at me, the "we are not amused" thought bubble hovering over his head.

"I'm sorry," I say, dashing a tear from my cheek. "I've just never heard the name Mangina. Is that a British name?"

"Italian."

I consider explaining what mangina means in American slang, but change my mind. I've already made some serious breaches of British etiquette; telling a staid detective that his surname is slang for a man who tucks his twigs and berries would be a right royal cock-up. Maybe cock-up isn't the best choice of words, either.

"Just so you know, Inspector," I say, omitting his surname, "I tried the usual avenues before following the prince. I contacted the Royal Communications offices at Clarence House and Buckingham Palace, but they didn't respond to my request for an interview."

"One wonders how they could have overlooked a request from a magazine as prestigious and thought-provoking as *GoGirl!* An egregious error, no doubt."

Really? Trash talk from someone named Mangina?

I am tempted to tell Mister Twigs-and-Berries what I think of him and his Keystone Cops, but I just want to get out of the station, hop on a ferry to France, and put the snooty Rubens with their crap air conditioning behind me. A hot Frenchman is waiting for me in a hotel in Paris…a posh hotel with real working air conditioning.

"Look, if you would just call my editor—"

"Louanne Collins-London?"

"Yes! So you have at least done a rudimentary investigation of my background. Thank God. I was beginning to think MI-6 only existed in James Bond movies."

"Tell me, Miss Grant, are you always so exuberantly candid?"

"Absolutely." I grin. "It is *rawther* a prerequisite of my occupation."

Accents aren't really my forte, but I think I *rawther* nailed the detective's clipped, snooty patois. From his pinched expression, I'd say he thinks I nailed it too.

"Now, if you would just call my editor."

"I have spoken with Ms. Collins-London already. She corroborated your story and vouched for your mental fitness, though I have my reservations."

"Then why am I still sitting here talking to you about my unfortunate penchant for dancing starkers?"

Now it's the detective's turn to wear a smug grin. "Call it an occupational prerogative."

"In other words, you were pissed off when you saw me reading your notes and decided to have a little fun intimidating the barking mad colonial?"

"Indubitably." He reaches for his notebook and slips it into his tweed coat pocket. "I would have been remiss in my duties had I released you without conducting a thorough interrogation."

Nothing pisses me off more than a chauvinist abusing his power to subjugate the "lesser" sex. I would love to release a blistering barrage from my verbal arsenal, but I am afraid Detective Inspector Hairy Man Parts would throw me in some dank cell and withhold basic necessities, like my ionizing flat iron and iPhone. One week without my flat iron and I would look like Shaun White, or Carrot Top—I always get those two confused. Either way, my hair is not made for hard time.

"Are you satisfied?" I smile sweetly. "Maybe not as satisfied as those peeping pervos at Buckingham Palace, but satisfied enough to release me? I still have a job to do."

"No, you don't."

My heart drops. "What do you mean I don't?"

"Ms. Collins-London assured me you would remain a safe distance from the royal family. Your article has been terminated."

I exhale. For a frightening second I thought Man Parts was going to say that Louanne Collins-London fired me.

"Right," Man Parts says, sliding the manila envelope toward me. "You will find inside this envelope the personal artifacts we confiscated from you upon apprehension—your mobile, watch, passport, wallet..."

Man Parts is still speaking, but all I hear is Charlie Brown Teacher Speak—*Wha wha whaaaa wha wha*. I seize the envelope, tear it open, and retrieve my iPhone, stopping short of rubbing the device and murmuring, "My precious."

"...after you sign the requisite paperwork, you are free to go."

While Man Parts retrieves the paperwork to parole me from the pokey, I snap a few prison selfies for my Twitter Feed and check my texts.

> *Text from Jean-Luc:*
> *See you at the train station, mon cœur.*

My phone rings, and the words Big Boss Woman flash on the screen. I jab the volume button and wait for the call to go to voicemail. I don't want to have a conversation with my editor with the po-po listening. Besides, I need a little time to do some damage control. Maybe if I think of a scathingly brilliant idea for a new story, Big Boss Lady won't pull a Henry VIII and axe my ass.

I slip the phone into the pocket of my trench and wait for Man Parts to spring me from the pokey.

Chapter 3

Petting a Bitch

Text from Camilla Grant:
It's Mum. News of your arrest is going epidemic. It's all over the Facebook. Anna Johnson brought over a casserole and a business card of the lawyer who represented Amanda Knox. Is it as bad as all that, Luv?

Text to Camilla Grant:
By "'that bad," are you asking if I am accused of stabbing my roommate in a pot-and-porn-fueled frenzy? If so, I must plead the fifth on the grounds my answer might incriminate me.

Text from Camilla Grant:
Don't get cheeky with me, Vivia Perpetua Grant! Anna Johnson said she read on the Twitter you were arrested for stalking Prince Harry. My daughter arrested! What will I tell Father Escobar?
Text to Camilla Grant:

Tell Father Escobar I am like the apostle Peter, wrongfully imprisoned by a cruel, heartless authority, freed from my shackles through the power of prayer! And there was much rejoicing!

My mother spends an inordinate amount of time worrying about what the neighbors think, especially that sanctimonious busybody, Anna Johnson. My mum transferred her appearances neurosis to me. I am pretty sure this occurred while I was still in the embryonic stage; however, my lack of shame after the aforementioned Wonder Woman Bathing Suit Incident pokes a hole in the nature over nurture argument.

Second, American English is not my mum's first language. She was born and raised in Manchester, so her comprehension and application of American slang and sarcasm is woeful. She thinks a video or picture that becomes popular via Internet sharing is called "going epidemic." She is indiscriminate in her use of the word *the*. For instance, my mum calls it "the Facebook" and "the cancer," but she drops the from sentences containing the word hospital, university, or museum. *Anna Johnson has the cancer and has to go to hospital. I read the news on the Facebook.*

Finally, although I take delight in tormenting her, my mum is the sweetest, most supportive mother in the world. She's a neurotic, kooky mess, and I love her.

I send my mum a reassuring text, sign the requisite paperwork authorizing my release, bid Man Parts a chipper cheerio, and exit Belgravia Police Station through a brightly painted blue door, squinting against the watery morning light. My eyes tear up, and I stand for a moment with my face turned to the sky. This must be what it's like for prisoners released from solitary confinement. Doing time has given me an appreciation for the psychological and physiological effects of incarceration.

My eyes finally adjust to the daylight. I look around, but don't see any familiar landmarks. I am on a narrow street facing a small park.

I could whip out my iPhone and use the CityMappers app to navigate my way back to the hotel, but walking would require more energy than I can muster. The stress of the last twenty-four hours has definitely taken its toll. I'm exhausted, humiliated, hungry, and in desperate need of hand sanitizer—the police cruiser that transported me from the Rubens to Belgravia Station reeked of piss and salt and vinegar potato chips, an unforgettably odiferous emanation that has attached itself to my trench coat.

I just want to take a shower, pack my bags, and retreat to the safety of France so I can lick my wounded professional pride—or a cone of *chocolat noir et noix de coco* from Berthillon, this fab ice cream shop on the Île Saint-Louis.

It's starting to rain as I cross the street. I follow the sidewalk bordering the park until I come to an intersection. The British might have crap air conditioning, but they are bloody brilliant when it comes to signage. Two large signs affixed to the building on the corner announce my arrival at Ebury Square and Semley Place. I haven't the slightest idea where Ebury Square and Semley Place are in relation to my hotel, but I somehow feel more empowered by the knowledge. I'm not hopelessly lost. I am at Ebury Square and Semley Place!

The rain is really coming down now, so I flip up the collar of my trench and run across the intersection to seek shelter beneath a green Europcar awning.

I look down Semley Place and see a larger intersection not too far away, so I make a run for it.

When I finally reach the busy intersection, I am soaking wet and wheezing like an asthmatic. I have lost the belt to my faux Burberry, and my leather boots are waterlogged. Without even glancing in a shop window, I know my previously straightened hair is now a giant kinky ginger Afro. My friend G said girls in London aim for an artfully disheveled look. Think bed-head style meets vintage store find. So I chose my wardrobe accordingly. Yeah, I'm pretty sure that cool girly-but-with-an-edge image is now merely a figment of my imagination.

I walk to the curb, notice one of London's iconic black cabs headed in my direction, and wave my arms in the air. The cab drives on.

I repeat the process. Several times.

I am standing on my tippy toes, waving my arms in furious, slightly psychotic circles, shrilly crying out, "Taxi! Taxi!" when a beautiful blonde grabs one of my arms.

"I simply cawn't bear to watch this ghastly display," she says. "Please, do stop before you hurt yourself."

As if to mock my *Soul Train* meets *Little House on the Prairie* look, Lady Posh is wearing chic black trousers and a Burberry trench. An authentic Burberry trench.

"I am trying to hail a cab."

"Obviously," she says, pulling me away from the curb and leading me to a spot farther down the sidewalk. "However, you are going about it all wrong. Did you notice those zig-zaggy lines painted on the road where you were standing? They indicated a pedestrian crosswalk. Drivers won't pick you up if you are standing at a bus stop or crosswalk."

I am about to respond with a self-deprecating joke when Lady Posh resumes her lesson on cab etiquette.

"Additionally, the cabs you were attempting to hail had their lights turned off. An extinguished light means the cab has already been hired."

"Thank you," I mumble.

"Not at all," she says, pronouncing "at all" as if one word. "Finally, one simply does not wave one's hands frantically in the air."

She gracefully raises her hand in the air and a cab materializes, pulling to a stop beside us. My humiliation is complete. Miss Authentic Burberry: 1, Faux Burberry: 0.

She opens the door and slides into the cab like a starlet maneuvering her way into a limousine.

"Get in," she says, smiling and patting the seat beside her. "We can share."

I collapse on the seat beside her.

"Where are you headed?" she asks.

"Rubens at the Palace."

"You do realize the Rubens is less than half a mile from here? Walking would be faster."

I think about the tattling hotel staff and the tall tales they told about me to the police, and my shoulders slump. I don't want to go back to that über-swanky, über-stanky hotel. Miss Authentic Burberry misreads my reaction.

"You look knackered."

"I am knackered." I glance at my iPhone. "Is it really eleven thirty? I wish I could hit the 'do over' button and forget this day ever happened."

"That bad?"

"Worse."

"Look," she says, glancing at her Cartier. "I have an appointment in one hour half. Why don't we have lunch and you can tell me what made this a do-over day."

I am not accustomed to friendly Brits. "Why do you care?"

"You look like you could use a friend." She smiles. "I am in the hotel business. Hospitality is my currency. I hate to see a tourist looking as knackered and defeated as you do right now."

"I could use a friend."

"We could all use a friend, my dear." She gives the cab driver an address and then turns back to me. "Do you like French cuisine?"

"Yes."

"Brilliant! I know a fabulous restaurant."

I glance at my frizzy-headed reflection in the cab window and wonder if Lady Posh makes a habit of treating less-than-artfully disheveled paupers to lunch. I wonder what she will say when she learns this pauper was just sprung from the pokey?

"Thank you for helping me hail a cab," I say, looking back at Lady Posh. "I am Vivia Grant, by the way."

"Vivia Grant? Not *the* Vivia Grant?"

I remember what my mum said about the news of my arrest going viral, and for one horrifying second, I imagine my name on a BBC News ticker tape. *American Vivia Grant arrested in London while wearing Burberry knockoff, accused of harassing Prince Harry.*

"Are you a columnist for *GoGirl! Magazine?*"

"Yes."

Lady Posh's cool, disinterested expression undergoes a radical transformation. She literally beams at me.

"Poppy Worthington," she says, thrusting her hand at me. "Pleased to make your acquaintance."

I shake her hand.

"I read your column. You're really quite funny."

"Thank you."

My phone begins vibrating and blinging as I get a series of texts and e-mails.

"Would you excuse me?" I fish my iPhone out of my pocket. "I'm expecting an important message."

"Not a'tall."

I key my password into my iPhone, tap the Safari button, and type Poppy Worthington into the search bar. Poppy might be a nice person, but she could be barking mad, too. What if she's luring me to some seedy place so a gang of hairy Russians can bonk me on the head, jab a needle into my vein, and then I wake up in some dimly lit brothel in Cambodia, or worse, a bathtub filled with ice and a gaping wound in my abdomen? Okay, so I sound paranoid, but I am a single woman traveling abroad. Also, I have a healthy fear of human trafficking and organ harvesters.

My search returns 7,980,000 entries. I click on the first, a Wikipedia page for one Poppy Whitney Worthington.

"Poppy Whitney Worthington is a British socialite, hotelier, and philanthropist. Great-granddaughter of Sir Nigel Worthingon, Member of Parliament and founder of Worthington Hotels, and Lady Isabella Whitney, acclaimed poetess...."

I scroll down the page.

"...an undisputed social leader of the posh London set, Poppy has been romantically linked to actor Tristan Kent, playboy-mogul Sir Richard Blanchard, professional soccer player Trevin Larks, and billionaire software designer Colin Hardy."

Holy Shit! Tristan Kent? He's hot!

Tristan Kent is famous for playing a badass Wood Elf in a blockbuster fantasy trilogy. I don't even like fantasy flicks, but I saw Tristan Kent's movies three times just so I could watch him skewer villainous creatures with his bow and arrow.

I continue scrolling and reading.

"...elected CEO of Worthington Hotels after the death of her father... Worthington Hotels cater to the wealthiest and most elite travelers... Declared losses... In an interview with Hoteliers Magazine, Ms. Worthington announced her intention to transform the Brand into a boutique chain, renovating and rechristening the hotels under the names Luxe, Worth, Pamper, Voluptuary, and Pander."

The Wiki page includes a collage of photos of Poppy all glammed up at different red carpet soirees. I quickly close the Safari app and open my texts.

Mum wasn't exaggerating. My jailhouse tweets and cellfies have provoked a ridiculous amount of texts, including one from my best friend, Fanny.

> *Text from Stéphanie Moreau:*
> *Congratulations! Getting arrested by Buckingham Palace Guards and tweeting "cellfies" makes your booze-fueled night with Jett Jericho look almost lame. Now get to Paris. Jean-Luc is waiting.*

Sixteen texts from my mum, which is shockingly low given her obsessive nature.

One text from stupid old Travis Trunnell, my crazy-hot one night stand from college who made a sudden unwelcome reappearance last year that effectively destroyed my engagement to my then-fiancé, Nathaniel Edwards III. Serendipity works in unpredictable ways, though. If Travis hadn't exposed my one, teensy-weensy, little lie—that I wasn't a virgin when I met my fiancé—Nathan wouldn't have broken up with me. And Nathan ending our engagement turned out to be the best thing to ever happen to me—besides my discovery of Spanx and the ionizing flat-iron. The humiliation propelled me to embark on a journey of self-discovery, to stop trying to be the Vivia I thought everyone expected me to be and to keep it real. If Nathan hadn't broken up with me, I wouldn't have met Jean-Luc.

> *Text from Travis Trunnell:*
> *Saw you were arrested. Lucky police. I'd like to put a pair of handcuffs on you.*

> *Text to Travis Trunnell:*
> *Never. Gonna. Happen.*

Travis Trunnell's brazen predatory behavior pisses me off. He frequently texts me flirty messages even though he knows I am committed to Jean-Luc. I have never encouraged him. Not even once.

If I were to be one hundred percent honest, I don't exactly discourage him, either. The sexy Texan still makes my pulse race. Remember when *Fifty Shades of Grey* exploded on the scene? Women were hiding books behind John Grisham novels, so they could read them on the subway and on the treadmill at the gym. Travis Trunnell is my *Fifty Shades.* He's my secret ego-stroking guilty pleasure.

Several friends and colleagues sent texts. Finally, I come to the two texts I have been dreading.

> *Text from Jean-Luc de Caumont:*
> *See you in Paris.*

> *Text from Louanne Collins-London:*
> *What happened? Call me.*

Both Jean-Luc and Louanne Collins-London sent texts containing only four words.

Four words.

Four words like daggers, pricking my guilty conscience. How could four little words elicit such shame?

The Prince Harry Debacle has called into question my professionalism and ruined my plans for a perfect Nicholas Sparks-worthy weekend in Paris. I've disappointed my boss and my boyfriend, and it's killing me. Keeping it real, though? I am not sure which is killing me more: bungling an important assignment or dashing Jean-Luc's hopes for an interlude *romantique.*

"Bad news?"

"What?" I look up to find Poppy studying me, her perfectly plucked brows knitted.

"You're frowning. Is it bad news?"

"Not yet."

"Personal or professional?"

"Both."

"Ah," Poppy says. "I see."

This British blue blood hasn't the slightest comprehension of the shit tsunami about to crash down on the shores of my life. Once again, I am going to have to grab onto a plank of wood, hold on, and hope for the storm to end.

Whoa! A powerful wave of déjà vu is washing over me. Was it really just a year ago when I found myself in a similar situation: on the brink of losing my job and man because of one stupid little lie?

I want to drop my face to my hands and sob at my apparent inability to break bad habits, but Poppy is staring at me.

"My editor asked me to write a piece on what it's like to be part of the young royal set. I told her I would because I didn't want to disappoint her, but I don't have any connections to young, hip royals." My words come out in a guilty almost-manic rush. "The closest I've ever gotten to royalty is the Duchess of Yorkie—and she bites me anytime I try to pet her!"

A small wrinkle appears on Poppy's porcelain smooth forehead.

"My mum has a domineering Yorkie-Poodle mix named the Duchess of Yorkie."

Poppy chuckles. "When do you leave London?"

"I don't know." I shrug. "I think I am supposed to go to Bath in a few days for the Jane Austen Festival—that is, if I still have a job."

"Pish posh!" She waves her hands dismissively in the air. "Why, that's plenty of time for someone as resourceful and clever as you to write a bang-up piece."

"I appreciate the vote of confidence, but I have a restraining order prohibiting me from getting within five hundred yards of any member of the royal family, and I really don't want to spend any more time in a London prison."

Poppy chuckles and presses her hand to the strand of pearls at her throat.

"Restraining order?"

Chapter 4

A Spotted Dick in the Mouth

Poppy clutches the door handle and stares at me with wide horror-film eyes.

"I'm not a serial killer." I look her in the eye. "I promise I won't eat your liver with fava beans and a nice Chianti."

I stop short of making the Hannibal Lecter slurp, because I am not sure my new friend is ready for full-on Vivia dramatics.

Poppy just blinks at me.

By the time I finish giving her a synopsis of my run-in with the Buckingham Palace Guards, she seems more relaxed.

"Misadventure seems to follow you wherever you go."

"Hashtag *understatement!*"

We laugh.

The cab pulls to an abrupt stop in front of a magnificent brick Georgian building. Poppy thanks the driver, hands him a twenty pound note, and turns to me.

"Shall we?"

I follow her out of the cab and up the stairs of the brick building. As we approach, a liveried door man snaps to attention with the bearing of a well-drilled soldier, back stiff, gaze fixed on a distant point.

"Good day, Miss Worthington."

"Good day, Archie."

"Where are we?" I whisper.

"The Luxe, one of the hotels in the Worthington chain," Poppy says, smiling. "I have a meeting here this afternoon, so I thought we might have lunch in Délais."

"Délais?"

"Our new French restaurant. It's opening next week, but the chef is doing a test run of a tasting menu. Would you mind terribly being a guinea pig?"

"Would I? Are you kidding me?"

"Am I to interpret your unbridled American enthusiasm as an affirmative?"

"Absolutely!"

Poppy laughs. She has a pretty cool laugh. It's not loud and unrestrained like mine, but a throaty, controlled, I-was-raised-in-a-finishing school kind of laugh.

I follow Poppy through the lobby, the sharp tap-tap of her Louboutins on the marble floor announcing our arrival like the drumroll that precedes Hail to the Chief. Poppy could be the President. She strides through the hotel with complete confidence and authority, smiling at guests. I can't help but wonder what people are thinking as they watch the cool, sophisticated blonde and her ginger minion.

If the Rubens is posh, Luxe is über-posh. The two-story lobby is Georgian London meets Contemporary LA, with an elaborate plaster ceiling and sleek midnight black velvet Chesterfield sofas—like Jane Austen and James Bond collaborated on the interior design.

Poppy leads me down a hallway, around a rope barrier, and through a set of plush velvet drapes.

"Welcome to Délais!"

The restaurant is swanky. Super swanky. With an elaborate plastered ceiling, glossy parquet floors, walls covered in an expensive silver metallic paper, and sleek black walnut tables, the dining room has the same Austen meets Bond vibe as the lobby. An eclectic collection of art covers one wall from ceiling to floor—photographs, portraits, landscapes, post-modern paintings.

"Wow!" I whisper, awed by the sumptuous candlelit scene. "This is outrageous."

"Outrageous good or outrageous bad?"

The waver in Poppy's voice prompts me to shift my gaze from the art wall to her face. She's nibbling on her perfectly lacquered lower lip, and a tiny crease mars her otherwise porcelain smooth forehead. I can't believe what I am seeing. This cool, collected, cultured woman has a chink in her confident armor. What could poised and polished Poppy Worthington have to stress about? It's not like she's toting a ginger 'fro and enough baggage to fill the Louis Vuitton flagship store.

"Outrageous good, Poppy!" I grab her hand and squeeze her fingers. "It's like you opened a restaurant and cool cocktail lounge in the Louvre."

She stops biting her lip, but specters of self-doubt still hover behind her eyes. If we were better acquainted, I'd hug her and say, *"Believe, Sister! 'Cuz you got it going on."* Since I'm not sure perfectly pressed Poppy would appreciate such an exuberant public display of affection, I give her hand another little squeeze.

"This is the first hotel to be renovated since I assumed control of the Worthington Brand, and I am taking it in a totally new direction. Many don't share my vision. They predict my changes will tarnish the Worthington's golden reputation."

Poppy's looks down at her lap.

"You're a visionary, Poppy. Visionaries always have detractors, those frightened by change. Look at Michelangelo."

"Michelangelo?" she says, looking up.

"He was a visionary—painting naked saints and sinners on the ceiling of the Sistine Chapel—and he had his share of detractors. The Pope took one look at the masterpiece and lost his holy mind. He didn't appreciate seeing St. Paul with his peter hanging out, so he ordered Michelangelo to paint fig leaves over the saints' and sinners' genitalia. True story."

"Thanks." Poppy sniffs. "But I am no Michelangelo."

"Oh, I am not so sure about that." I glance around the restaurant. "You're an artist, Poppy Worthington, and this is your masterpiece."

"You can't know how much your praise means to me. You're precisely the demographic we had in mind when we designed Délais."

"Me?"

"Yes, you. Young, hip, well-traveled, and well-educated. Traditional values, but with a slightly irreverent approach to life."

Hip? *Me*? In my trying-too-hard London ensemble? I don't think so. "You got all of that from watching me hail a cab?"

Poppy chuckles. "And reading your column for the last year."

"Well, I am not sure if I deserve such praise, but Délais definitely nails the young, hip, cultured vibe."

Poppy's eyes fill with fresh tears.

"Oh, bollocks!" She murmurs, quickly blinking. "It's our GM. I mustn't let him see me all weepy."

I shove my hand into my purse and fish around. I whip out a bottle of Visine just as an officious looking man wearing a Saville Row suit, and smug expression, saunters up.

"Allergies are the worst. Here." I hand the Visine to Poppy. "Two drops per eye usually does the trick."

"Thank you." Poppy slips the bottle into her pocket.

"Good Morning, Miss Worthington," Saville Row says. "Might I have a word?"

"Certainly, Malcolm." She turns to me. "Would you excuse me a moment?"

"Of course."

While Poppy takes care of business, I whip out my iPhone and compose a text to Big Boss Woman.

> *Text to Louanne Collins-London:*
> *Thank you for springing me from the pokey. It was a mortifying misunderstanding. Am already working on another story that should be equally as enthralling. Super excited. Will call with details as soon as possible.*

All right, I'll admit it; I lied to my editor when I said I had connections to the royal family, and I just lied to her again when I said I am working on an enthralling story. I have no idea what I am going to write about. Something tells me Louanne Collins-London wouldn't appreciate a thousand-word piece on my extremely tenuous connection to Prince Andrew's naughty ex. And I don't think she would accept a rags-to-riches story about a plucky young hairdresser with a dream, who started off in a grungy chop-shop, but ended up styling the tresses of a disgraced Duchess.

GoGirl! readers are young, stylish, professional women who want to read smart, sassy, sexy pieces about life beyond their borders. Louanne Collins-London tells me they want to vicariously visit posh resorts, exclusive clubs, and offbeat shops. They want me to take them on adventures kayaking the Amazon, joining an archaeological excavation in Cairo, or hiking the Highlands. They want to meet larger-than-life characters—like spoiled debutantes, entitled movie stars, and jet-setting celebrities—but through my slightly distorted lens. They don't want to read about my mother's cousin's hairdresser.

> *Text to Jean-Luc de Caumont:*
> *I am going to be a little late.*

> *Text from Jean-Luc:*

I read your tweets and was about to launch Operation Rescue Vivia.

Tweet to Jean-Luc:
Ha ha! No rescue needed, my French cowboy. The hostiles have released me.

Text from Jean-Luc:
Does that mean I should unpack my six-shooter?

Text to Jean-Luc de Caumont:
Keep your weapon holstered, partner—at least for a little bit longer ;)

Text from Jean-Luc de Caumont:
Would you like me to come to London?

Text to Jean-Luc:
No! I'm just going to grab something to eat and then I will be on the next train, plane, or ferry out of this miserable moldering country. I'll send you my arrival info as soon as I have it.

Text from Jean-Luc:
See you soon, mon cœur.

We've barely taken our seats in one of the banquettes when Poppy says, "Do you really have a court injunction prohibiting you from approaching the royal family?"

"Yes."

"Did you spend time in prison? Truly?"

"Yes."

"You're quite serious, aren't you?"

"Yes."

"When?"

"This morning. In fact, I had only just been released from Belgravia Station when you found me on the street flagging a cab."

Poppy presses her hand to her throat again and takes an audible swallow.

I give her the low-down on my bogus rap, and by the time I am finished telling her my story, she is dabbing tears of laughter from her eyes.

The sommelier arrives with a bottle of Château Doisy-Daëne, removes the cork, pours the golden liquid into two glasses, and then silently retreats into the shadows.

"A toast," Poppy says, lifting her glass. "To Prince Harry!"

"Huzzah!" I laugh. "To Prince Harry!"

Poppy and I spend several minutes getting acquainted, and you know what? She's really cool. She's not the uptight etiquette Nazi I feared she would be. She didn't even flinch when I sipped my wine without swirling, sniffing, or checking for legs—a ritual that remains mystifying despite Jean-Luc's many attempts to educate me of the wonders of wine.

"I was probably setting my price tag too low—as my BFF Fanny likes to say—but I didn't understand why someone as polished and poised as you would want to hang with me until..."

Filter Vivia! Filter! Damn my unfortunate habit of articulating my every thought.

"Until you discovered I am a sad, neurotic mess with premature crow's feet?" Poppy finishes my sentence.

We both laugh.

"I think we shall be great friends, Vivia." Poppy raises her glass. "That is, as long as you leave the hailing of cabs to me."

A short dark haired man strides confidently up to our table, his strong Gallic nose tilted at an arrogant angle. I recognize the haughty expression immediately—the upturned nose, the slightly hooded eyes indicating boredom and disdain. *Il est Français*!

French haughtiness used to piss me off. Now, I find it endearing and humorous.

"*Bonjour*, Mademoiselle Worthington."

"*Bonjour*, Michel," Poppy says, prattling on in flawless French. "*J'espère que cela ne vous dérange pas que j'ai amené un ami avec moi aujourd'hui...*"

I nod my head as if I understand what Poppy is saying even though I am only able to translate every third word. Despite Rosetta Stone's emphatic promise—"*You'll start communicating quickly and have fun doing it!*"—I butcher the French language like Michel with a side of beef. I want to learn to speak French fluently—I really do—but I think I have Language Alzheimer's. Jean-Luc or Fanny will teach me a word. I will practice saying the word, repeating it several times a day, but as soon as they quiz me, my mind goes blank, and I stare wide-eyed, mouth agape.

Both Michel and Poppy are staring at me. I am too embarrassed to admit I zoned out and have no idea what they asked me, so I whip out one of the few French phrases I have managed to master.

"*Je voudrais commander un café au lait, s'il vous plaît.*"

Poppy blinks. Michel stares as if I were a fly in his béchamel. I have been on the receiving end of that expression—that patronizing, my-family-home-*ees*-older-than-your-country expression—more times than I care to admit.

"*Je voudrais commander un café au lait,*" I nervously repeat.

I would like to order a coffee with milk. I learned that handy phrase while listening to Earworms, a French language CD that uses catchy tunes and repetition. I don't know how handy the phrase is, actually, since I don't even drink coffee.

"Michel asked if you had any food allergies, Vivia," Poppy explains. "Though I am certain we can get you a coffee with milk."

Prickly heat spreads from my cheeks to my toes like a California wildfire. I want to go limp, slide off my chair, and pretend I am suffering from a fit of the vapors. Victorian women worked the vapor swoons, so why can't I? Generally speaking, the Victorians creep me out, but I could get behind a swooning revival.

"I'm sorry," I mumble. "My French is rusty."

Michel rolls his eyes. "Pfft."

What the...? Did he just pfft me? I might not speak fluent French, but I can translate pfft. He just dismissed me as a creature beneath him. Pfft means, "Naturally, you are just another sad, ignorant *Américaine.*"

I am tempted to tell the little chef to stick his ladle in his pompous French ass, but I don't want to embarrass Poppy. Instead, I tell him I am allergic to mushrooms. Ha! That oughta throw a little cayenne into his crock-pot. What French chef cooks sans mushrooms?

Michel narrows his eyes.

I totally lied. I am not allergic to mushrooms—not in the strictly, grab-an-EpiPen-STAT, medical sense—but I do gag and retch like a cat yukking up a furball whenever I am forced to feast on fungi. It's not a pretty site.

Michel pivots on one foot and stalks back to the kitchen.

Poppy rolls her eyes. "The French really take the biscuit, don't they? They're self-impressed and right temperamental. They completely disintegrate if we don't wax poetic about their Camembert or rhapsodize over every bottle of Burgundy they uncork."

I think of Jean-Luc. I always think of Jean-Luc when someone mentions France, or speaks in French. Thinking of Jean-Luc—his ripped, tanned body, his smoldering gaze—always makes my chest constrict. The thought of him literally takes my breath away.

"My boyfriend is French."

"Cor!" Poppy's cheeks flush apple red. "I forgot you have a French boyfriend! I am sorry if I offended you."

"No worries," I laugh, thinking about Luc's obsession with Taco Bell and John Wayne movies. "Jean-Luc isn't your typical Frenchman."

"No, he certainly is not."

I frown. How does Poppy Worthington know about my boyfriend?

Poppy reads my thoughts. "I follow your Twitter account. You've tweeted about him."

I don't know if I should feel flattered or slightly creeped out. A year ago, my friend G tweeted a photo of me hanging on the beach in Cannes with Jett Jericho. The photo went viral. I'm talking Ebola sized viral. My Twitter followers jumped from 362 to 193,000. Big Boss Woman checks my numbers each month and sends me gleeful texts.

Text from Louanne Collins-London:
1,178 more followers this month. You're starting to give Jenna
Marbles a run for her money. Tweet! Tweet! Followers = readers.

I've never taken the numbers seriously. My Twitter Followers have never seemed real to me. They are just nameless, faceless entities with disembodied voices who respond to or RT my ramblings. It's not like *@BottleBlonde @AtomicDawg @112UserNotFound* or *@DuchessofBainbridge* are real friends—not drink-champagne-cocktails-until-you're-drunk-enough-to-get-an-ass-tattoo friends. They're my *faux amies*.

It's weird to think of Poppy as one of the disembodied voices. I can't wrap my mind around someone as smart and chic as Poppy Worthington taking time out of her important *shed-yule* to read one of my tweets about seeing Rachel Zoe licking a cracker wrapper in the Milan airport, let alone committing details of my private life to memory.

"Hello! Vivia?" Poppy waves her hand in front of my face. "You've gone all polka dots and unicorns."

"Polka dots and unicorns?" I frown. "Oh! You mean zoned out?"

Polka dots and unicorns. The British are hilarious. I am so working that into my next conversation with Fanny or Jean-Luc.

"I'm sorry, Poppy," I say, smiling. "I feel a little guilty."

"Guilty? Why?"

"I was supposed to meet Jean-Luc in Paris this weekend for..."

Poppy waggles her eyebrows. "A shag fest?"

"I was going to say for our first anniversary celebration, but shag fest works too."

I dig Poppy. I know dig is a 1950s word, but deep down I've got an inner Beatnik that's aching to bang a bongo while composing bombastic poems about my spiritual journey.

"You can still meet him in Paris," Poppy says brightly. "British Airways have flights leaving every hour."

"I'll hop a flight this afternoon, but my heart's not totally in it."

Poppy tilts her head and her sleek angled bob spills over her shoulder. "Why not?"

I shrug. "I am going to spend the whole weekend stressing about blowing the Prince Harry story. I should probably scrub my shag fest, stay in London, and conjure up another story."

"You're a smashing writer, Vivia." Poppy smiles. "I am certain you will get it sorted out."

"I hope so!" I don't share Poppy's confidence. "I can't afford to lose another writing gig. I have a chocolate addiction that needs regular fixes."

"You aren't going to lose your job over one lost story."

"I might." My voice is wobbling like a newborn colt. "Unemployment is high. The economy sucks. It's only a matter of time before my boss realizes readers don't want to hear about my frivolous wanderings."

"Have you lost the plot?"

"What?"

"Are you crazy? You're a bloody brilliant writer. Your boss knows you're a valuable commodity. She wouldn't sack you over one cocked-up story."

"Really?"

"Abso-bloody-lutely!" Poppy slams her fist on the table. "Set your price tag high, Vivia, and others will appreciate your value."

I feel like stomping my feet, raising my hands, and saying, *"Preach, Sister!"* Poppy's little sermon is the same one I gave myself last year when I was picking up the pieces of my shattered life. I have a habit of setting my price tag too low.

"Thanks, Poppy."

"Of course. Now stop frowning. No job—or man—is worth risking wrinkles."

"Don't risk the wrinkles. I like that mantra."

"You may have it."

I laugh. "Thanks!"

Michel arrives bearing two plates. "I formulated zee menu as a general formulates zee battle plan," he says, nose thrust high in the air. "I have brazenly selected flavors to assault your senses. I wish to take you unaware."

Now that's a frightening thought. Ratatouille taking me unaware. Ugh.

With great pomp and pageantry, Michel presents us each with a plate of what appears to be pureed bologna floating in a sea of snot or cat food floating in bile.

"For the first course, I have prepared *canard pâté de foie avec de la mousse de pomme de terre.*"

Duck liver pâté with potato foam. Did I miss something? Is food supposed to be foamy? I don't remember Guy Fieri saying anything about foamy potatoes. Potatoes can be sliced and deep fried in peanut oil or mashed and mixed with heavy cream and butter, but not foamed. How does one foam a potato?

I stare at my plate skeptically before taking the tiniest of bites. Then, I take another bite— just to confirm my first impression. The verdict? Duck innards floating in potato bile is actually good…like *crazy* good. The pâté is smooth, buttery, with just a hint of brie, and the potato foam is so delicious I am actually reconsidering a rendezvous with ratatouille. Jean-Luc is loyal, sweet, and insanely hot in bed, but I'm pretty sure he can't make potato foam.

Michel returns with our next course: deconstructed *coq au vin* with a beaker of warm, fruity Rhône Valley grenache. It's like grandma went into the kitchen and whipped up some comfort food—assuming the grandma was Coco Chanel. Michel's *coq au vin i*s classic but modern, complicated yet straightforward.

"This is amazing, like a symphony in my mouth" I murmur, forking another piece of chicken and dipping it in the wine sauce. "Michel is a culinary virtuoso."

"He is, isn't he?"

Michel returns with our choice of desserts: Profiteroles filled with Bourbon vanilla custard and drizzled with spicy Mayan dark chocolate sauce or a spotted dick in crème anglaise.

I confess. I have a simple palate. Until I accepted the *GoGirl!* gig, my most adventurous foray into the world of exotic cuisine was Mr. Foo's

Spicy Chicken—eaten with disposable chopsticks from a white take-out carton. Michel has broadened my gastronomical horizons.

I am torn between two lovers. Profiteroles or spotted dick? Which one should I choose? I want them both. Why, oh why, can't I have my cake and eat it, too?

Mistaking my hesitation for disinterest, Michel starts to step away from the table. Uh-uh Michel. Don't even play.

"Wait!" I shout. "I want your spotted dick!"

Sweet Aunt Jemima! There's a phrase I never thought I'd say. Poppy pretends to blot her lips with her napkin, but I know it's only to hide her smile.

Michel serves the spotted dick and hurries back to the kitchen, presumably to puree a mushroom digestif as a chaser for my spotted dick.

"Vivia, I've just had a scathingly brilliant idea!"

"Scathingly brilliant idea?" I pause between bites of warm, spongy pudding soaked in crème anglaise to stare at my new friend. "Haley Mills. *The Trouble with Angels*, right?"

"Yes! I love that movie."

"Me too!"

Poppy and I grin at each other like two love sick teenagers—the way new friends smile when they discover common interests or experiences.

"Okay." I pop a golden raisin in my mouth. "Let's hear it, Hayley. What's your scathingly brilliant idea?"

Poppy forks a chocolate covered profiterole into her mouth. She's nearly finished her dessert. Thank God she's not one of those "I'll just have a glass of water and watch you eat dessert" kinda girls. Score! Another thing we have in common.

"You need a bang-up story, right?"

"Yes."

"I might have one for you."

Oh man! I should have known something was up when a complete stranger offered me a comped lunch at a chi-chi restaurant. She probably wants me to write a promo piece about her restaurant.

"Look, Poppy." I put my spoon down and push my spotted dick away. "*GoGirl!* strictly forbids employees from receiving anything of monetary value gratis, even meals. I would be happy to write an article about Délais, but then I must insist on paying for my lunch."

"What?" Poppy frowns—though, maddeningly, not a single wrinkle appears on her face—and then chuckles. "You think I want you to write an article about the restaurant? Don't be absurd."

My face warms. I suddenly feel absurd. Why would someone as posh as Poppy Worthington care if I wrote a silly little article about her world class restaurant? I mean, it's not like *I* hobnob with Tristan Kent and Sir Richard Branson.

"I would be absolutely delighted if you wrote an article about Délais, but that is not what I was suggesting. I would never impose upon our friendship in such a way," Poppy's brow knits together for a moment. "I was invited to a party by an American cable station tonight and thought perhaps you would like to be my plus one."

"Really? Which station?"

"BravaTV"

"Brava? Ugh!" I literally have to stifle my groan. "I hate reality television. It's totally ruined my viewing experience. Reality TV is like a hostile alien invasion, taking control of our airwaves and subjugating the masses with its hypnotically insipid message, and BravaTV is the mother ship. Real Housewhores of Brooklyn. Georgia Belles. Score a Bachelor."

Filter, Vivia! Filter! Damn me and my ever-moving mouth. From the look on Poppy's face, I've looked her gift horse in the mouth. Shit. I kicked her gift horse in its damned mouth.

"I am concerned our budding intimacy might restrict you from speaking with candor." Poppy grins. "Do tell me how you really feel."

"I'm sorry."

"Not a'tall. I find your forthrightness refreshing. British women aren't nearly so uncensored. We choose our words with great care, often to devastating effect, and we hide behind false smiles."

"It sounds exhausting."

"It is."

A shadow moves over Poppy's pretty features, like a dark amorphous cloud floating before the sun. I wonder if Poppy, with her jet-setting connections, feels as lonely as she looks.

"Why is Brava hosting a party in London?"

Poppy shifts in her seat.

"They're celebrating the success of their new series, Brash Brits."

Ladies of London? I imagine expressionless women with ridiculous fascinators perched atop their heads sipping tea while discussing the weather. Yawn.

"I haven't heard of it."

"They've been courting me for months now." Poppy leans in and lowers her voice to a whisper. "They want me to be on the next season. Can you imagine?"

I stare at her with my mouth hanging open. Cultured, classy Poppy Worthington the next Bravalebrity? Isn't that one of the signs of the apocalypse, right before the appearance of the horsemen?

"Anyway," she says, "it supposed to be a big, splashy affair. They've invited several celebrities. David and Victoria Beckham. Wynona Pathlow. Hugh Grant. Bishop Raine."

"Bishop Raine?"

"Yes. Why?"

Is it too soon to confess my unadulterated affection for bad boys like Ronnie Radke of the band Falling in Reverse and the sexy leather-clad comedian Bishop Raine? I think it might be.

"Readers enjoy articles about celebrities like Bishop Raine because he's smart, politically astute, and funny."

"You should come with me."

"Are you serious? That would be awesome." I hop to my feet. "Oh, Poppy! I could kiss you."

Poppy holds up her hand. "I'm British. I don't do kisses."

I laugh. "How about hugs?"

Poppy grimaces. "Only on terribly special occasions."

I laugh again and am about to pull perfectly pressed Poppy into a sisterly squeeze when I remember my interlude *romantique* with Luc. I hunch my shoulders and exhale slowly. I'm like a slow leaking balloon.

"What?" Poppy asks. "Oh, yes, the shag fest."

"The shag fest," I repeat, crinkling my nose. "What should I do?"

"Don't ask me." Poppy holds up her hands. "I will not be responsible for the French dis-Connection. It's your decision."

Poppy is totally cool, but I wish Fanny were here. Fanny would know exactly what to do. Fanny always knows what to do. My goal-setting, type A, itinerary-drafting best friend would organize another story and have me on a plane headed for Paris before sunset.

"Let me just check something." I pull out my iPhone.

I open Safari and type Ryanair into the search bar. Maybe all of the flights to Paris are already booked, which would mean I am stuck in London until morning—and if I am stuck in London until morning, why shouldn't I go to Poppy's party?

"If you are checking on a flight to Paris, don't bother."

I look up from the glowing screen. "Why not?"

"I'll have my assistant book you a seat on a British Airways flight out of Heathrow." She whips out her smartphone and taps the screen. "How about the six fifty flight? You will arrive in time for breakfast."

"Oh, thank you, but I can't ask you to do that."

"Too late." She slips her phone back into her purse. "It's done."

Either Michel slipped a few mushrooms into my spotted dick or I'm already suffering pangs of guilt, because my stomach aches.

"I'll still have three days and two nights with Luc," I say, trying to rationalize my selfish decision. "Besides, we would have been asleep for most of the night anyway."

I mentally calculate the profit versus the loss and decide it's worth the risk. Luc might be a tiny bit irritated, but Big Boss Lady will probably give me a raise.

"Okay, I'd love to be your plus one, Poppy."

"Splendid," Poppy says, standing. "Now, we really should do something about your hair."

Chapter 5

Hips Don't Lie

Text from Camilla Grant:
It's your mum. I finally joined the Facebook. I was going to like the donut shop's page, but I hit enter too soon and typed Happy Ho instead of the Happy Hole Donut Shop. Can you believe there are 173 Happy Hos on the Facebook? I am thinking of friend requesting one and inviting her to church.

Text to Louanne Collins-London:
Fab news! I've been invited to the Brava party celebrating the first season of their new show. Bishop Raine, Wynona Pathlow on guest list. Would you like me to write a piece about it?

Text from Louanne Collins-London:
Sure.

I am not sure which text fills me with more dread: my mother's expressed desire to send a friend request to some random perky prostitute or Louanne Collins-London's tepid one word response to my exciting Brava party invite.

Sure.

Maybe I am reading more into it, but Louanne's text was distant and dispassionate.

Would you like a cup of Earl Grey?

Sure.

Wanna listen to Josh Groban's new album?

Sure.

How could an editor of a hip and happening magazine be so blasé over a splashy, celeb-filled party piece?

"Because you totally blew the Prince Harry story and now she's blasé about you," whispers my inner Regina George.

Yes, I have an inner Regina George. The manipulative, deceitful, belittling queen bee in the movie Mean Girls talks smack, giving my self-esteem Ray Rice beat downs. Don't judge. I'll bet you have an inner Regina George, who makes you feel like crap because of your thighs/boyfriend/job/laugh. We all do. Some are just better at silencing their Reginas before she inflicts real damage. My Regina is telling me I am going to lose my job.

Fishing in my pocket, I pull out my iPhone and scroll through my contacts until I come to Jean-Luc de Caumont. I select his name and his tanned, handsome face pops up on my screen above his contact info. I look at his thick eyelashes framing his smoldering brown eyes and suddenly feel weepy.

What if I jeopardize my relationship with Luc for some silly insipid story about Bravalebrities, and Louanne still fires me?

I select his mobile number and hold my breath. The phone rings five times before sending me to voicemail. A lump forms in my throat as I listen to Luc's deep voice and smooth, sexy French greeting.

"Bonjour. C'est Jean-Luc. Veuillez me laisser un message et je vous téléphonerai aussitôt que possible. Merci."

*"Bonjour, Mon Cowboy. C'est moi…*Vivia," I say, my mood and tone falsely chipper. Spending the evening at some narcissism and martini-fueled soiree with a bunch of self-impressed Flat Stanleys suddenly seems pointless, shallow, and tragically selfish. "Something has come up here and I won't be able to make it to Paris tonight. I'm catching the British Airways flight leaving Heathrow tomorrow morning at six fifty. Luc, I'm…really…sorry."

By the time I speak the last sentence, my voice is as painfully thin and shaky as Rachel Zoe. I wonder what Luc will think when he listens to my message. To borrow a Zoe-ism, I must have sounded bah-nan-ahs, starting off airy and ending up weepy. Torn between my career and romance, I feel like I am having a bipolar breakdown.

Jesus, Mary, and Joseph Gordon Levitt! Did I really just quote Rachel Zoe, a woman I find about as annoying as woolly boogers on a cashmere sweater?

I look in the mirror at my pale, gangly legs, bare beneath them hem of a black tent dress with white puritan collar and cuffs, and then up at my red-rimmed eyes.

"How is that Alexander McQueen working for you, Vivia?"

True to her word, Poppy is getting me "sorted out"—rather, she is having her devoted minions sort me out. She put me in a taxi and gave the driver directions to her favorite hair salon for an "emergency wash and blowout." My ginger fro has been flat-ironed, glossed, and pulled into a sleek, chic high ponytail. Now I'm in Demimonde, her cousin's ironically named chi-chi boutique.

"Umm." I blink away my tears, open the purple velvet curtains, and do a little spin. "What do you think?"

Carolena tilts her head, and her chestnut curls spill over her Versace bustier. I only know the dress is a Versace because Fanny pinned a picture of it to her "Covet It" board on Pinterest.

"It's too..." She struggles to find the perfect word to describe the part hippie, part habit dress swathing my body.

"Ecclesiastical?"

"No."

"Voluminous?"

"No." Carolena studies me intensely. "Insolent," she finally says. "The gown is simply too insolent. It does rude things for your figure."

How can you not love a woman who uses a word like insolent to describe a—I lift the price tag and gasp—two thousand three hundred and thirty five dollar dress?

Who would pay two thousand three hundred and thirty five dollars for a dress that looks like a Project Runway unconventional challenge gone wrong? An image of Tim Gunn standing with his hands pressed together in a downward triangle pops into my head and his Snagglepuss voice plays in my ear, *"For this challenge you will be sourcing your materials at a convent. Make it work, people, and if all else fails, pray!"*

I grapple for the side zipper, anxious to remove the ludicrously overpriced dress before I break out in a cold sweat and ruin it.

Carolena reaches over and slides the zipper halfway down.

"Thank you."

"Not at all."

She pronounces at all just as Poppy does, blending the two words together to form a single *veddy* British-sounding portmanteau.

I step back into my fitting room, close the velvet curtains, and carefully remove the dress, hanging it on the padded silk hanger. Seriously, who spends two thousand dollars on a simple dress?

Fanny. Poppy. Carolena. My friend G.

Heiresses spend thousands of dollars on a single garment. I, however, am not an heiress, and even if I were an heiress, I wouldn't spend two thousand three hundred and thirty five dollars on a dress! I am quite happy making it work in skinny jeans and my vintage Guns N' Roses T-shirt.

"Hand me that beastly thing and try this instead."

She sticks a slinky mini dress between the curtains. I take the heavy beaded dress and hand her the hippie habit.

"I have the perfect shoes for that dress," Carolena declares. "A beaded mini-dress simply demands a marvelous pair of heels. Wait for me to get them. I won't be a minute."

Silver and gold bugle beads cover the mini dress like sparkly, swingy fringe. It's very Gatsby-esque. It's Daisy Buchanan circa now. Classic, but current.

I slip the heavy beaded gown over my head and do a little shimmy. The beads capture the light like a disco ball, creating a constellation of stars on the fitting room walls and velvet curtains. It's mesmerizing.

I summon my inner-Shakira, shaking my hips side to side. The beads make a pleasant rhythmical noise similar to a rain stick when it's turned upside-down. It's like having my own backbeat, a hip personal soundtrack. Shakira. Shakira.

Inexplicably, unbelievably, I recognize the pangs of love at first site. I am falling in love with a dress—a designer dress that probably costs more than my entire collection of my Rock Ts and skinny jeans. How can this be happening? I'm not a fashionista like Fanny and Poppy.

Take it off, Vivia. Take it off while you still have the strength.

It's not just the sparkly beads that make this dress so fantastic. The gown hugs my body, amplifying my assets—bosom—and minimizing my deficits—slight muffin top—*merci, pain au chocolats!*) The fringy beads conceal the evidence of my recent over indulgences without making me look like a shapeless Teletubby.

I do another little shimmy, and the metallic beads bounce tiny circles of light all over the fitting room walls.

Look away, Vivia. Look away from the light.

I can't. The beads are whispering to me, casting a mind-altering spell with their hypnotic song: "Why such stress? Just buy the dress. Buy the dress! If you use your Visa you can buy the dress. Make us shake and shimmy whenever you want. Buy the dress."

"Vivia?" Carolena's voice comes to me from a distant place. "Vivia?" she repeats. "I know you're in there because I can hear the beads clattering together. Do you like the dress?"

I pull the curtains back and give the beads a little shake.

"Oh, baby, the hips don't lie," I sing, mimicking Shakira's vibrato.

Carolena stares at me blankly.

I swivel my hips and make wavelike motions with my arms, to no effect. Poppy's posh cousin continues to stare at me blankly, her perfectly painted pout hanging open, strappy heels dangling from a single crooked finger.

"The hips don't lie?"

Nothing.

"Shakira, Shakira," I sing.

"Right then." Carolena snaps out of her reverie. "Don't do that. Ever. Especially not tonight, at Boujis."

Heat flames my cheeks as I suddenly imagine what I must have looked like to the staid Brit, singing and shaking to Shakira.

"Is it posh?"

"Very."

"Lots of beautiful people?"

"Loads."

My inner-Regina buzzes in my ear, telling me I'm an idiot for going to a Brava party, that I am not posh, not one of the beautiful people, not even a Bravalebrity.

"Maybe I shouldn't go to Boujis."

"What? Why not?"

"Hello, Carolena," I say, thrusting my hand out. "My name is Vivia Perpetua Grant. I am a brash, clumsy American with a penchant for raunchy rock music and spicy Chinese takeout. I am not posh."

"You're posh-*ish*."

I tilt my head and give her my best get-the-fuck-outta-here look.

"Well, you're beautiful."

I roll my eyes.

"You are," Carolena argues, handing me the strappy heels. "I would kill for your legs and your hair."

"My hair?" I bend over and slide my feet into the high heels. "You're joking. It's an ugly rusty blond and frizzy. I have a ginger 'fro."

"Have you lost the plot entirely?" Carolena walks over and spins me around to face the mirror. "Look at yourself! Gorgeous hair, endless shapely legs. You will fit in with the beautiful Boujis crowd."

"Thanks, Carolena. That's kind of you to say."

"Not at all." She looks at me in the mirror. "Now, do you like the dress?"

"Are you kidding me?" I shimmy my hips with each syllable. "I would shank my best friend for this dress."

"What is shank?"

"Never mind." I laugh. "It means I covet this dress."

"Does that mean you would like to buy it?"

"Would I?"

Carolena frowns."Yes, would you?"

"Are you kidding? I would love to buy this dress. I would wear it for the rest of my life—to the grocery store and the gym and my wedding—or at least until all the beads fell off. Only…"

"Only?"

"Only…" I reach under my armpit to feel for a price tag, but can't find one. It's probably so expensive—one of those, if you have to ask, you can't afford it dresses. "I am not sure I can afford it."

"Oh, biscuits!" Carolena waves her hand like she's brushing crumpet crumbs from the tea table. "You look brilliant! I wager you feel fairly brilliant, too. Please say you will take the dress?"

I do a mental balancing of my checking and savings account. If I dip into my travel contingency fund and forgo *pain au chocolat* for a year, I might be able to afford my Gatsby-esque gown.

"It depends."

"On what?"

"On the price." Ain't no shame in admitting the truth. No fronting. I am a Grant, not a Rockefeller. "I can't afford a two thousand dollar dress."

Carolena glances over her shoulder and moves closer, lowering her voice to a conspiratorial whisper. She confesses one of her customers purchased the dress and returned it.

"She said some of the beads came off in her hand." Carolena rolls her eyes. "Absolute rubbish."

"Why do you think she returned it?"

"I sold the same dress to her cousin's wife. The two don't get on, you see."

I didn't see. If my cousin's wife wanted this dress, I would risk life and limb wrestling her for it. My cousin's wife is five-foot-four and weighs one hundred and ninety eight pounds, so I would literally be risking life and limb.

"Couldn't you have refused the return?"

"I could have, but she is an important customer." She widens her eyes and lowers her chin, as if the gesture conveys more than her words. "An extremely important customer."

"The kind of customer with loads of connections?"

"The sort of customer with a sterling antecedent."

"A royal?"

Carolena closes her eyes and turns away.

"Tell me, Carolena. Did a royal wear this dress? I am going to die. You have to tell me. Please?"

She opens her eyes and fixes me with an implacable stare—a stare that says, "You can toss me in the tower and threaten me with the rack, but I shan't answer your inquisition."

My mind whirls as I try to imagine which royal princess or duchess or highborn lady slipped into my slinky shimmy gown.

"I can't sell a gown in my store now that has been worn. I was going to sell it to a vintage boutique in Notting Hill, but maybe we could strike a bargain?"

"What sort of bargain?"

Who am I kidding? I would give her my virginity for this dress. That is, if I hadn't already given my virginity to Leo Crandall, Travis Trunnell, and Nathan Edwards. Yes, I told more than one man he took my virginity. Just call me the perpetual virgin.

"Buy the shoes, and I will sell you the dress seventy percent off."

I assume the dress costs as much as the hippie habit and mentally calculate thirty percent of two thousand three hundred and thirty five dollars. I suck at math, but even I can know the number is big, too big for my budget.

"That's super generous, Carolena, but if this gown costs as much as the Alexander McQueen, I won't be able to afford it."

"It doesn't cost as much as the Alexander."

"How much?

"Since the Louboutins are last season and the dress has been worn, how about I sell them to you for…"

Carolena's words turned to Charlie Brown adult drone shortly after she said Louboutins. Jesus, Mary, and Gianni Versace! Louboutins are crazy expensive. Carolena obviously mistook my plastic spork for a silver spoon.

"Vivia?" She waves her hand in front of my face. "Hello, Vivia? Are you away with the fairies?"

"Sorry? How much for the dress and shoes?"

"Two hundred and seventy five pounds."

It's a little over four hundred and twenty five dollars. That's two pairs of Ugg boots, a pair of skinny jeans, and a couple orders of Mr. Foo's Spicy Chicken and Noodles plus tax. Or one hundred and eighty *pain au chocolats* from my favorite Parisian patisserie.

"That must be one deep discount."

"Do we have a deal?"

One hundred and eighty days without my morning *pain au chocolat* in exchange for the sexiest, slinkiest, most mesmerizing dress I've ever shimmied in and a pair of Louboutins? Yeah, that's a deal I think I can make.

"Abso-bloody-lutely," I say, borrowing a Poppy-ism.

Chapter 6

French Kissing in the UK

Carolena was wrong. Boujis isn't posh. It's über-posh. The club is the nocturnal playground for the beautiful creatures inhabiting an exclusive netherworld of privilege and pedigree. Millionaire playboys, anorexic supermodels, golden-haired heiresses, bored bluebloods, and megawatt celebrities gather nightly to mingle and mate to an electropop soundtrack. Celestial bodies floating in a neon cloud tinged with perspiration and Chanel No. 5.

As befits Poppy's noble lineage, we arrived late and took a place in the VIP lounge—a long leather banquette situated beneath a wall of tiny light bulbs flashing Boujis in turquoise, purple, and hot pink. She ordered two bottles of Veuve Clicquot and introduced me to her crew of countesses, celebs, and CEOs, before a gorgeous blond with a Rugby player's honed body led her to the dance floor.

I am sweating-balls nervous. The VIP lounge in an über-posh London nightclub is so not my scene. I am just plain old Vivia Perpetua Grant. Ugg-wearing, Groupon-using, Vivia. I haven't had silicone implanted in my breasts or Botox injected in my face. My sisters jiggle and my forehead moves when I smile.

The savages smell my fear. Two emaciated brunettes seated to my right keep eyeing my last-season Louboutins and fixing me with tight smiles.

They move in for the kill before I can escape to the bathroom.

I liberally lubricate my rusty courage with Poppy's expensive champagne. By the time I have finished my flute, I am feeling smooth, mellow, and as entitled to be chilling in the VIP lounge as any other member of Poppy's privileged posse.

"The Parisian is insane, isn't he?" says the brunette with slicked back hair. She looks like one of rhythmless models in the old Robert Palmer "Addicted to Love" video. "He is barking mad."

"Excuse me?"

"Martin."

I stare blankly. Apparently, I am supposed to know mad Martin.

"Martin," the second brunette repeats. "Solveig."

"I'm sorry. Who is Martin Solveig?"

"The DJ."

Her unspoken "duh" hangs heavy in the electropop charged air.

"Oh, yeah," I say, shrugging. "He's great."

I want to say, *"He's an awesome DJ, but it's a shame he's spinning monotonous electropop with an uninspired, pretentious Eurotrash backbeat."*

But I don't.

"What do you think of what he's doing to Röyksopp and Robyn?"

"Who?"

They exchange looks.

"That song"—the Robert Palmer brunette points at the speaker above our heads—"is by the band Röyksopp and Robyn."

"What do you think of the way he is mixing Röyksopp and Robyn with an old Blondie song?"

The rolled eyes and outraged little exhalations tell me they don't really care what I have to say about Milksop and Robin.

"Honestly?" I say, a little drunk.

They both nod like bitchy twin bobbleheads.

"I hate electropop. Immensely. I would rather listen to Ronnie Radke sing "The Drug in Me is You," or Josh Todd sing "Crazy Bitch," or Austin Carlile sing the Teletubby theme song. Rock. Classic rock. Metal. Post-hardcore. That's my kind of music. Not this seizure-inducing series of synthesized lines mixed with electronic drum beats and cold, dead robotic vocals. This is the ambient sound in a Star Wars flick. It's mindless, soulless."

"Here! Here! Heed the words of wisdom ushered forth from the lips of the beautiful, albeit brash, American," says a warbling voice that is more Mockney than Cockney, an affected upper-middle class British accent that one might expect from a cheeky street urchin with posh pretentions.

I squint, hoping to put a face with the voice, but can't see through the neon-tinted smoke machine haze. Out of the darkness comes a tall tattooed familiar form.

It's Bishop. *Freaking*. Raine.

Hair teased and sprayed to resemble a cockatoo, eyeliner smudged around his eyes as if applied by a prepubescent Emo girl. Paisley silk shirt unbuttoned to his navel, half tucked into nut-hugging black leather pants. He's rebel rocker-cum-Jesus. And he's crazy sexy.

"You are an American?" he asks.

"California Girl."

The bobbleheads gasp at my inadvertent Kitty Kat reference, because Bishop dated the singer early in his career and the pair engaged in a tabloid war after their breakup. Bishop stares at me, stony-faced.

"You know what they say about California girls?" I shouldn't reference Kitty Kat's song again, but some wicked inner demon is prodding me with his pitchfork. I always blather when I am nervous, and having Bishop Raine's sexy smoldering eyeliner-ringed gaze fixed on me is making me very, very nervous. Not because he is a celebrity, but because he's really cute. "California girls are unforgettable."

Nobody laughs. The bobblehead bitches turn away from me. Someone coughs. Everyone avoids making eye contact. Finally, Bishop laughs.

"So I've been told."

He barely takes a breath before launching into a monologue about electropop.

"Electropop is a reflection of society's ennui. It's indicative of a larger problem within our culture; our inability to emote, to connect, due, in large part, to social media."

Bishop has a frenetic energy, speed talking, shooting words at me like bullets from a machine gun. It's exhilarating.

"It is pervasive, encroaching, disjointing, transforming us from free-thinking, autonomous individuals into blind, self-destructive lemmings, too ignorant to realize what is happening and too lazy to thwart it."

This leather clad Rasputin with kohl-smudged eyes and eighties glam rock hair has completely enthralled Poppy's posse. Even the bobblehead bitches are nodding and murmuring with cult-like rapture. I dig Bishop's bohemian chic ramblings, not because he's a celebrity, but because I genuinely dig people brave enough to be different and intelligent enough to translate their motives for being different. Nevertheless, I am not enraptured.

"What bullshit!"

Bishop makes a rolling motion with his hand, indicating he would like me to proceed with my scintillating rebuttal.

"I don't believe social media is responsible for society's downfall any more than I believe the president spends his spare time parting the Red Sea."

"Wha'?" Bishop slides onto the booth beside me, leaning his lanky body in close, nudging the bobbleheads away. "You don't believe the American Messiah spends his free time performing miracles?"

"Not unless you consider perfecting his golf drive a miracle."

"Ooo, lookee here," he squeals, black eyes flashing. "We have ourselves a rare and endangered beast: a jaded conservative."

"Hardly!" I snort.

"You're not a jaded conservative, then?"

"Jaded? A little. Conservative?" I tip more champagne into my flute, toss it back, and fix Mister Bishop Sexy Raine with my naughtiest expression. "Only out of the bedroom."

He chuckles.

What the Jesus, Mary, and Gyrating Stripper am I doing? Am I really flirting with Kitty Kat's ex-boyfriend?

Poppy arrives, glowing and breathless.

"Bishop, darling," she says, pressing a kiss to his whiskered cheek. "How are you? Have you been introduced to my friend Vivia?"

Bishop's lips turn up in a mischievous grin. "No, actually, not formally."

"Bishop, this is my soon to be dear friend, Vivia Grant." Poppy leans against the banquette, inadvertently giving the entire posse a peek down the front of her silky black jumper. "Vivia is from San Francisco."

"So, Vivia from San Francisco, what are you doing on this side of the pond?" Bishop asks. "What brings you to Londontown? A butcher, a baker, a candlestick maker?"

"Vivia is a magazine writer," Poppy says. "A brilliant writer, in fact."

"Really?" Bishop leans forward. "How splendid! Did you feel that palpable shift in the atmosphere? Vivia from San Francisco just elevated the IQ level of the room. Perhaps this evening won't be an endless parade of vapid nitwits ensconced in ignorance and glitter."

As if on cue, two beautiful blond barmaids wearing little more than British and American flag pasties on their nipples approach. The one wearing the American flag pasties holds a smartphone.

Bishop ignores them.

British Flag Pasties clears her throat. Bishop looks at the barmaids. The barmaids burst into piercing squeals.

"Yeah, I know." Bishop fixes them with a toothy grin. "I feel it too."

I snort.

"Um, Mister Raine," American Flag Pasties says in a breathy Marilyn Monroe-esque voice. "Can we take your photograph for the Boujis Blog?"

"For the blog, you say?"

American Flag Pasties giggles again, and the tassels hanging from her nipples sway back and forth. British Flag Pasties flutters her glitter-encrusted false eyelashes.

"Well then," Bishop says, leaping to his feet, "of course you may take a snappy. Anything for art."

He grabs my hand and pulls me up to stand beside him.

"You may steal my soul with your smartphone device, but only if Vivia Grant is also in the photo."

British Flag Pasties flutters her bovine falsies at Bishop again, but I can tell she's pissed. If there were a thought bubble hovering over her head right now, it would read, "Ohmygod, like, we only take snappies of, like, famous people."

American Flag Pasties hands her smartphone to Poppy before positioning herself beside me, lips pursed duck-like, hand on hip, breasts thrust forward. British Flag Pasties drapes herself over Bishop.

"On three," Poppy says, her voice barely carrying over the ear-throbbing electropop. "One...two...three..."

Poppy pushes the button and a bright flash of light momentarily blinds us. She hands the phone back to American Flag Pasties.

"Would you mind sending me a copy of that photo?" I ask American Flag Pasties.

"Absolutely," she says, smiling. "Type your e-mail into my phone and I will send the photo to you right now."

I take her phone and type *PerpetuallyVivia@yahoo.com.*

"Thanks." I hand her phone back. "I really appreciate it."

An electropop beat later, the Patriotic Pasties have melted into the crowd.

"We are living in a sequin-encrusted virtual prison," Bishop says, sliding onto the booth beside me. "A sequin-encrusted prison where the economic elite hog along in plump luxury—destroying the planet as they go—and the destitute starve for sustenance of edification. We must stop this."

"I wish you would have told me that before I opted for this mini-dress!" I joke, giving my dress a little shimmy and shake. "I don't wish to imprison you with my sequins."

"I surrender." Bishop presses his wrists together. "Perhaps a sequins-encrusted prison is just the fing."

A cocktail waitress bearing a glass of iced water with a twist of lime appears, pasties pointing. She squats gracefully and hands Bishop the iced water.

"Fank you," Bishop says.

"You're welcome, Mister Raine." She arches her back until her pasties nearly poke Bishop in the eye. "Can I bring you anything else?"

The implication is as clear as the glass of iced water. Forget the lime twisted water; I'm the tall glass of something you're looking for, Mister Funny Man. My cheeks flame with heat and I look away, pretending the action on the dance floor is suddenly all-absorbing.

"Does it bother you?" I ask, after the waitress leaves.

"Wha'?" Bishop's eyes are wide with feigned incomprehension. "The notion of being imprisoned within your sequined dress? Not a'tall."

Poppy and her posse laugh. Bishop laughs, but shards of pain glint behind his sparkling eyes.

The bobbleheads roll their eyes at me and change the subject by asking Poppy a question about Délais. While Poppy and the bobblehead bitches chat, the rest of the posse hit the dance floor.

Bishop looks back at me, piercing me with his laser gaze. "Does wha' bother me?"

"That people work so hard to grasp something that is not real."

"Wha'? Are you saying I am not real?"

"No," I say, suddenly sober and sad. "You are real, but your rock star, sex machine, celebrity persona is not."

"Wha'? Are you saying I am not a sex machine?"

He focuses a two-thousand-watt grin on me, and the champagne-induced warmth spreads from my cheeks to my thighs. His flirtatious manner and approachable sex appeal really discombobulate.

Just when I think he's not going to answer me, Bishop launches into a rapid-fire monologue, blitzing me with a barrage of archaic words and revolutionary notions on the vacuous world of celebritydom.

"The phenomenon of celebrity exists to fill a void created by an appalling lack of morals. A pantheon of over-valued, over-paid, over-worshiped celebrities exists because the populace craves fame. They crave fame because they feel lost in the monotony and pointlessness of their existence. They feel lost because the world feels vast and empty. Fame, their brushes with fame, makes them forget we are essentially alone, moving through the universe without purpose or aim. Someone meets a celebrity, a celestial body who has been lifted far above their tiny world, and for a moment, they feel a flicker of purpose, passion, and connectivity."

He pauses, takes a sip of water, and fixes me with a probing, questioning stare.

"Yes," I say, fixing him with an equally probing stare. "But how does the vacuousness of celebritydom make you feel? How do you feel when a desperate being moves into your orbit just so they can feel less alone?"

"Are you interviewing me? Is this for public consumption or merely your own edification?"

Holy Sheisterburger! Bishop Raine just called me out.

"I would be lying if I said I wouldn't give my right breast to land an interview with you, but that's not what this is about. I'm genuinely interested in your answer. Me," I say, pressing my hand to my heart. "Vivia Grant the woman, not Vivia Grant the writer."

"Sacrificing your right breast in the pursuit of knowledge is a trifle extreme, luv," Bishop says, grinning again. "How would you like to make a bargain?"

"A bargain?"

"A barter, trade, swap, quid pro quo…"

"Yes," I say, laughing. "I know what a bargain is. What did you have in mind?"

He leans in close and his whiskered lips brush against my ear. "Here's the fing. I will answer your question and grant you the coveted interview, and all you have to do is give me the tiniest of kisses."

"Wha'?" I say, imitating him. "Trade my journalistic integrity for a single story?"

"Journalistic integrity? Isn't that an oxymoron?"

I slant him a withering look.

He raises his hands in the air. "Kidding. Kidding."

Poppy sticks a fresh glass of champagne in front of my face, which is akin to tossing a bucket of water on Mister Bishop Sexy Raine's smoldering mojo vibes. He's pretty damned hypnotic with his intellectual mumbo-jumbo and his I'll-rip-your-clothes-off-with-my-teeth gaze.

"Here." She presses the glass into my hand. "You look entirely too serious for this venue."

"Thanks." I toss the champagne back in a single swallow and handing her my empty. "It's just what I needed."

"Okay, California Girl," Bishop says. "You can have your interview sans kiss."

"Really?"

"Really." He grins. "Now, fancy a dance?"

Wait! What? Did Bishop Raine really just ask me to dance? This can't be happening.

Bishop stands, pulls me to my feet, dips me low, and plants a big, wet kiss on me. His tongue pushes between my lips, briefly, and I taste lime. The world starts spinning like a Boujis disco ball. I am vaguely aware of a pop, a flash of light, and then Bishop's tongue withdraws, and I am standing, slack-jawed and wide-eyed.

"What just happened?"

"Bishop kissed you," one of the bobblehead bitches says, her lips curling in a fake smile. "And we hate you."

"You hate me?" I blink. "Because Bishop kissed me?"

I am nonsensical. My world is still spinning, and I don't know how to make it stop so I can get off. All I can think of is Luc. What he would say if he knew I was in a posh club macking with Bishop freaking Raine.

"Don't be ridiculous," the other bobblehead says. "We don't hate you because Bishop kissed you; we just hate you."

"Shut up, Katrine!" Poppy snaps.

"We're just kidding."

"Well then, you've rather missed the mark, because nobody else is laughing."

Poppy pierces each of the twins with a don't-fuck-with-me-or-I-will-stab-you-with-my-Louboutin-heel stare until they apologize.

"No worries," I say, teetering on my new heels.

"Come on, Vivia," Poppy says, linking her arm through mine. "Let's take a walk."

We weave our way through the crush of sweaty perfumed bodies, but another of Poppy's friends intercepts us before we reach the loo.

"You go on, Vivia," Poppy says. "I'll join you in a minute."

I leave Poppy near the dance floor and hurry to the loo. I can feel my Dior lip gloss smeared around my mouth, shiny, sticky proof of Bishop Raine's unexpected oral assault.

I hear my best friend's voice in my head.

"Was he worth the Dior?"

Yes. Yes, he was.

Chapter 7

A Right Royal Cock-Up

Text to Stéphanie Moreau:
OMG! You'll never guess where I am or what just happened!

Text from Stéphanie Moreau:
In some swanky hotel in the 7ème, having sexy time with your gorgeous boyfriend?

Text to Stéphanie Moreau:
No! In the loo at Boujis, a posh London club. Bishop Raine just French kissed me.

My phone rings so loud, I nearly drop it in the toilet. Poison's "Talk Dirty to Me" echoes in the tiny stall. That's right, Bret Michaels singing old school hairband rock. Electropop? Whatever. I jab the red circle on my iPhone screen to answer the call.

"Hello?" I whisper.

"Why are you still in London? What do you mean you were French kissing Bishop Raine? Where is Jean-Luc? How does he feel about you French kissing some sleazy comedian?"

Fanny is the most supportive and loyal friend ever. When my ex-fiancé broke off our engagement on the eve of our wedding and got me fired from my job at San Francisco Magazine, Fanny methodically picked up the shards of my shattered life and helped me superglue them back together. She even rode shotgun on my biking "honeymoon" through Provence and Tuscany.

Second, she can be a relentless interrogator. I am talking Spanish Inquisition relentless, putting-you-on-the-rack-and-stretching-your-limbs-like a-rubber-band relentless.

"Vivian? Hello?"

Fanny calls me Vivian because she thinks it's more sophisticated than Vivia. Like Vivian Leigh.

"I'm here," I whisper. "Bishop is not sleazy. He's actually kinda nice."

"Bishop?" Fanny's French accent is unusually thick, a sign she is teetering on the precipice over the valley of Truly Pissed Off. "Bishop is it? So now you're on a first name basis with Bishop Raine? I can think of another man you're on a first name basis with: Jean-Luc de Caumont, your boyfriend. Remember him?"

"Wow!" I pull the phone away from my ear and stare at the screen as if I might find the explanation for Fanny's anti-Bishop tirade. "I had no idea you had such strong feelings about Bishop Raine."

"*Je m'en fiche!*"

I don't care! I whistle low and long. Her transition from thickly accented English to full-on French means I am in deep trouble.

Fanny might be Team Luc, but her reaction is a bit overblown. It's not like I ditched my boyfriend to become a Bishop Raine groupie. I didn't pawn my MacBook and buy an old VW Van so I could follow Bishop from gig to gig.

"Calm your culottes, Frenchy! No need for a revolution," I chuckle, in a dismal attempt at levity. "I am flying to be with Luc in the morning, and the British boy will be but a distant memory."

"I still don't understand why you are in some club in London, French kissing the sleazy comedian, instead of celebrating your one-year anniversary with your boyfriend in Paris. What is this really about, Vivian?"

I tell Fanny about my right royal cock-up with the Prince Harry story, my time in the pokey, and Big Boss Woman's vaguely displeased text.

"Normally, I would choose Jean-Luc every day of the week and three times on Sunday, but after tanking the Harry story, I thought I could save face by going back to my editor with a dishy tell-all about London's reality TV stars." I take several breaths before launching into my final argument. "Choosing Poppy's party over Luc's love-in was a shrewd career move. If I am going to go out, I might as well be on top, and not wallowing in a pit of humiliation over a failed story."

I speak the truth, but deep down something niggles at me. Something else kept me from leaving London, from joining my crazy-hot boyfriend in Paris for some crazy-hot sexy time, but I don't know what that something else is.

Fanny mutters something in rapid French.

Despite countless hours of Rosetta Stone brainwashing, my ability to translate spoken French is no better than a deaf and dumb Inuit. I think she said, "Lord help me teach the old monkey to make funny faces," but I don't know what an old monkey has to do with our conversation or why she would want to teach it to make faces.

"Who is Poppy?"

"Poppy Worthington. Heiress of the Worthington Hotels fortune?"

I wait for Fanny to respond, the muffled thumping of the electropop playing in the background.

"She's a British socialite. She dated Sir Richard Blanchard and Tristan Kent, remember?" I hold my breath and wait for Fanny to say something. Six muffled thumps later, I finish my story. "We met on the street outside the police station. I was trying to hail a cab, waving my arms and jumping up and down like an idiot. Poppy took pity on me. She taught me the proper way to hail a cab."

"What the…" Fanny emits an explosive pffft. "The proper way to hail a cab? Did you really just say that?"

"We have different rules for hailing a cab in London," I say, defensive of my new friend. "She was only trying to help."

"She sounds pretentious."

"Anyway," I say, ignoring the jab. "I told her about my royal cock-up and she invited me to a party at Boujis. It's hosted by Brava TV. Her cousin, Carolena, is the newest Bravalebrity on some show called Ladies of London."

"I still don't understand why you decided to spend the evening with some uppity snot instead of Luc."

The hinges on the bathroom door squeal and the explosive sound of electropop reverberates off the smoked glass partitioning the stalls.

"She is not a snot!" I whisper, cognizant of the stranger on the other side of my stall door. "She's really nice, actually. I think you'd like her."

Fanny mumbles something in French.

Now it's my turn to sit quietly and wait for Fanny to speak, because she will speak. Oh, she'll speak.

"What is going on, Vivian? Why are you letting some sleazy comedian stick his tongue down your throat when you should be with your boyfriend? Has your career become more important than your relationships?"

An exhalation explodes from my lips as if someone delivered a swift uppercut to my solar plexus. I have experienced this sensation before— the breath-robbing, gut-wrenching blunt force trauma caused by one of Fanny's carefully aimed verbal assaults. I remind myself that brutal bluntness and tactless honesty are merely byproducts of her French ancestry. After all, her sharp, pointed questions often needle my conscious and prod me toward deeper introspection.

"Of course friendships matter more than my career," I say, shifting my iPhone from one ear to the other.

"Really? Because I can't remember the last time we had a real, meaningful conversation. Ever since you took that *GoGirl!* job, you've been AWOL in the friend department."

Ouch! Another one-two jab to the solar plexus.

"I'm sorry if you've felt neglected. I've tried to keep in touch with you. I called a bunch of times, but with the time difference and my crazy itinerary—"

"Is Poppy on Facebook and Twitter?"

"What?" Fanny's abrupt change of subjects confuses me. "I don't know if Poppy is on social media."

"Well," Fanny sniffs. "I hope for her sake she has an active Facebook account. God knows, you can't be one of Vivia's friends unless you're active on Twitter, Tumblr, Facebook, and Instagram."

Ding! Ding! Sound the bell Mickey; Rocky is down for the count. This unprovoked boxing match has left me dazed and bewildered. I am flat on my back, prostrate and gasping for breath, but Fanny's still doing her float-like-a-butterfly-sting-like-a-bee victory dance.

"Being a magazine columnist, traveling the world, meeting interesting people. This is my dream."

"It's not your dream, Vivian," Fanny snaps. "Writing a novel about Mary Shelley is your dream—at least, it was before that stupid photo of you and Jett Jericho went viral and you became famous."

"Okay, maybe being a travel columnist for a chick magazine wasn't my dream before, but it is now," I argue, my voice rising. "I am living a dream, and I don't want it to end. If you were a real friend, you would stand by me—"

"Pffft."

"Don't you pffft me!"

"Why? What are you going to do? Send me a strongly worded tweet?"

I let out a low, long whistle to keep from saying something I will regret. She's starting to piss me off.

"Look, Fanny," I say, struggling to control my temper. "I get it. You're not a touchy-feely, I-get-your-pain-sister-kinda gal, but do you have to be so blunt?"

We remain silent for several seconds. When Fanny speaks again, some of the bitter has leeched from her tone.

"I am worried about you, Vivian," Fanny says, pronouncing my name with her nasal French accent. "You have a good thing with Luc—a great thing—and I am afraid you are taking it for granted. I saw how devastated you were after your breakup with Nathan. It killed me to see you in such pain. I supported you—"

"I know you did, Fanny," I say, the piss and vinegar gone from my tone. "And I appreciate it."

Fanny makes a noise low in her throat, a dismissive noise that translates, "Please, it was nothing."

"The love you felt for Nathan was but a drip in the wineglass compared to what you feel for Luc." Fanny's voice is suddenly hoarse. "You might not realize it yet, but it's true, *ma cherié.* I've never seen you as happy as you are when you are with Luc."

An image of Luc holding a sign with the words "You fill my heart with music, Vivia Perpetua Grant" in the arrivals terminal at the Vienna airport, a musician dressed as Mozart playing the violin behind him, flickers in my brain. Luc. Sexy, smart, sometimes-sappy, larger–than-life romantic gestures, Luc. Luc does make me happy. Crazy happy.

"I love Luc. I do." My voice is thick with emotion. "But I love my job, too. I might not have imagined myself a travel columnist, but I have always wanted to be a writer and I love writing travel pieces. I am not ready to trade my suitcase for a stroller. You know what they say, first comes love, then comes marriage, then comes popping Prozac over the baby carriage."

Fanny chuckles. "Oh, Vivian."

"I am not kidding!" Fanny's verbal jabs have loosened secret feelings I have been too frightened to release before this moment. "My mum could have had a brilliant career as an artist, but she gave up art to marry my father, support him in his career, and raise me. I don't want to be my mother, Fanny."

I love my mum, dearly, but I don't want to follow in her domestic footsteps, suppressing my creative spirit, abandoning my goals, in the name of marital bliss. I won't be subjugated by any man...not even Luc.

"Your mum is wonderful, Vivian. Truly."

"Yes, but deep down she's not happy. She knows she could have had a brilliant career. That's why she keeps such a frantic, frenetic pace, rushing between Zumba and poetry readings and Bible study. Her creative spirit has withered and cries out for nurturing."

"Have you ever thought your mum didn't really want an art career? That if she did, nothing, not a domineering husband or an energetic child, would have kept her from painting?"

I exhale again. This is all too deep, too emotional for Boujis. I can't ponder weighty life issues to an electropop soundtrack.

"Luc and I have only been dating for a year—long-distance dating. We have had a whirlwind romance—champagne in Chamonix, bootie calls in Belgium—and I'm not ready for it to end."

"You can't go on dating long-distance forever, Vivian."

"Why?"

Fanny sighs. "If you love Luc-ious, forget the Downton Abbey set and get to Paris."

I grit my teeth. I hate when people refer to Jean-Luc as Luc-ious. It's a stupid, demeaning name coined by one of my Twitter followers after I tweeted a photo of Luc, tanned and shirtless, sailing off the Amalfi Coast.

"I am still on assignment, working on a story. Jean-Luc will wait."

"French men don't wait."

Chapter 8

A Conscious Uncoupling

I sink down and take a seat on the commode. Have I become self-absorbed? I have missed a few of Fanny's phone calls over the last few months—and I've only seen her once since taking the *GoGirl!* gig.

It suddenly occurs to me that I don't know what is going on in my best friend's life, who she is dating, how she spends her Saturdays now that I am not in San Francisco. Fanny is right! I have become a wee bit self-absorbed. Tears prickle my eyelids.

"Vivia? Are you okay?"

Oh shit! It's Poppy. I don't want posh, powerful Poppy to see me weak and weeping. I swipe the tears from my cheeks and open the door, the brightest, phoniest smile plastered on my face.

Poppy narrows her gaze.

"If you think you are fooling me with that smile, you really must be away with the fairies." She tilts her head, and her chic blond bob spills over her bare shoulder. "Whatever is the matter?"

My bottom lip trembles. I can only shrug like some sad six-year-old. Poppy reaches into her Lucite clutch, pulls out her Dior Addict Lip Gloss, and offers the tube to me. I shake my head and tears spill down my cheeks.

"Blimey!" She tosses the lip gloss back into her clutch, puts her arms around me, and pats my back, crooning, "There, there."

I knew it! I told you my instinct about Poppy was spot-on. Behind her stiff upper lip British exterior beats the heart of a warm, huggy California kinda girl. The kind of girl who invites you to a posh party, helps you score discount Louboutins, and shares her Dior Addict with you. Poppy pats my back one last time.

"I must paint a rather pathetic picture."

"Abso-bloody-lutely."

Poppy grins, unabashed, and I can't help but laugh. Her unflinching, unapologetic manner reminds me of Fanny, which makes me feel somehow better and homesick all at once.

"Thanks," I say. "I must look positively wretched, because you broke your No Hug rule."

Poppy grimaces. "Yes, well. I believe I said I don't do kisses." She takes the lip gloss out of her bag again and swipes the bright pink wand over her full lips. "Hugs are permissible, once annually, or on extremely special occasions. You just received your annual hug. You're welcome."

She has such a serious Churchill-esque expression on her face.

"I am serious." She turns away from the mirror and hands me her lip gloss. "Now, care to tell me what catastrophic event has you weeping in a loo stall instead of dancing your arse off?"

While I hit the high notes of my tragic opera, Poppy repairs the water damage to my face, dabbing my cheeks with a puff from her compact. I wait for her to tell me to ignore Fanny's advice, to concentrate on my career, because, after all, she is the CEO of a major hotel chain, but she doesn't.

"Whenever I am struggling with a difficult decision, I try to follow the advice my father always gave me. Would you like me to share my father's advice?"

"Yes."

"When life roars at you, find a quiet place and listen to the whispers in your heart. They will not lead you astray." Poppy lips quiver.

I sense loneliness settling around her like an Armani poncho.

"What does your heart whisper, Vivia?"

Luc. *GoGirl*! Luc.

Maybe I have a schizophrenic heart.

"Are you kidding me?" I joke. "Who can hear a whisper over Martin's mad electropop remixes?"

Poppy doesn't push me.

"Come on, Bishop is worried he offended you. Perhaps you can assuage his guilt." Poppy tosses her compact back into her clutch and snaps it shut. "Besides, Mandy Cohen wants us to do a shot with her, and Prince Harry just arrived with a new blonde."

* * * *

Bishop is deep in conversation with some leggy blonde, but he grins when he sees me. The blonde flips her hair back and I realize she is Wynona Pathlow. She's holding an untouched martini and fiddling with the plastic spear impaling the fat olive in her glass.

I take the flute of champagne Poppy offers me and pretend not to listen to Bishop and Wynona's conversation

Bishop proselytizes to Wynnie about his call for a nation-wide abstinence from voting to draw attention to the "massive economic disparity perpetuated by a preexisting paradigm which is quite narrow and only serves a privileged few and ignores the disenfranchised and discarded lower class."

Wynnie appears to be more interested in her olive than Bishop's plan for a New World Order. And who can blame her, really? When you're pipe cleaner thin, a single olive must look like a veritable feast. I'll bet that single olive contains more calories than she consumes in a day. I stare at her hard and send a telepathic message.

Go on, girl. Binge. Eat the olive. You can run a marathon tomorrow to make up for it.

Wynnie looks up, and we make eye contact. She stares right through me. Poor thing. Malnutrition must be impeding her vision.

I have to wrap both hands around my champagne flute to keep from Yelping the nearest Italian joint and having a pizza with extra olives delivered to Boujis in care of Wynona Pathlow.

When Bishop stems the flow of his Niagara Falls-sized monologue long enough to take a sip of his lime water, Wynnie releases her grasp on the olive spear, rises majestically, and leaves without uttering a word.

"Looks like you and Wynnie just had a conscious uncoupling," I say, referencing the ridiculous phrase the actress used to announce her divorce from her husband, Chris Morgan.

Bishop looks at me and grins.

"You fink?"

"Abso-bloody-lutely."

"Good," he says, rubbing his hands together. "My divinely inspired though wholly devious plan worked."

"What plan?"

Bishop finishes his lime water, deposits the glass on a low table in front of us, and leans over to confess his wicked, wicked little secret.

"The former Missus Morgan is an insufferable prig who believes serving on the board of a homeless charity nulls and voids her grossly lavish lifestyle."

"Harsh."

"Reality is often harsh, luv," he says, leaning back and crossing his long, lanky leather-clad legs at the ankles. "Wynona lives in a self-perpetuated, self-gratifying, delusive fantasyland wherein dispensing wisdom to the masses on where they might purchase pricey monogrammed knickers qualifies as a philanthropic act."

"Isn't it hypocritical to criticize a system that has brought you untold fortunes and fame? You fault Wynona Pathlow her lavish lifestyle, but I remember reading you flew to India first class, cruised Jaipur in a Mercedes Benz, and rented an elephant to serve you peanuts or something."

"Balderdash!" Bishop slams his fist down on his knee. "That is complete and utter rubbish. I loathe peanuts."

We laugh.

"Poppy tells me you are madly in love with a Frenchman. Is this true?" He doesn't wait for my answer. "What a bloody shame! I rather fancy shagging someone with a firm grasp on grammar."

Hold up. Did Bishop Raine just say he wanted to shag me?

"I don't know what I find more flattering: your expressed desire to shag me or your bizarrely worded praise of my vocabulary."

He tosses his hair and laughs.

"Nice tattoo," I say, briefly touching the Sanskrit symbol inked on one of his forearms. "What does it mean?"

Bishop explains the significance of the symbol and asks me if I have any tattoos.

The blush that stains my cheeks is reflexive. Although a year has passed since my wild night in Cannes, when, fuelled by copious champagne cocktails and Jett Jericho's compelling philosophy, I staggered into a tattoo parlor and came out inked.

"Oh-ho!" Bishop cries gleefully. "Methinks I smell a tramp stamp."

"I don't think so."

"No?"

"No."

"Out with it." He makes a regal rolling gesture with his hand. "Regale me with the tale of your descent into debauchery, sparing none of the sordid details."

With Poppy listening, I tell Bishop Raine about one of the most humiliating events of my life.

"I lied to my ex-fiancé and told him he was my first lover. A few days before our wedding, we were at our favorite wine bar when we ran into Travis Trunnell, an arrogant jackass I slept with while I was in college."

Bishop waggles his eyebrows and grins. I can almost hear the "Yeah, baby, yeah," in his head.

"Travis brought his drunk, idiotic college roommate to the wine bar with him that night. Drew." I wrinkle my nose when I say his name.

"Drew remembered me and told Nathan, my ex, all about my late night booty call with 'his boy' Travis."

"You dirty girl!" Bishop crows.

"Not really," I protest, my cheeks warming. "Nathan ended our engagement. Naturally, I was devastated, but my best friend convinced me to go on the honeymoon anyway."

"Did you?" Bishop asks.

"Did she?" Poppy grins and raises her champagne flute in tribute. "Abso-bloody-lutely."

We clink glasses.

"I was on the beach in Cannes, nursing my broken heart and a few champagne cocktails, when I met Jett Jericho. He gave me this whole speech about transformation and regeneration, about going down in flames and rising up from the ashes."

Bishop snorts and rolls his eyes.

"What? His speech was very empowering."

"Go on, Vivia. Tell the rest of the story."

"Anyway," I continue, trying to ignore Poppy's posse, listening with rapt attention. "Jett said—"

"Jett said!" Bishop scoffs, rolling his eyes again.

"Jett said I needed to do something bold, something brave, something that would symbolize my regeneration."

The bobbleheads slant me a withering we-are-so-bored look, and I suddenly question my wisdom in sharing a story about a time when I was totally off my game, fragile and confused.

"Go on, Vivia," Poppy encourages. "Tell him the best part."

"Long story short, I was drunk and Jett was persuasive—very persuasive. I woke up the next morning with pink hair and a tattoo."

"Come on then. Don't be shy." Bishop sits up, leans forward, and rests his elbows on his knees. "Let us have a look at the life transforming tattoo."

"Shut up."

"Wha'?" Bishop cries. "Only a wretched, heartless tease would begin a joke with no intention of sharing the punch line."

"I can't."

I fix him with an intense let-it-go-please stare, but he merely grins his wicked, wily, charming grin.

"Go on then. How bad can it be? Show us."

I lean close to Bishop, cup my hand around his ear, and whisper, "I can't show you my tattoo because it is located in a private area."

Bishop looks at me, eyes wide, mouth agape. I know what he is about to say before he even moves his sexy lips.

"You tattooed your privates? You are a dirty girl!"

The bobbleheads stare at me, noses crinkled, lips curled in disgust. The ripped Rugby player cracks his knuckles and grins. Poppy slaps Bishop.

"Stop it, Bishop! Leave Vivia alone!"

"Don't blame me," Bishop cries in mock outrage. "Blame Jett Jericho and his perverted persuasive philosophy. What possibly possessed him to convince Vivia to tattoo her privates? I always thought he was a trifle… outré!"

"Very funny!" I laugh. "Almost as funny as that scene of you shoving baggies of heroin up Sage Roman's ass in *Audition at the Apollo*."

"Ouch," Bishop says, reaching his hand around his back. "Could someone pull the knife out of my back? Brutus?"

A cocktail waitress arrives with a new bottle of champagne—compliments of Boujis and Brava TV—and Poppy's posse loses interest in my ass tat tale.

Bishop, however, does not.

"So what did you have tattooed on your bum? An inspirational saying or culturally significant symbol?"

"It's a cartoon sushi roll."

"A sushi roll?" Bishop tilts his head and squints as he tries to unravel the mystery of my ass tat. "Is that a metaphor for humanity's cohesion and inter-dependence?"

"No."

"Ah-ha!" Bishop laughs, slapping his knee. "You were being esoteric in using the sushi roll, right? It wasn't meant to be literal, but rather abstract. Sushi is often served with Agari, green tea. Agari literally translated means, 'Rise up.' Ergo, sushi represents your rise from the ashes, regeneration."

His explanation of the meaning behind my sushi roll ass tat is so fucking brilliant and so much more inspired than the real meaning, I am tempted to agree with him.

"Nope."

Oh my God! I've never felt more infinitesimally insignificant and ignorant as I do right now—speaking to Bishop Raine about my ridiculous cartoon sushi roll tattoo.

"Well," he says, leaning back and crossing his ankles again. "Are you going to illuminate, enlighten, edify me with the significance of your transformative tattoo?"

I tell him about Raw, the sushi restaurant I worked at to help pay my college tuition, and about the ridiculous T-shirt with cartoon sushi rolls and the slogan, "I like it Raw" that I had to wear. I tell him how much I loved wearing my Raw T-shirt because the naughty, stupid slogan made me giggle like a fifteen-year-old, and how much my ex-fiancé hated, I mean gut-level-loathed it.

Bishop listens quietly, his gaze fixed on my face like two black laser beams.

"So what you're saying is your fixation with cartoon sushi rolls was originally motivated by your indentured servitude to crass commercialism, but when you met the illustrious and enlightened Mister Jett Jericho, your fixation underwent a transmogrification into a symbol, an icon, if you will, representing liberation from the matrimonial shackles that threatened to strip you of your individuality." Bishop takes a deep breath. "In essence, the sushi roll now represents your rebellion against the subjugation of your sex."

Transmogrification? Fuck me. If I weren't in love with Luc, I would hock my MacBook, buy a VW Van, and follow Bishop freaking Raine around the world just so I could listen to him utter brainy words like transmogrification. He's a word nerd's orgasmic dream.

"Yes." I cross my legs and twist my ponytail around my finger. "That is precisely what I was saying."

Chapter 9

Sex, On My Mind

By the time I teeter out of Boujis and into Poppy's waiting limousine, I am as giddy as Wynona Pathlow at an olive farm. I have consumed enough expensive champagne to make my un-tattooed private parts feel warm and fuzzy—shit, even my non-private parts feel warm and fuzzy. I did shots with Mandy Cohen, the president of BravaTV, and persuaded her to allow me to interview the cast of Brash Brits. I negotiated an interview with Bishop Raine. And I have pretty much sealed the deal on an eternal and abiding friendship with Poppy Whitney Worthington.

The promised interviews have restored my battered pride and salvaged my career. Bishop's shameless flirting has stroked my ego and left me feeling rawther horny. Who needs a British Airways flight? I am so high I could float to Paris!

We are about to pull away from the club when someone raps on the limousine window. The window magically opens and Bishop leans in, grinning and reeking of sex appeal.

"Fancy a lift, Bishop?" Poppy asks.

"Brilliant."

He doesn't wait for the driver to open the door for him—scoring major unpretentious points with me—folding his long, lanky body into the limo and closing the door behind him.

Poppy moves to the seat opposite, leaving Bishop and me to sit together.

I can feel his hot leather-clad leg pressing against my bare thigh. Despite my rock star fixation, I've never felt a man in leather and it's kinda sexy. I wonder if I could get Luc to wear a pair of leather pants?

I snort.

"Wha'?"

"Nothing. Sorry."

"I'll bet you are a Scorpio, aren't you?"

I look at Bishop. "Yes, how did you know that?"

"You're mysterious, sensual, charming, and a little crazy—hallmarks of a Scorpion." The limousine passes beneath a street lamp and golden light shines on Bishop's shaggy tasseled hair, making him look like a fallen angel. "And…I googled you."

Bishop Raine googled me? How is that even possible? Maybe someone slipped a roofie in my Veuve Clicquot and I am stoned out of my mind. Maybe I am hallucinating. Or, maybe I am still in the pokey. Maybe another inmate shanked me and I am tits-up. Maybe Bishop really is an angel, and this limo is taking me to that big party in the sky.

My head suddenly feels too heavy for my neck, my eyelids too weighty to keep open. I have not been roofied or shanked. I am tipsy—which sounds ever so much nicer than drunk. I close my eyes, rest my head, and listen to Bishop's hypnotic voice as he chats with Poppy. His warm leather-clad leg pressed against mine, the limo's rhythmic sway, and the patter of raindrops on the roof lull me to a very warm, very happy place.

"Vivia? Vivia, darling, you need to wake up now," Poppy whispers, gently shaking my shoulder. "We've arrived at the Rubens."

I try to open my eyes, but I feel like Dwayne "The Rock" Johnson deadlifting four hundred pounds. My eyelids are that heavy.

"I don't want to go to the crappy old Rubens. Please don't make me. They're a bunch of meanies." My words come out tangled, my tongue thick and furry like I inhaled Poppy's faux fur shrug in my sleep. "Can't I just sleep in your limousine?"

Bishop laughs. A bloody booming laugh.

"Shhhh."

When I open my eyes I see why Bishop's laughter sounded so unusually loud. My head is resting on his shoulder—and I have drooled, a little.

No! This isn't happening. This. Is. Not. Happening. I sit up and lift my head off of Bishop's shoulder.

Sober now. Completely sober.

Well, almost sober.

"Sorry about that," I mumble, making a quick swipe of my damp chin.

"Not at all." Bishop grins.

"Bishop, be a darling, won't you?" Poppy opens her door, and raindrops plop on the leather upholstery. "Help me walk Vivia to her room."

Bishop opens his door, hops out, and holds his hand out to me. I stare at his long, slender be-ringed fingers and wonder what the mega-Zen, sober star thinks of my sloppy antics. My bruised pride will not let me take his hand. I have my dignity.

"Thanks," I say, looking up at him. "I've got this."

Bishop steps back, and I step out of the limo.

Either I drank more tonight than I realized, or London's Public Works Department installed moving sidewalks while I was in Boujis.

I miss the curb completely. Bishop wraps his arm around my waist and pulls me to him, saving me from making a humiliating face-plant on the moving sidewalk.

Sweet Christian! What a sight that would have made—me spread eagle on the sidewalk, Louboutins kicked off, sparkly dress around my waist, while Buckingham Guards secretly snapped pictures from the palace windows.

"Steady on, California Girl," Bishop whispers, his lips brushing against my ear. "Maybe you should have stuck to lime water."

His whiskers tickle and I giggle.

"Right then," Poppy says, linking her arm through mine. "Onward and upward."

I am still giggling when I spot a tall, muscular man standing in the rain, collar of his black trench coat turned up, framing his angled, handsome, dark face. A raindrop pelts my right eyeball, the world turns blurry, and I blink until the Mr. Gorgeous Trench Coat comes back into focus.

Holy. Shit.

"Luc!" I pull out of Bishop's grasp and stumble over to my boyfriend, throwing myself into his arms. "What are you doing here? I didn't expect you."

Luc hugs me and then steps back. His gaze flicks from me to Bishop and back to me again.

"Obviously."

If the shock of finding my boyfriend standing in the rain outside my hotel wasn't sobering enough, his cool, pseudo-accusatory tone is like having a bucket of ice water poured on my face. Now this is a right royal cock-up.

"Luc," I say, gesturing towards Poppy and Bishop, "these are my friends, Poppy and Bishop."

Did I just classify Bishop Raine as a friend?

"Hey mate." Bishop holds out his hand. "You must be the Frenchman."

Thank you, Bishop.

Luc shakes Bishop's hand.

"Viv is barking mad for you," Bishop says, winking at me. "You're all she talked about tonight. Luc. Luc. Luc."

Viv? Shut up, Bishop! Shut up!

Luc smiles, but it is one of his tight, I-am-tolerating-you-for-propriety's-sake expressions. Luc is unfailingly polite and polished. Sometimes, it makes me feel gauche.

"A pleasure to meet you, Luc." Poppy links arms with Bishop and pulls him back to the limo. "We'll leave you two alone. Talk to you soon, Vivia."

Luc wraps his arm around my waist to steady me. We walk into the hotel, cross the lobby, and get into the lift. I expect Luc to pin me to the wall and give me a little love in an elevator, but he just stands beside me staring at the control panel.

I peek at him out of the corner of my eye and my heart dips to my heels. Damn, he's fine. His hair, damp from the rain, is tousled. I want to reach over and brush the hair from his tanned forehead.

"I missed you." I reach for his hand and lace my fingers with his. "A lot." His hand is so cold. "Were you waiting a long time?"

I look at him full-on and my heart dips again.

"Long enough."

He pierces me with his smoldering gaze—only it's not a sexy smolder; it's an angry smolder. Stubble covers his angular jaw, giving him a slightly dangerous appearance.

"Luc, you're not jealous of Bishop are you?"

"Should I be?"

The elevator dings and the doors slide open. A liveried porter is waiting to board the elevator. He steps aside, letting us pass.

Luc follows me down the dimly lit hall. I fumble in my purse, trying to find my room key. My hands are shaking so much my lip gloss and iPhone fall out of my purse and onto the floor. Luc scoops them up and dumps them back into my purse. He sticks his hand in my purse, pulls out my room key, and slips it into the lock.

"*Après vous*," he says, holding the door open. "*S'il vous plaît.*"

Formal French. He is pissed.

I step into my room, turn on a small lamp, and stare at the bed. A massive bouquet of pink roses, tied with a black bow, rests on my pillow.

"Did you bring those with you all the way from Paris?"

"*Non*," Luc says, shaking his head. "I phoned the Concierge from the airport."

Luc. Generous, thoughtful, larger-than-life romantic gestures Luc. Maybe Fanny's right. Maybe I should ditch the writing gig, marry Luc, and have a herd of dark-haired French babies.

"*Merci beaucoup, mon amour.*"

Even in Louboutins, I have to stand on my tiptoes to press a kiss to his lips. He tastes good—like rain and romance—and smells good, too.

Luc stops kissing me so suddenly, I have to put out my hands to balance myself. He moves over to the sitting area and shrugs out of his trench coat. He tosses his coat on the couch and takes a seat in a wingback chair. Luc is always impeccably dressed, but tonight he is GQ-sharp in a black pinstriped suit, crisp white shirt, and charcoal tie.

He leans back, stretches one leg out in front of him, puts an elbow on the arm of the chair, and presses a finger to his temple, staring at me in a way that is both erotic and disconcerting.

Sometimes, when we reunite after several weeks apart, I feel like a schoolgirl—nervous, shy, and awkward. Standing in the middle of my hotel room in a skimpy, sparkly mini-dress and nosebleed high Louboutins, buzzed from doing shots with Mandy Cohen, my legs feel long and gangly and I don't know what to do with my hands.

"*Parlez-en à moi*, Vivia?" Luc's low, husky voice is like foreplay, slow and seductive. "*Qu'est-ce qui s'est passé ce soir?*

"What happened tonight?" I repeat his question in English, a feeble stalling tactic. "What do you mean?"

Luc stares at me.

My nerves kick into overdrive and I start blathering. I tell Luc about Detective Inspector Mangina, the bogus stalking charges, my serendipitous encounter with Poppy, Big Boss Woman's ominous-sounding text, the Brava party, and scoring interviews with the newest Bravalebrities and Bishop Raine. Omitting only one teensy-weensy detail—Bishop sticking his tongue down my throat—because it's a trivial detail, really.

I mean, Bishop's kiss meant nothing. Nothing. The kiss was probably just all part of his Yeah, Baby-Rock Star shtick. Sticking his tongue down someone's throat is just his enthusiastic Mockney way of saying hello. That's my story, at least, and I am sticking to it.

Luc is still staring at me, like he knows I am holding back, like he knows Bishop and I played hide-and-seek with our tongues in the VIP lounge at Boujis.

Ridiculous. He couldn't possibly know. Could he? Maybe he can smell Bishop's cologne, or lime water, or my rotten stinking guilt.

Please God, please let me get away with this one little indiscretion and I promise I won't kiss another man as long as we both shall live. Amen.

Luc's lips pull up in a wicked, sexy smile. He crooks his finger and beckons me come.

Thank you, Jesus!

Chapter 10

Sex, Lies & Louboutins

"*Mon Dieu*," Luc whispers against my mouth. "Do you know how damned sexy you look in that dress? I can't decide whether I want to rip it off you or make you wear it for the rest of our lives."

Our lives. My stomach flips. My stomach always flips when Luc kisses me, or looks at me, or talks to me, or…

He is still sitting on the wingback. I am straddling his legs, my miniskirt pushed high on my thighs, my arms around his broad shoulders. Not to be pervy or anything, but I fell in love with Luc's backside the first time I saw it riding at the head of my "honeymoon" bike tour. Broad shoulders, tapered waist, sculpted ass, muscular legs flexing with each push of the pedal. Just remembering that day makes me horny.

I scoot closer to him, press my breasts against his chest, and flick my tongue over his lips. If that's not an invitation to tear my beaded dress from my body, I don't know what is.

Luc groans low in his throat. "Wrap your legs around me."

"I thought you'd never ask," I murmur, wrapping my legs around his lean waist. "What took you so long?"

Luc grins.

He carries me to the bed as if I am nothing more than a sparkly dress and pair of empty Louboutins, his arm muscles flexing around me, his broad hands cupping my bum.

He removes one hand from my bottom and sweeps the flowers off my pillow. And then we are on the bed, frantically tearing at each other's clothes, driven by a feverish desire to press our bodies together.

I try to kick off my heels.

"*Non*," Luc moans, against my mouth. "Leave them on. They drive me wild."

We make love—Luc still in his suit, me naked except for my Louboutins—until our bodies are slick with perspiration and our chests heave from the exertion.

Luc falls onto the bed beside me and we listen to the sounds of our ragged breathing and London's late night traffic outside the window. Drowsy from the champagne, wrapped in a contented post-conjugal relations cocoon, I am about to drift off when Luc gets out of bed.

"Where are you going?" My words tangle together.

"I will be right back, *mon cœur*." Luc leans down and kisses me, his tongue circling my lips. "I just have to get something."

When he climbs back into bed beside me, he has removed his suit, turned off the lamp, and closed the curtains against the loud London night sounds. It's dark, but I don't need the light to recognize my lover's hard body.

He pulls the blankets over us and I snuggle against him, resting my head on his shoulder. It's the best pillow in the world.

"Happy Anniversary, *mon cœur*," Luc says, pressing a kiss to my temple. "One year ago today, you walked up to me in your ridiculous pink riding gear and walked away with my heart."

I love when he kisses my temple and I love when he calls me *mon cœur*. My heart.

"Happy anniversary, Luc. I love you."

"When you didn't show up in Paris, I was afraid maybe..." He clears his throat. Several seconds pass before he speaks again, his voice thick with emotion and heavily accented. "I was afraid you had fallen out of love with me."

Tears fill my eyes. I have been a crap girlfriend, leaving Luc alone in Paris on our anniversary to pursue a story about shallow fame-whore reality television stars.

"That's not possible, Luc." I roll onto my side, facing him. "I will love you forever."

Luc is strong, confident, and in possession of just a little of the arrogance that comes with being a noble-born Frenchman, so seeing him being vulnerable feels strange. I am usually the vulnerable, anxious, emotionally needy one.

"Does that mean I don't need to worry about you running off with Bishop Raine?"

Ouch. What is that sharp pain in my chest? Guilt?

Before we met, Luc was engaged to a French woman who cheated on him and then told him she had only wanted to marry him because of his title, so I shouldn't be surprised at his fears about my fidelity.

"Bishop?" I laugh softly and nuzzle his cheek with my nose. "Why would you even worry about him?"

"I know all about your secret affection for the rock men."

"The rock men?"

I rest my head on Luc's chest and listen to the steady thump-thump-thump of his heart. His tanned, muscular chest smells like male sex. He always smells good.

"Ronnie Radke. Chet Michaels."

"Bret," I laugh, kicking my heels off and pressing my cold feet against Luc's warm legs. "Bret Michaels."

"So you admit it, then? Your secret passion for the rock men?"

"Rockers," I correct, trailing a path through Luc's chest hair with my finger. "In the past, I did have a crush on some rock stars, but that was before you."

"*Bon*," Luc murmurs, pressing another kiss to the top of my head. "I was starting to think I would need to buy a pair of those hideous leather pants and learn to play the electric guitar."

"No leather pants?" I laugh. "*Merde*! Now what am I going to get you for Christmas?"

"I can think of a few things," he chuckles, slapping my bare bottom. "None of them involve me wearing leather."

We both laugh. When Luc speaks again, his tone is serious. "Vivia, I need to say something."

"Mm-hmm?" I yawn and wiggle closer to his warmth. "What is it?"

"I don't like the idea of you going to clubs and spending the night drinking with strangers."

What the Fred Flintstone? My eyes snap open. I squint, trying to read his expression shrouded in the darkness, to determine if he meant to sound like a circa-1950s domineering husband.

"What does that mean?"

"Only..." Luc hesitates.

"Yes?"

"You are a beautiful, bubbly woman, traveling alone in a foreign country. I wouldn't want anyone to misinterpret your open and friendly nature as, as..."

"As what, Luc?"

"Flirtation."

This is how it begins. The slow, steady loss of my independence in exchange for a wedding band. First comes love, then comes marriage, then comes popping Prozac over the baby carriage.

Indignation and outrage bubble inside me, threatening to boil over. I am tempted to scald Luc for possessing such a chauvinistic attitude, but I remember my flirty exchanges with Bishop and turn down the heat of my indignation to a slow simmer.

"Let me understand this, you are telling me not to do my job because someone might misinterpret my behavior as slutty?"

"*Non!*" Luc holds me tighter. "I am not saying that, *mon amie*. I would never say that."

I relax a little.

"What are you saying then?"

"*Merde! J'ai fait une bourde.*" Luc runs a hand through his hair. It's a Luc-ism I love. "That came out wrong."

"I'll say."

"What I meant to say is, please be careful." He squeezes me. "I could not live with myself if anything terrible happened to you."

I kiss his collarbone and promise not to do anything stupid or needlessly dangerous.

We fall asleep, foreheads together, legs and arms entwined.

Sometime just before dawn, Luc rouses me from a deep champagne-induced sleep by kissing me. He is on top of me, using his arms for support, but I can feel his erection pressing firmly against my abdomen.

"Again?"

"Mmmhmm."

"So soon?"

"It's never too soon, *mon cœur*."

He slides down the bed and puts his head between my legs, kissing my thighs, teasing me with his tongue, his teeth, until I grab him by the hair and pull him back up.

"Now, Luc," I moan, wrapping my legs around his waist. "Make love to me now."

He pushes inside me slowly, inch by thick, throbbing inch, all the while murmuring endearments to me in French. I climax before he pushes all the way inside me—a deep, powerful, dizzying orgasm that stirs a torrent of emotions within me.

"Luc! Luc!"

I say his name over and over, tears spilling down my cheeks. I hate when I orgasm-cry . It makes me feel like a weak, clingy female.

"I am here, *mon cœur*," he whispers in my ear, wrapping his arms around my waist, holding me tight against my body. "If you want me, I will always be here."

Chapter 11

I Kissed a Girl

I wake a few hours later to the sound of my iPhone blowing up. I assume the incessant blinging is my mum texting me her usual maternal inquiries and admonitions. Don't forget to go to Mass. When are you moving back to San Francisco? Are you ever going to settle down and give me grandbabies?

I open my eyes, blinking as bright mote-filled light streaming from between the curtains blinds me.

"*Merde*," Luc mumbles. "*Je déteste ce telephone.*"

He rolls to his side, affording me a delicious view of his lovely backside, and grabs my purse from the floor. He rolls back and hands me the purse.

"Please make it stop, *mon cœur.*"

I pull my iPhone out of my purse, enter my passcode, and stare in shock at the text and e-mail icons.

Seventy-two texts. One hundred and three e-mails.

I haven't gotten this many messages since the Jett Jericho photo went viral.

Oh shit!

Oh fuck!

A cement lump forms in the pit of my stomach as I try to recall details from the previous evening. Boujis. Booze. Bad music. Nothing terrible happened, did it?

A flashbulb pops in my brain and a still frame of Bishop bending me over his arm and thrusting his tongue between my lips comes into focus.

Oh shit!

I click open the text message app and my fears are immediately confirmed. Somehow, the world has learned of my indiscretion.

So much for answered prayers!

Text from Camilla Grant:
Vivia, it's your mum. Anna Johnson posted a photograph on
the Facebook of you kissing that raunchy comedian. She said it's
gone epidemic. Again, Vivia? Again?

No. No. No. No. This isn't really happening. Not again. And what the
fuck is wrong with Anna Johnson? My mum's arch nemesis and nosy
neighbor must have me on Google Alerts.

Text from Stéphanie Moreau:
Whatthefuckwereyouthinking? Have you seen the picture yet?
Has Luc seen the picture? You do realize he was going to ask you
to marry him this weekend?

What the what? I look at Luc, dozing beside me. Luc is going to
propose this weekend? He said something in a text, but I didn't take him
seriously. I thought he was just teasing. I shift my gaze to the nightstand,
to a small blue velvet box resting on the nightstand. A ring box.

Oh my freaking God! Luc *is* going to propose. To me. This morning.
Tears fill my eyes and clog my throat.

Text from Poppy Worthington:
I feel positively dreadful! This is my fault. Please call me. I
will do anything I can to make this right with your Frenchman.

Maybe the situation isn't as bad as I imagine. I type "Bishop Raine
photo kiss" into the search bar. My search reveals a surprising—or
unsurprising—number of relevant photos, including a small poorly-
lit snapshot of Bishop kissing me. The headline above the photo reads,
"Bishop Raine's New California Girl." I click on the link and speed-read
the article.

Bishop Raine's New California Girl
By James Adair
Bishop Raine kissed a girl and he liked it! Kitty Kat's ex
was spotted creating fireworks in one of London's hot-hot-hot
nightclubs last night with a sexy redhead.
According to an eyewitness, Raine pinned the girl against the
wall and kissed her passionately for several minutes.
Another anonymous witness identified the redhead as GoGirl!

columnist Vivia Grant. This witness said Ms. Grant was the
aggressor, not notorious womanizer Raine.
"She flirted with him all night," the anonymous witness said.
"She called him a sex machine and said she wanted to imprison
him in her mini-dress."
Raine has had a reputation as a...

The rest of the irresponsibly researched and poorly written article is a recap of Bishop's dating history. Frankly, I don't give one Sanskrit tattoo that he dated a supermodel and Yoga guru. All I care about is the egregious attack on my character and what Luc will say when he reads the yellow journalism.

I did not call Bishop Raine a sex machine, nor did I say I wanted to imprison him in my mini dress. As if!

Text to Poppy Worthington:
Do you know who took the photo and how it ended up on the
Internet?

I know the answer before Poppy's text hits my phone: the bobblehead bitches. Who else would have snapped the humiliating picture and sold it to the tabloids? Wynona Pathlow?

Text from Poppy Worthington:
Trust me, I am on it. You just focus on fixing things with your
handsome Frenchmen. Leave the rest to me.

I haven't known Poppy that long, but my gut tells me when she says she is on it, she is on it.

Text from Travis Trunnell:
It was hard enough for me to wrap my mind around you being
with a French bike guide, but Bishop Raine? Really, Vivia? You
are trying my patience, woman.

I grit my teeth. Stupid old Travis Trunnell knows Luc is a Professor of Literature at the University of Montpellier and acts as a bike guide for his brother's tour company only on occasion, but he insists on demeaning him just to piss me off.

Sweet San Antonio! I ain't got time to play with the Texan. Not now. Not when Luc is moments from waking up and finding out his "sexy redhead" is a shameless hussy, a brazen flirt who swapped spit with a Rock Man.

Maybe he won't find out. Maybe...

My phone blings again, alerting me to an incoming text.

Text from 44 20 7834 6600:
Let's get together.

Text to 44 20 7834 6600:
Who is this?

Text from 44 20 7834 6600:
Your favorite hypocritical, elephant renting, peanut eating, French kisser.

Poppy must have given Bishop Raine my phone number.

Text to 44 20 7834 6600:
Wait a minute! I thought you didn't eat peanuts?

Text from 44 20 7834 6600:
(Insert laughter) Very good, California Girl. You were paying attention. This probably isn't the best time, but if you still want that interview.

Text to 44 20 7834 6600:
Now? Seriously? I am in bed with my boyfriend—soon to be ex-boyfriend after he sees the photo of us kissing.

Text from 44 20 7834 6600:
Relax, luv. It was just a kiss. Do you do yoga? You should.

I sneak a peek at Luc. It was just a kiss. A stupid, unexpected, though not wholly unappreciated, kiss. I don't think Luc will see it as just another kiss, though.

Text from 44 20 7834 6600:
Let me know when you want to do that interview. I know this

great place that plays electropop. I'll bring the lime-water. You bring those sexy shoes. Kidding.

Text from 44 20 7834 6600:
Not really.

I am about to power off my iPhone when I get another text.

Text from Louanne Collins-London:
Congratulations! Thanks to your latest stunt Vivia Grant and GoGirl! Magazine are trending on Twitter. Huge circulation increase. #Raise #Bonus P.S. Need 2000 words by COB Friday. Next assignment & travel details to follow.

Luc reaches over, takes my phone, slides the mute button to silent, and tosses it on the floor.

"Forget that 'orrible phone." He pulls me onto his naked chest. "Nothing on Twitter is as important as what is happening in this moment."

He pronounces Twitter the French way—Twee-ter—which usually makes me giggle, but not this time.

Luc frowns.

"What is it?"

"What?" I ask, stalling. "What is what?"

"You are frowning, *mon cœur.*"

I stare into his green-brown eyes, eyes I have lost myself in dozens of times in the last year, eyes looking at me with concern and limitless love.

What have I done?

Tears spill down my cheeks and onto Luc's chest. He sits up quickly. I sit up, crossing my arms over my naked breasts. I've never felt more vulnerable.

"Vivia, what is it? Tell me, please."

I try to speak, but the words evaporate in my throat before reaching my mouth. Shifting emotions play across Luc's handsome face. Concern. Confusion. Fear.

How do you tell your boyfriend you kissed another man? What is the proper way to break such news? I am pretty sure it doesn't involve being naked and in bed.

"I need to tell you something."

I snatch Luc's shirt off the floor, stick my arms in the holes, secure a few buttons, and begin pacing the length of the room. Luc watches me, one eyebrow raised, lips pressed in a grim line. His stoic expression reminds me of Detective Inspector Mangina, and soon I am blabbering like a stool house pigeon.

"It was only one stupid kiss. One kiss. I wouldn't even mention it, because it's no big deal, but someone took a photo and now it's on the Internet, and it's becoming, like, a big freaking deal."

I stop pacing and face Luc. I am waiting for him to laugh and tell me it's no big deal, but he doesn't laugh, doesn't exonerate me. He just stares at me standing at the end of the bed, wrapped in his shirt, my hair hanging in tangles.

"You kissed Bishop Raine?"

"No."

"You let him kiss you, though?"

I shrug, letting my arms dangle beside me, Luc's long sleeves hiding my hands.

"Let me see it, Vivia."

"See what?"

"The photo."

I dart a guilty glance at my iPhone on the floor beside the bed. Resistance is futile, really. The photograph, uploaded last night, has gone "epidemic," spreading to blogs, e-zines, and all manner of social media. I am beaten.

I bend down and retrieve my traitorous iPhone. Opening the Twitter app, I find a tweet of the photo with the least offensive hashtags and hand the iPhone to Luc. He stares at the image on the screen, clenching and unclenching his jaw.

He chuckles, but the sound isn't easy or natural.

"No big deal."

He drops my iPhone on the bed, stands, and shoves his legs into his trousers.

"Luc," I plead, resting my hand on his tanned, muscular forearm. "Let me explain, please."

"You don't need to explain."

"I didn't cheat on you, Luc." My voice cracks. "You have to believe me!"

Luc makes an indignant noise in his throat.

"Is that why you think I am upset? Do you truly believe I am worried you cheated on me with that…that…" Luc runs his fingers through his hair. It's a Luc-ism I love. "…self-impressed, mediocre actor who is famous for his marriage to…"

He stops speaking and shakes his head slowly. The gesture conveys just how pathetic he finds me.

"What then? What is it, Luc?"

"You're a smart girl, Vivia. You'll figure it out."

He narrows his gaze on my face. When he finally speaks again, bewilderment laces his voice.

"What are you doing, Vivia?"

"What do you mean?"

"Going to nightclubs. Getting drunk. Letting a stranger kiss you. Wearing skimpy mini-dresses and designer shoes. This is not you, Vivia."

"It's my job, Luc." I cross my arms over my breasts because his words make me feel like a big, fat fake. "And as I recall, you didn't mind the skimpy dress and shoes last night!"

Luc's mouth drops open. He doesn't need to say, "Really, Vivia? That's your response?" His expression says it…and more.

"What happened to settling down and committing yourself to serious writing?"

"What are you saying? My *GoGirl!* articles aren't serious?"

Luc stares at me and shakes his head.

"For the last six months, you've been telling me you looked forward to the day when you could settle down somewhere and work on your Mary Shelley novel. What was that? More romantic fiction?"

Ouch!

"I do want to settle down and write my novel. I am sick of living out of a suitcase, washing my clothes in bathroom sinks, sleeping on lumpy hotel beds…"

I don't totally hate my *GoGirl!* gig. Sure, some aspects of my job suck, but it comes with some pretty incredible bennies, too. Meeting new people, eating in swanky restaurants, learning about different cultures. How many people can say they've attended the Geisha Academy in Kyoto, Japan or been on a private tour of the Palace of Versailles's hidden rooms?

"I don't know what to believe anymore. What happened to keeping it real? What do you really want, Vivia? The truth."

"The truth is…the truth is…"

Shit! I am so used to telling people what they want to hear, spinning colorful stories to entertain; I don't even know the truth.

The truth is: I love wearing ripped jeans and Ugg boots, but I also love how I feel when I am wearing skimpy designer dresses and sexy, red-heeled Louboutins. I want to write serious literary fiction, but writing light, breezy travel articles is a blast. I love Luc and miss him terribly when we are not together, but I am not ready to settle down yet. I always thought I would have a gaggle of kids, but now...not so much.

Luc clenches his jaw. "Maybe we should take a break."

"A break? What does that mean?"

In the history of relationships, the phrase "on a break" is surely the most ridiculous sentiment ever uttered. Either you are together or you're not...no in-between. I feel confident about only a few things in this world: a handbag doesn't need a Prada tag to make you feel good, Ronnie Radke is the sexiest rocker alive today—next to old-school Bret Michaels— spicy noodles and Red Beach champagne cocktails can ease the pain of a broken heart, and "on a break" is synonymous with over, *finis, finito, terminado*.

Luc is wearing his socks and shoes, has retrieved his coat and tie, and is standing across from me with an expectant look on his face.

I'm slow on the uptake. I think he is searching for the words to explain what he meant when he said we should take a break. Finally, I realize what he wants: his shirt.

Removing your boyfriend's shirt and standing naked before him as he bids you *adieu* is about the most humiliating experience.

Ever.

Covering my breasts with my cupped hands, I watch Luc walk out the door and out of my life.

Forever.

Chapter 12

Dirty Tweeter

Steven Schpiel @TheWholeSchpiel
How to get 15 Minutes of Fame: Write intelligent articles?
Nope. Do the dirty with #BishopRaine? Score. #GoGroupie

Steven Schpiel @TheWholeSchpiel
Busted! @PerpetuallyViv was engaged to handsome
Frenchman when caught macking #BishopRaine. #AdieuFidelité

Steven Schpiel @TheWholeSchpiel
#BishopRaine spotted in London jewelry store buying gaudy
baubles. Prezzies for his sexy redhead? #GoGirl

Steven Schpiel @TheWholeSchpiel
Yikes! Paps snap @PerpetuallyViv leaving London hotel
wearing loose top. #BabyBump #Cravings (Click for pic)

I shouldn't do it, but I can't help myself. Slapping one hand over my eyes, I splay my fingers enough to see my MacBook screen, and click on Steven "Muckraker" Schpiel's link.

Jesus, Mary, and Joseph Pulitzer!

Schpiel's pap snap is a grainy photograph taken only a few hours ago, when I ducked around the corner for a big-ass bottle of Thatchers Hard Cider and some fish and chips. I am wearing black leggings and an old gray fisherman's sweater pilfered from Luc's closet. My snarly hair is hanging loose around my shoulders, and I am clutching the big, greasy white fish and chips bag to my chest like a homeless waif—or a woman trying to disguise a burgeoning baby bump.

Damn Steven Schpiel! Damn, damn, damn him to the deepest, darkest, smelliest bowels of Hell. A rancid little turd like him deserves to spend eternity inhaling noxious fumes and suffering the agony of having his flesh slowly singed from his rotten bones.

The bitchy little gossip hound would dig up dirt on his own mother if he thought it would get him a trended tweet.

Mothers. Mum.

Oh, shit! What is my mum going to say when nosy old Anna Johnson posts that picture of me on Facebook? What will Luc say? And Fanny? And my dad?

I drop my head to the desk and try not to think of what my dad, a Professor of Theology at UC Davis, will say when he discovers his daughter might be carrying Bishop Raine's lovechild.

Well, Pops best step off.

He has nothing to say. Nothing. Not after he left my mum and shacked up with a kooky vegan who collects creepy porcelain dolls with soulless eyes. She tries to foist her carob and bean-paste brownies off on me, but I'd rather bust a move with mom in Hip Hop Abs than eat one of those bricks. I wonder how long before Meadow, the kooky vegan, mails me bean-paste brownies laced with folic acid?

I still can't wrap my mind around my fire-and-brimstone father forsaking his marriage vows to live in sin.

This is serious. Really serious.

I grab the hotel phone receiver, jab the button for room service, and order two more bottles of Thatchers and a carton of Häagen Dazs Chocolate Raspberry Truffle.

"Will that be all, Miss Grant?"

"Yes—" I am about to hang up when I remember the pap snap. What if another pap follows the waiter to my door? "No. Wait!"

"Yes?"

"Just leave the tray outside my door."

"Outside your door, Miss Grant?"

"Yes."

He hesitates, and I imagine him gesturing to a pack of camera-toting paparazzi huddled nearby.

"As you wish."

Ten minutes later, a soft rap on the door lets me know my baby-bump inspired binge-fest has arrived. I creep over to the door and peer through the peephole in time to see the waiter walking away.

I wait until he disappears around the corner before whipping the door open, pulling the tray into my room, and slamming the door shut again.

I am six songs into my "When I Am Blue" playlist and halfway through my second bottle of Thatchers when my iPhone starts ringing. Which of my curious friends is calling to get the 4-1-1 on my scandal *du jour*? Maybe I should just send the call to voicemail.

I flip the phone over and look at the caller ID flashing on the screen. Louanne Collins-London.

Oh, shit! Could this day get any worse?

That's rhetorical. No, no it couldn't.

I take another swig of Thatchers for strength and answer the call.

"Cheers, Ms. Collins-London."

"Vivia, dear"—she laughs—"it's Louanne, remember?"

No, I don't remember. Calling Big Boss Lady by her first name feels as wrong as French-kissing Steven "Rancid Turd" Schpiel.

"I am just finishing my piece on last night's Brava party and will send it to you soon." I cross my fingers in a childish effort to cancel out my lie. "It's fab, really fab!"

"Yes, yes." Big Boss Lady switches the call to speakerphone. "I have Rawlings here. He has a few questions for you."

This can't be good. Rawlings is head of HR.

"Good Morning, Miss Grant."

"Mr. Rawlings. How are you?"

"I'll get right to it, Miss Grant." Rawlings must be leaning over the speaker because his voice suddenly explodes out of my iPhone. "Your position as a travel columnist involves a certain amount of risk, and is, at times, physically demanding. How confident are you in your ability to continue meeting those demands?"

I knew it! I am being sacked, shit-canned, fired, given the axe, made redundant. Big Boss Lady—Louanne—probably thinks I am cuckoo for Cocoa Puffs. Sane, credible journalists avoid arrest—except for those barking mad reporters who sneak into communist countries—and they definitely don't have their names bandied about by gossip columnists like Steven "Rancid Turd" Schpiel.

"I am quite capable of performing my duties. Nothing's changed. I swear!"

The pause in conversation stretches. Papers rustle. Big Boss Lady's ubiquitous gold Tiffany bangles clank together as if she's waving her hand or writing. Finally, Rawlings clears his throat.

"Are you quite certain? We do not expect you to put your health, or the health of your unborn child, at risk. No story is worth—"

"Jesus, Mary and—" I exhale all of the air from my lungs in one violent burst. "Thank you for your concern, Mr. Rawlings, Ms. Collins-London—"

"Louanne, dear."

"Louanne, I am not pregnant."

Another pregnant pause. Eek! I inwardly cringe at my poor word choice.

"I. Am. Not. Pregnant." I am trying to hold it together, keep it professional, but my voice cracks and tears fill my eyes. "You have to believe me. Please."

"We believe you, Vivia." Louanne takes the call off speakerphone. "Steven Schpiel's assistant called here asking for confirmation about your pregnancy. I told Rawlings the story was bunk, that my girl is far too clever to get herself into such a messy situation."

My spine turns to jelly and I sink back against desk chair. Louanne Collins-London called me her girl. She called me her girl and said she believes me.

"Thank you," I sniffle.

"Nonsense," Louanne says. "Now, let's talk about your next assignment."

"Okay."

"I am sending you to Scotland. I want you to explore Edinburgh for offbeat tourist attractions. Don't give me two thousand words on the castle or tartan weavers. Give me the Vivia perspective. Think young and quirky. Can you do that?"

"Absolutely."

"After that, you'll be heading to a working sheep farm in the Highlands."

"A sheep farm?"

"That's right. A sheep farm."

Louanne's other line rings and she puts me on hold. What the bloody hell am I going to do on a sheep farm? Sheer those little wooly boogers? Milk them? Do they milk sheep? Sweet lamb chops! I just hope Louanne doesn't expect me to slaughter a sheep.

"Vivia? Are you still on the line?"

"Yes."

"Apparently, girlfriend vacations to working farms are en vogue thing among the twenty-five to forty-five female demographic. Cattle ranches. Goat Farms. Working in a vineyard. Who knew?"

"It's not the Ritz."

Louanne chuckles. "No, it is not."

"Is that it?"

"I realize this is short notice, but do you think any of your girlfriends might be able to join you on the farm?"

"Shearing sheep?"

"Yes."

I imagine sleek Pantsuit Poppy standing in a pile of sheep shit and snort. Something tells me Miss Worthington Boutique Hotels would politely decline my invitation to the sheep soiree. If Fanny hadn't called me self-absorbed, I would ask her to catch the redeye and help me rustle up some little lambs. Now, I am afraid she would take my invitation as an implication that her life wasn't as important as mine.

"I don't think so."

"Well," Louanne says. "If you change your mind and think of someone you would like to join you on the farm, send me a text and I'll have Travel make the arrangements."

"Yes, ma'am." I type "sheep farm attire" into my web browser. "How long will I be working the farm?"

"Eight days."

Eight days? Shearing sheep and shoveling shit? Is she serious? I guess every assignment can't be champagne and Boujis.

Louanne taps her keyboard, and I wonder if she is searching the net for appropriate sheep shearing attire too.

"Is that all?"

"No, I have one other assignment."

"Please don't say you want me to join a fishing vessel. I hate fish, unless they're battered, fried, and served with extra salt."

Louanne is silent.

"Louanne?"

"Sorry. I was just thinking, your fishing vessel story has some merit."

I sputter. Just because I am on a first name basis with Big Boss Lady doesn't mean she's ready for my back-sass.

"I am kidding, Vivia." Louanne's other line rings again. "Listen, dear, I have to take this call. I don't have time to brief you on the other story, so I'll send you an e-mail with the details. Gotta go."

She hangs up. I stare at my computer screen, at the images of women wearing plaid wool jackets and dark jeans tucked into shiny rain boots. I am thankful to have a boss as supportive as Louanne Collins-London and an amazing job that allows me to write and travel the world, but I can't help feeling blue. In the last twenty-four hours, I've lost the love of my life, argued with my best friend, and had an unflattering pap-snapped photo posted all over the Internet. The entire world thinks I am a celebrity groupie carrying Bishop Raine's lovechild. Okay, maybe not the entire world, but at least half.

After Nathan dumped me, I worried I would become a shriveled old spinster, shuffling around in my housecoat and slippers, mumbling song lyrics to my herd of stray cats. Landing the *GoGirl!* gig and a hot French boyfriend chased the fear away—or so I thought.

My old fear never really went away. Like a stalker lurking in the shadows, it waited for my most vulnerable moment to strike.

I envision a lonely future *sans* love, *sans* children, *sans* rescue poodles. Someday soon, my *GoGirl!* readers will grow up. They will stop reading my ridiculous column about my ridiculous exploits. Vivia Grant will stop being a trending topic.

Oh my God! I am a living Tweet—humorous and relevant only until someone more entertaining comes along.

Chapter 13

Getting Knocked Up

By the time I write and submit *A Right Royal Cock-up: How to get arrested and knocked up in London in twenty four hours or less*, my Brava/Boujis article, I have finished the third bottle of Thatchers and listened to my entire "When I Am Blue" playlist...twice.

It's only seven o'clock and I am a mess. Mascara rings my eyes, I smell like fish and chips, and I am stupid weepy drunk.

I should take a shower and sleep off my weepy hang-over, but I don't always do the best things. Instead, I drunk-dial Luc...repeatedly.

"*Bon Shwah*, Lukie-Pookie." I fall back on the bed, holding the phone to my ear. The scent of Luc's sultry cologne clings to his pillow. "It's me, Vivia, again. Just wanted to say goodnight. So, goodnight."

I hang up.

I dial him again just to listen to his voice-mail message. Hearing his deep, sexy voice makes me miss him. My throat tightens. I am wailing like a child before he utters *au revoir*.

"Luc. Luc. Luc?" I don't know what I want to say so I repeat his name until something comes to me. "I am sorry, Luc. Really sorry. *Je suis desolée*, Luc."

As soon as I hang up, I think about how pathetic that last message sounded. So, I dial him again.

"This is the last time I will call you. I promise. I just wanted to shay—" I pause because my tongue feels thick, my eyelids heavy. I yawn, rest my head on the desk and close my eyes. "—I'm just so tired..."

My phone beeps in my ear and I wake with a start.

"Luc?"

A confused moment passes before I realize the beep signified the end of my message. I dozed off and Luc's voicemail disconnected me.

"How ironic."

I dozed off and Luc's voicemail disconnected me. That could be a metaphor for what's been happening in my life. I dozed off, became complacent in my relationships, and now my boyfriend won't talk to me and my best friend is disappointed in me.

I toss my phone aside, bury my face in Luc's pillow, and sob. Great, loud, racking sobs, dredged from the darkest, most wounded places in my soul, places I thought healed. In my head, I play snippets of the sad break-up songs on my "For When I Am Blue" playlist. Snippets that speak of heartbreak and surviving by the grace of God. Snippets of Adele, Christina Perri, Toni Braxton, and Katy Perry.

I should follow the advice of my sisters in suffering: pick myself up, put one foot in front of the other, and go on, but right now lifting my head from the pillow feels like more effort than I could possibly manage.

I almost don't hear the wailing guitar riff that is my ringtone.

"Luc?"

"Fanny."

"Fannnnnyyyy!" I sit up and hug my knees. "I miss you so much, Fanny. You are my best, best, best friend and I miss you. I made a cock-up of my life again. Luc won't talk to me. Everyone thinks my muffin top is a baby bump. I have to go to a Scottish sheep farm and shovel shit. And I am drunk."

"Yes, you are."

"Yes, I am."

"What's going on, Vivian? Have you been cheating on Luc with Bishop Raine? Are you pregnant?"

Fanny asking such a preposterous question is painful proof of the yawning gap between us. When I lived in San Francisco, we saw each other almost every day and shared all of our secrets. Back then, Fanny never needed to ask what was happening in my life because she lived it with me—the cool, calm cosmopolitan Ethel to my Lucy.

Fanny listens to the rambling, weepy, over-dramatic narrative of the blackest moment in my *histoire d'amour tragique* without interjecting. When I finally finish speaking, she lets out a low, long whistle.

"You were right about one thing."

"What's that?"

"You, *ma chérie*, have royally cocked-up your life."

"Again."

"It *is* becoming a trend."

My gaze drifts to the blue velvet ring box on the nightstand. "He was going to ask me to marry him."

"I know," Fanny whispers. "He booked a suite at L'Hotel."

The opulent L'Hotel is one of the most famous hotels in the world. Oscar Wilde, Princess Grace and Prince Rainier of Monaco, Richard Burton and Elizabeth Taylor have stayed in the hotel. L'Hotel has a long history as a setting for romantic rendezvous.

"L'Hotel?" It hurts to breath. "I didn't know."

"That's not all."

Of course that's not all. Luc, grand romantic gestures Luc, would have planned a breathtakingly romantic weekend to celebrate our engagement. I can't resist picking at the scab.

"What else, Fanny?"

"Are you sure you want to know?"

"Yes."

Fanny hesitates.

"Tell me, please."

"He contacted the artists who created Le Mur Des Je T'aime and got them to agree to paint a special temporary message on the wall that reads, 'Marry me, Vivia.'"

A raw sob bursts from my lips. Le Mur Des Je T'aime, a wall in the 18th arrondissement created by two artists and emblazoned with the words "I love you" in 250 different languages, has become a meeting place for Parisian lovers. I wrote an article about it for the magazine.

Fanny waits until my pathetic sob simmers to barely audible weeping. *"Je suis desolée, ma chérie."*

"What am I going to do, Fanny?" I swipe my runny nose with the back of my hand. "How can I fix this?"

Fanny is silent for a long time. Finally, she says, "You might not be able to fix this one, Vivian. French men are late to commit, but when they finally do, it's deeply and completely."

That's my girl. Brutally blunt Fanny.

"He might have been able to forgive and forget if you were just a fuck buddy, but he chose you to be his wife, the mother of his future children." Her French accent is thick as she explains the nuances of the French male psyche. "French men have liberal views when it comes to affairs, but they are consummate traditionalists when it comes to marriage. They fall into bed with many, but love only one."

"So what are you saying? I should give up? Write our relationship off as a lost cause?"

I grab a fistful of Kleenex from the box on the nightstand and twist them into a rope.

"Are you ready to make a grand gesture?"

"Absolutely!"

"Are you ready to give up your job and brushing elbows with the celebrities to settle down with Luc?"

"Rubbing."

"What?"

"It's rubbing elbows with celebrities, not brushing elbows."

"Whatever." Fanny snaps. "Just answer the question. Are you ready to quit your job, fly to France, and beg Luc to forgive you?"

"Beg Luc's forgiveness? For what?" I crush the Kleenex in the palm of my hand. "I didn't do anything wrong. I didn't cheat on him. It was a kiss, Fanny, one stupid over-in-a-flash kiss, that meant nothing. Nuh-thing."

"To you."

"What?"

"It meant nothing to you, but that kiss wasn't 'nuh-thing' to Luc," she says, mimicking me. "A world-famous comedian with a reputation as a lothario shoved his tongue down your throat...in public."

"So what are you saying?" I begin shredding the Kleenex to bits. "Is this, like, some strange French sexual custom? You can cheat as long as it is not in public or with someone who is socially inferior? If Bishop had pulled me into some dark private supply room and stuck his tongue down my throat, would it have been okay then?"

"Probably not."

I swipe the Kleenex bits onto the ground and press the palms of my hands to my eyes.

"What are you saying then? I don't understand."

Fanny exhales slowly. When she speaks again she measures her words, as if talking to a dim-witted child. "I am saying this, my dear stubborn but not obtuse best friend: You have wounded and humiliated Luc, made him look like a—" I hear Fanny snap her fingers, something she does when she is trying to think of an elusive English word "—le mari trompé."

"*Le mari trompé*? I don't know what that means."

"La! It means the husband of an adulteress, a man duped."

"Cuckold?"

"*Oui*! Cuckold."

"I did not cuckold Luc!" I leap to my feet, but the room tilts at a precarious angle so I fall back onto the bed. "Cuckold implies I intentionally deceived him. Fuck, Fanny! I confessed the kiss to him. I did not betray Luc."

"I know you didn't, *chérie*, but he doesn't. Someone posted a photograph on Twitter of his fiancée kissing another man and made him a laughingstock. Luc has become an embarrassing hashtag. Hashtag Jilted Frenchman."

"I'll admit, Jilted Frenchman is not a good moniker, but then neither is Fame Whore." Tears stream from the corners of my eyes into my hair. "I've ruined everything special between Luc and me, but I didn't do it on purpose. I love him."

"I know."

"What would you do?"

Fanny snorts.

"What?"

"I am the last person to give advice about relationships. My last date took me to some nouvelle Mexican pop-up, ordered a pork and bean dish smothered in onions and an expensive bottle of Pinot Noir. Seriously. Who orders Pinot Noir with Mexican food? He ate his food, chugged most of the wine, belched, and then staggered off to the bathroom. The *bâtard* never came back!"

"He stuck you with the check?"

"*Oui.*"

Fanny's had a rotten string of luck with men. She dated a self-absorbed bodybuilder nicknamed Mick the Midget for three months before discovering the mini-rage monster used steroids. After Mick, she dated a gorgeous proctologist who had an abnormal obsession with anal sex. He kept trying to persuade Fanny to give him a little "anal action" by telling her crude jokes, like, *"Oral sex makes your day, but anal sex makes your hole weak."*

I realize again how disconnected I have let myself become from my best friend.

"I'm sorry I haven't done a better job at staying in touch. I've been a crap friend. You were right when you called me self-absorbed."

"Pffft." I close my eyes and see Fanny waving her petite hand dismissively. "Forget what I said. I was being a jealous, judgmental bitch last night."

"You were."

We both laugh.

"Why? What's up?"

"It's not important. Let's finish talking about you."

This is a classic evasion tactic Fanny employs to avoid talking about her deeper feelings.

"I am sick of talking about me." I switch the phone from one ear to the other. "What's been happening in your life? What was your mini meltdown really about last night? I mean, besides trying to prevent me from trashing my relationship with Luc?"

"I don't know." Fanny's voice wavers. "I don't know what I am doing with my life, Vivian. I don't have a purpose. My career is stagnating. My love life is the mold on top of the stagnant water. You have a purpose, a successful career, and hip new friends. I guess I was jealous and afraid you were replacing me."

I feel as if someone whacked me in the chest with a croquet mallet. Fanny never reveals weakness or tender emotions. She's the toughest, most confident, the most self-contained chick I know.

"Replace you? You're kidding, right? You're irreplaceable, *ma puce*."

Ma puce is French for my flea. It's a term of endearment, but also an allusion to her diminutive size.

Fanny does one of those laugh-cry things. "But you've really bonded with Poppy."

"I have, but that doesn't mean she's replaced you."

"Good." Fanny's voice is steady. "Now what's this about you going to Scotland to shovel sheep shit?"

I quickly fill Fanny in on the details of my Chick Trip to a sheep farm in the Highlands.

"Why don't I meet you in Scotland and we can shovel sheep shit together?"

"You?" I laugh as I imagine Fanny leaving the comfort of her trust-fund-funded swank apartment for a week in a rustic cottage. "You hate farms and animals and manual labor and footgear without high heels."

"Yes, but I love Scotland."

"When were you in Scotland?"

"I've never been to Scotland, but I'm certain I'll love it. Buff men in kilts. Woolen mills with deeply discounted sweaters and scarves. Sipping Drambuie in a smoky pub. Walking the gorse-covered paps in the rain." Fanny releases a rare, girly sigh. "What's not to love?"

"Look at you, waxing poetic."

"I've been watching Diana Gabaldon's *Outlander* on Starz and I've developed a wee bit of a crush Sam Heughan, the Scottish actor who plays Jamie Fraser."

"You? Watching a romantic drama series on cable television? Okay, who is this and what have you done with my cynical best friend?"

Fanny chuckles. "It's your fault! Always leaving those silly romance novels about and making me watch *Under the Tuscan Sun* two dozen times."

"Uh-uh! Don't even go there. Not *Under the Tuscan Sun*. That movie is sacrosanct. It is the—"

"—*Holy Grail of all Rom-Com movies*. I know. I know."

And this is why Fanny is my best friend. She tells me what I need to hear, not what I want to hear. She calls me Vivian instead of Vivia because she believes I am more glamorous than my name, like an old Hollywood screen siren. She is always willing to ride shotgun on my wild adventures. And she respects my Rom-Com Theology, even if she isn't a believer herself.

"I miss you, Fanny."

"I miss you, too."

"You'd really use your vacation days to help me shovel sheep shit?"

"*Absolument.*"

I let out a sigh of relief. Fanny will help me sort my life out. Good old, type A, take-charge Fanny.

"Vivian?"

"Yes?"

"I want to say something to you but I don't want to upset you. May I speak candidly?"

"Do you speak any other way?" I laugh, but inside I am bracing myself for the Fanny one-two punch. "Go ahead. Hit me."

It's what I love about Fanny. She doesn't know the meaning of pulling punches.

"Remember last year, when Nathan found out you lied about your virginity and broke up with you?"

"Yes."

"Well, what did you learn from that experience?"

"Not to lie about being a virgin?"

"*Non.*"

"Not to fall in love with a pretentious prig?"

"Vivian! Would you be serious?"

I inhale and let it out in one long, cleansing exhalation.

"I learned that I need to keep it real, to be myself, the self I have always wanted to be, not who I think others want me to be."

"Are you keeping it real?"

Ouch. My stomach clenches as if someone delivered a swift jab to my bellybutton. I try to think of an answer while I catch my breath, but I am saved by the knock.

"Someone's at my door, Fanny. Maybe it's Luc. I've gotta go!" I run my hands through my snarly hair in a futile combing effort.

"Okay," Fanny says. "I'll text you my flight information as soon as I make reservations."

"No!" I give up finger combing my hair and pinch my cheeks for color. "Big Boss Lady said *GoGirl!* would pay for your tickets. I'll text you the deets as soon as I hear back from Travel."

Another knock at the door.

"Gotta go!"

"*À bientôt!*"

I hang up and toss the phone on the bed. Cupping my hand around my mouth, I do a quick breath check. Fab! Only a hint of fish and desperation. No time to brush my teeth, I run to the bathroom, squirt some toothpaste in my mouth, and use my tongue as a toothbrush to scrub my furry, fishy teeth and gums. I use E-mail Diamant Rouge l'Original, thick red clove-scented toothpaste capable of masking the most odiferous oral emanations.

I stumble over to the door and press my eyeball to the peephole. My heart drops to my feet with a thud.

I open the door.

"Hello, Poppy." I lean against the door to keep upright. "You might not want to come in because I am stinky drunk and you are not." I look at her expensive pantsuit and shake my head. "You're always so smooth and shiny. How do you keep from getting wrinkles in your pantsuit? Are you a witch? Are those magic pants? Did Dumbledore teach you a secret wrinkle-removing incantation?"

Without missing a beat, Poppy waves her hand in the air and says, "Wrinkulus Arresto!"

Watching Perfectly Pressed Poppy pretend to wave a wand and recite a wrinkle-banishing incantation is frankly funnier than my wasted ass can stand. Once I start laughing, I can't stop. I laugh until I double over, clutching my aching side.

When I finally stand and wipe the tears from my cheeks, my breath is coming in ragged asthmatic hiccups. I take several deep, measured breaths, before looking at Poppy.

She is standing in the hallway, hands on hips, head tilted to one side, eyes narrowed. She looks so much like a grown-up, blonder Hermione

Granger that the hysterical laughter I just swallowed, bubbles back up my throat and bursts from lips.

"W…w…wrinkulus A…arresto!" I repeat, waving my hand over my rumpled leggings.

"I'm glad to amuse." A small wrinkle furrows her brow. "It wasn't that funny, though, Vivia."

"Yes it was," I chuckle.

"Hmmm." Poppy breezes past me, leaving a contrail of expensive perfume. She strides over to the desk and lifts an empty Thatchers bottle. "As I thought, you're pissed. Wicked pissed."

"No I am not," I say, shutting and leaning against the door. "I *was* wicked pissed…especially at Turd Boy, but now I am just numbly resigned."

Poppy deposits the bottle back on the desk and wipes her fingers on a pristine white hankie she pulls from her pocket.

"Who is Turd Boy?"

"Steven Schpiel." To my horror, spittle flies out of my mouth and lands on Poppy's perfectly pressed lapel. "Rancid little gossip columnist Steven Schpiel of The Whole Schpiel."

"Drunk, Vivia. Pissed means drunk."

"Oh! Well then——" I push away from the door, walk to the wingback, and collapse in a most unladylike manner, my legs spread and head lulling back against the wing. "I might be a teensy-weensy bit pissed, but the deliciously anesthetizing effect is beginning to wear off."

That I said anesthetizing without stuttering or stumbling is proof of my rapidly approaching sobriety.

Poppy walks to the sofa and perches herself on the very edge of the cushion. She reaches into her massive designer handbag and pulls out a bottle of champagne and a newspaper.

"It looks as though I have arrived at the perfect time, then."

She hands me the silver-plated bottle.

"What is this? Why are you handing me a bottle of"——I turn the bottle around and read the label——"Dom Perignon?"

"To celebrate."

"Celebrate? Celebrate what?" I stare at the silver metallic label on the pricey bubbly. "The spectacular end to my spectacular love affair?"

"No."

"What then?"

"This." She opens the newspaper to a back page and waves it under my nose. "Read."

My eyes take several seconds to focus enough to read the tiny print. It's a society gossip page.

"'Heiress Phoebe Stainsbury, England's Billion Dollar Baby, dropped a Nagasaki-sized bomb Tuesday evening, sending shockwaves through London's poshest posh set, when she announced her engagement to Tottenham plumber—'"

"Not that article!"

"Why Aussies make the best nannies?"

"No." Poppy points to an article on the opposite side of the page, tapping the paper with her long, perfectly polished red fingernail. "This one."

I gently place the bottle of Dom Perignon on the table and read the title aloud.

"Altered Reality: Boujis, Raine, and Brava...."

Poppy grins at me over the top of the paper.

"Go on," she urges. "It's all good. I promise."

The society piece runs for one column and offers a squeaky-clean, bright-as-a-soap-bubble take on the glam Brava/Boujis party. I speed read the article, skimming over the less pertinent details, until I come to an anonymous quote that makes me snort.

"Is this true?"

"Is what true?"

"The bit about one of the bobblehead bitches dating Bishop before his marriage to Kitty Kat?"

"Excuse me? Bobblehead bitches?"

"Those two electropop-loving, Robert Palmer groupie throwbacks that spent the evening making snarky comments and rolling their eyes."

"Katrine and Bianca?"

I roll my eyes. Of course their names would be Katrine and Bianca, not bourgeois names like Tina or Michelle.

"Yes."

The article says Katrine Kline is a back-up singer who worked with several famous pop stars. Of course she's a singer! She couldn't be a maggot farmer or a zit-popping esthetician, even though either one of those would be an appropriate vocation for her.

"Are you the anonymous source who said, 'Poor Katrine! She came to the party hoping to get back together with Bishop, but he was only interested in promoting his next film'?" I can't contain my cackle. "'Her flirt-fail was truly cringe worthy.' Did you say that, Poppy?"

Poppy grins. "I can neither confirm nor deny it."

I vault off the chair and throw my arms around Poppy, crushing the newspaper between us.

"No hugs, remember?" Poppy laughs and tries to pull away. "You received your annual hug, you greedy cow."

"Right." I step back. "Sorry."

"Keep reading."

Taking the paper from Poppy, I settle back into the wingback chair and finish reading the article. The columnist references the Kiss Heard 'Round the World, explaining it away as another one of "Raine's attention-seeking showman antics" and describes me as the unwitting victim to his over-zealous greeting.

Poppy's quote jumps from the page. She identifies me as a *GoGirl!* columnist and says I am madly in love with my French boyfriend, Jean-Luc de Caumont.

"Ex."

"Sorry?"

"Ex-boyfriend, almost fiancé."

"You can't be serious."

"I wish I weren't. Luc broke up with me this morning."

"Have you called him? Get him on the phone. I'll explain everything."

"I tried texting and calling him, but my calls went directly to voicemail." I force a brave toothy grin. "Maybe I should change my Twitter handle to Perpetually Single."

Poppy frowns. "Don't be ridiculous."

"Maybe you are right. Perpetually Single has too many characters."

"No." Poppy squints as she stares at my mouth. "What's wrong with your teeth?"

"Why?" I lean forward. "What's wrong with my teeth?"

"They're pink!"

I have a flashback to the morning after my wild night in Cannes, when I woke up and discovered I had an ass tat and pink hair. The pink hair turned out to be a temporary dye job. Why would my teeth be pink? Then I remember my toothpaste.

"No worries." I lean back, pull my knees up, rest my chin on them, and grin. "It's just my toothpaste. It's French."

"French? But of course." Poppy rolls her eyes. "What do the French know about toothpaste?"

"Says the British pot to the French kettle."

We both laugh, but mine is hollow, slightly-forced. Mentioning Luc, seeing his name attached to mine on the society page, has poured salt on my oozing, wounded heart.

Poppy notices the tears in my eyes and reaches over to squeeze my hand. "Have you eaten anything?"

"Fish and chips this morning."

Poppy wrinkles her nose. "That explains it."

"Do I offend?"

"A little." Poppy stands and claps her hands. "Let's go, mate! Take a soak. Make yourself pretty again. We will eat dinner and hatch a scathingly brilliant plot to win your man back."

I don't know what I did to deserve this crazy-good Karma in the form of another generous take-charge friend in my life, but it couldn't have arrived at a better time. Maybe the universe recognized Steven Schpiel's column was like dropping a whopping heap of shit on top of me and sent Poppy as a shit pile counterbalance. Yin and yang.

I grab clean jammies and underthings from my suitcase and head to the bathroom, pausing at the door as a prickly thought needles me.

"Poppy?" I turn around, holding my flannel frog prince jammies to my chest like a shield protecting my vulnerable heart. "I get why I need you right now, but what's your angle?"

"What do you mean?"

I clutch my jammies tighter. "Why are you being my friend? You're rich, successful, well-connected, and incredibly pulled together. You must have a crazy long contacts list full of international bluebloods."

"That's a bit harsh, isn't it?"

"What? Saying you have loads of friends?"

"No." Poppy shakes her head. "The implication that you are a sad charity case is harsh."

"Well, I haven't exactly put my best foot forward. In less than twenty-four hours, I have been arrested for stalking, gotten wicked pissed twice, and become an Internet laughingstock. That's hardly an impressive pedigree."

Poppy tilts her head and the long bangs of her sleek, angled bob fall over one eye. I wonder if the mannerism is a defensive action, like hugging flannel jammies?

"Trust me, being born with wealth and a title doesn't make one morally superior or imminently more desirable friend material."

I just don't buy Poppy's poor-little-rich-girl story. My journalist's bullshit meter is pegging at Not the Whole Story.

"You're friends with lingerie models, world famous actors, billionaire businessmen, and jet-setting heiresses. Why would you want to be friends with me, Burberry knock-off wearing Vivia Grant from Davis, California?"

I expect Poppy to make another bubblegum-cracking, wise girl retort—she's very Lauren Bacall-esque or Katherine Hepburn when she played the witty privileged socialite in *The Philadelphia Story*—but she raises her gaze and lowers her voice.

"I want to be friends because you have something none of my other friends"—she raises her hands and makes air quotes with her fingers when she says friends—"have."

"What's that?"

"Sincerity."

"Me? Sincere?" I snort. "I'm too busy holding this successful, confident, got-it-all-together, perpetually entertaining Vivia mask in front of my face to be sincere."

"You see? You just proved my point."

"I don't see. I just admitted I am a big muffin-topped phony, too concerned with impressing my boyfriend, my boss, and the twits on the Twitosphere to keep it real. How did that prove your point?"

"An insincere person would never admit to wearing a façade." Poppy's eggshell fragile smiles appears for a second.

I recall my earlier impression of a lonely young woman.

"The people in my life wear masks without even knowing it and they don't care a bloody damned whit about impressing others. They only care about themselves."

The silver champagne bottle catches my eye. I don't know how much the bubbly cost, but the shiny laser-engraved label hints at an eye-popping price tag. Who gives an expensive bottle of champagne as an apology gift to a virtual stranger? Several answers pop up. Rich. Generous. Lonely. Desperate. Serial killer. Maybe I can cross serial killer off the list of potential motivators. I doubt the bottle of champagne is all part of some complicated, nefarious plan to lure me into the bathtub so Poppy can jab a needle into my neck, shoot a potent, immobilizing sedative into my vein, and then surgically remove my organs. Miss Prada Poppy doesn't strike me as an organ harvester.

"Are you lonely, Poppy?"

Poppy inhales until the silver buttons on her suit coat threaten to pop. Several deep seam-straining breaths. When she speaks, her single-word answer conveys an unspoken soliloquy of pain.

"Yes."

Words fail me—me, the professional wordsmith, the tireless Tweeter, the perpetually verbose. Fortunately, Poppy finds her words.

"Have you ever had that feeling you were forgetting something important, but you just couldn't remember what? You walk around your house looking in each room. You check your calendar and your messages. But you never figure out what it is."

"Sure."

"I feel like that all of the time."

"Alzheimer's doesn't run in your family, does it?"

Poppy doesn't speak and I curse myself for my stupid, inappropriate humor.

"I'm sorry." I stop hugging my pajamas. "That was a thoughtless joke. I make those sometimes, when someone is suffering and I can't find the words to make them feel better. Crap humor is my reflex."

Poppy brushes my apology away with a flick of the wrist. "I don't know what I am searching for, but…"

"But what?"

"Posh tea parties, Polo in the Park, winter holidays in Gstaad and St. Tropez, shopping in Paris, and socializing with the posh set isn't it."

"It doesn't exactly sound unsatisfying, not when you consider most of the world spend their lives hustling to afford tea from Starbucks and winter vacays to Disneyworld."

"I sound like one of those clichéd spoiled rich girls, don't I?" Poppy doesn't wait for me to respond, but hurries on in a whiny, self-mocking tone. "*Don't judge me. My life is soooo hard. Toting a Louis Vuitton full of couture clothes from Heathrow to Charles de Gaulle is really hard.*"

"You don't sound that spoiled."

Poppy arches a skeptical eyebrow.

"Okay, maybe only a trifle ungrateful."

"I am grateful for my cosseted childhood, elite education, and familial connections. If it weren't for nepotism—" She shrugs. "Somehow, my life just doesn't feel enough."

"Enough or satisfying?"

She tilts her head and wrinkles her nose as she considers my question. "Satisfying. You know what I mean?"

I shake my head. I don't really understand. Poppy has all of the advantages youth, money, connections, intelligence, and beauty. She's never had to hustle to make rent or been forced to subside on cheap Chinese take-out.

"Have you ever gone to a patisserie because you craved a chocolate éclair?"

"Seriously?" I tilt my head and grimace. "Have *I* ever gone to a patisserie for a chocolate éclair? Have you seen the pap snap of my muffin top? I didn't get that from sipping kale smoothies, girlfriend."

Poppy chuckles softly. "You don't have a muffin top, Vivia."

"White lie appreciated. Now finish your analogy."

"It's like when you really want a chocolate éclair, but the patisserie is out of éclairs so they suggest a mille-feuille instead. You don't want to appear ungrateful, so you take the mille-feuille, smile, and say *merci*, but deep down you are still longing for the éclair." Poppy's smile wobbles on her face. "I feel like my life is the mille-feuille. I have no reason to complain, but I still feel unhappy and yearn for something…else."

"I get you, Poppy."

"Really? You do?"

"I do," I say. "I should be happy that a man as wonderful as Luc wants to spend his life with me. Most women would be content, but I still yearn for something else."

"Another man?"

I shake my head.

"What then?"

I shrug. "I don't know. I just know the idea of giving up my job and settling down in the South of France to be the wife of a university professor terrifies me." I sigh. "But this is not about me right now; it's about you. What's your éclair, Poppy? What would make you stop yearning?"

"I don't know, but I have a feeling you are going to get me sorted out."

"Me?"

"Yes, you."

I chuckle self-consciously. "Why me?"

"You are brave and audacious."

"Please, don't hero-worship me, Poppy." I hug my jammies again. "You'll only be disappointed."

"I am British. I don't hero worship." Poppy crosses her arms. "You are searching, just like me, but you search boldly, unapologetically. You might not always take the right path, but at least you take it. I am still plodding along the same track, too frightened to deviate."

"I am not the trail blazer you imagine me to be," I confess. "If my ex-fiancé hadn't been a vindictive ass and used his family connections to get me fired from *San Francisco Magazine*, I probably wouldn't have ever left California or lucked into the *GoGirl!* gig."

"Luck, huh?"

"Serendipity."

"If nothing else—you are refreshingly honest. I need honest friends, people who will tell me the truth, not bow and scrape because they're in awe of the Worthington name. My grandfather used to say, *'There are two kinds of friends: those who tell you what you want to hear and those who tell you what you need to hear. If you are fortunate enough to find a friend who tells you what you need to hear, keep that one, Pop.'"*

Chapter 14

Sex in the Shitty

Submerged in a steaming tub of almond-scented bubbles, I worry the intense déjà vu I am experiencing is a sign of a deteriorating mental state.

I once interviewed a controversial psychologist who published a paper in which he suggested people who claim to experience déjà vu suffer from serious mental disorders. When I asked him about people who claimed to remember things from previous lives, he dismissed them as mentally ill and suffering from temporal lobe epileptic fits.

If Dr. Déjà vu could read my thoughts right now, he would put me in a hug-,me jacket and cram a few Lithium down my throat, because I definitely have the sensation of having experienced this moment before. A stupid lie. Public humiliation. Broken heart. Repeat.

At least one thing is different: the last time my life imploded—when Nathan dumped me for not being a virgin—I obsessively checked my phone for e-mails, tweets, texts, and Facebook posts from him. I looked for a slender thread of hope to grasp onto, a brief message promising me life would return to normal.

Not this time.

What's the point? Luc is probably gone. Forever. Maybe we will cross paths one day—in the airport in Zurich or Athens. He will be walking toward me, his muscular arm thrown around the shoulders of some petite, chic French woman. I will freeze in place, bracing myself for the inevitable devastating moment when he looks up and notices me. He will look right through me before turning and pressing a kiss to his lover/wife's forehead, a tender, fleeting gesture with an eternally devastating impact.

I slide down until my chin sinks beneath the bubbles and close my eyes. The future scene flickers in my brain like a sad romantic drama or a sappy music video. It's a Taylor Swift video, which is apropos since we are never, ever, ever getting back together. Like ever.

My inability to maintain a stable long-term committed relationship should come as no surprise. I am Vivia Grant, daughter of a faithless theology professor.

Holy Shit! After a year of soul searching and horizon broadening experiences, I still have more baggage than a Louis Vuitton store.

Poppy is straight up cracked if she thinks I am brave.

I'm not brave. Not a bit.

I am terrified.

I am afraid to end up like my mom. I am afraid of pinning my hopes and dreams on a man, sacrificing my goals to help him achieve his, spending my days quietly, thanklessly building a life he will take for granted. Then, he will look at me from across the table one day and say, "When you're finished passing the green beans, I'd like a divorce, *s'il vous plaît.*"

Who knew I had so many trust issues? I guess my parents' divorce really did a number on me.

I emerge from the bathroom half an hour later, my pink, puckered, almond-scented skin scrubbed clean of Luc's touch and the unpleasant aroma of fried haddock. The hotel's luxurious lotion can't mask the desperation emanating from my pores, though. My emotions are swinging like a pendulum from mildly-hopeful to extremely-despondent.

"There now," Poppy says when she glances up from her iPhone and notices me standing in the doorway. "You look a billion pounds better, less knackered. Love the pajamas, by the way. Are those frogs?"

I nod like a toddler and the towel shifts, slipping over my right eye. "They're frog prince pajamas."

"The legendary frog prince." Poppy chuckles wryly. "I've snogged a bloody pond full of frogs and still haven't found my prince."

I remember the Wikipedia entry about Poppy dating Tristan Kent and Sir Richard Blanchard and wonder if those are the frogs she's referencing.

"Did you really date Tristan Kent?"

"Come sit down and we will have a proper chin wag." She takes a seat in one of two chairs on either side of the table. "I ordered dinner while you were in the bath. I do hope you like herb-roasted chicken."

"I love roasted chicken, but I don't remember seeing it on the room service menu."

I sit across from Poppy, lift one of the silver domes, and inhale curls of herb scented steam.

"I didn't order it from room service. I thought you needed a proper meal, not quail eggs on rye toast, so I phoned my favorite bistro."

Poppy's generosity and thoughtfulness bring tears to my eyes. Of course, discovering I had run out of smoothing serum for my hair brought tears to my eyes, too. So I'm thinking I am pretty much an emotional wreck.

"Thank you, Poppy. I can't tell you how much your kindness means to me right now."

"Nonsense."

She moves her hand as if brushing crumbs from the table. Stiff-upper lip, no hugs Poppy has returned.

The herb-roasted chicken is a thing of beauty, and if I weren't starving, I would whip out my iPhone and snap some food porn for my Instagram feed. The chicken rests on a mound of smashed red potatoes surrounded by a moat of creamy gravy. A bowl of mushy peas accompanies the chicken.

Between bites of chicken and sips of iced lemon water, Poppy tells me about her brief romance with the only man who could rock tights and pointy ears. When I ask her if Tristan was a good kisser, she dabs her lips with her napkin and changes the subject. If our friendship weren't still in its infancy, I would ask her if the Wood Elf ever showed her his wood or if he ever used his arrow to make her quiver. Ha! The raunchy double-entendres could roll of my tongue for hours.

We're nibbling blackberry tartlets when Poppy says, "I found the article exonerating you on the newspaper's website. What if we send a link to Jean-Luc?"

I shrug. "I don't think it will matter."

"We could try."

"He probably wouldn't even open my e-mail."

"What if I send it? Would that help?"

"I don't think so." I push my dessert plate away in an effort to stop the muffin-top spread. "Fanny says French men are slow to commit and even slower to forgive when they believe they have been betrayed."

"Where is the plucky, eternally optimistic, glass-half-full, Vivia? The audacious Prince Harry-stalking Vivia who cycles from Provence to Tuscany, parties with Jett Jericho, goes to Kyoto to learn how to be a geisha?

"Vivia Perpetua Grant of San Francisco, California died this morning after being stabbed in the heart with gossip columnist Steven Schpiel's poison pen." I speak in a low, soft voice and press my hands together in prayer. "In lieu of flowers, donations can be made to Victims of Media Bias and the North American Spinster Society."

"Don't be ridiculous!" Poppy rolls her eyes. "Schpiel hasn't killed you, only momentarily wounded you. You're down and stunned, but you will come back stronger because you are fierce. Fierce Vivia."

"I don't feel fierce."

"Shake it off."

"Excuse me?"

"Shake it off," Poppy sings, giving me jazz hands and performing a strange little seated twerk. "Ah ah ah."

I snort with laughter. "What was that?"

"My Taylor Swift impersonation."

"Hold up! Back that little twerk train up, Miley. Did you just say Taylor 'Bubblegum and Ponytails' Swift?"

"What's wrong with Taylor Swift? I love Tay Tay!"

"Oh my God!" I slap a hand over my eyes and groan. "Did you just call her Tay Tay?"

"It's an affectionate nickname coined by the Swifties."

"The *Swifties*?" I drop my hand and stare at my new friend as if she just confessed to being a foot fetishist. "Who are the Swifties?"

"Taylor Swift fans."

I let out a whistle and widen my eyes.

"Ooookay then."

"All right Judgmental Judy"—Poppy puts her hands on her hips—"what's wrong with Taylor Swift?"

"What's wrong?" I laugh hysterically. "Her music is little whiny bubblegum country-pop about her myriad of bad love relationships."

"Have you ever actually listened to her songs?"

"Pfft," I roll my eyes in a spot-on Fanny imitation. "Have I listened to her songs?"

"Have you?"

"How could I not listen to her songs? We are never, ever, ever, ever, like ever, ever, ever getting back together, like ever, ever must have played on the radio six trillion times the first month the song was released."

Poppy holds up a finger. "That's one song. Name another of her songs."

"What is this Tay Tay Trivia?"

"One. Name just one song."

I close my eyes and pinch the bridge of my nose. Think. Think. I think so hard my brain aches, but I can't remember a single Taylor Swift song.

"Ha!" I open my eyes and snap my fingers. "She sang that song about Jesus being the co-pilot."

"Jesus Take the Wheel?"

"Yeah, that's it!"

"Wrong. That was Carrie Underwood."

"They're both blond country singers. Gimme a break."

"You've never actually listened to her music, have you?"

"Not by choice," I admit. "And you can add that to my obit."

"When I am melancholy, I make a pot of tea and listen to Taylor Swift songs. What do you do, Vivia?"

"I eat gourmet junk food like Mr. Foo's Noodles and Torchy's Tacos and crank Black Veil Brides, Falling in Reverse, Tempting Fate, or Countless Good-byes."

"Countless Good-byes? That sounds so sad."

"They're an awesome Finnish Metalcore band with a crazy hot drummer."

"Awesome?" Poppy laughs. "You are so American."

"Yes, yes I am!"

"Well nothing is more American than Taylor Swift." Poppy grabs her iPhone. "Just listen to four songs. If it doesn't change your feelings about her, I will never mention her name again. Deal?"

"Four?"

"Three."

"Deal." I hold my hand out and Poppy shakes it. "Three songs. Cue 'em up."

Poppy starts with "Back to December," a mournful, haunting song about a girl begging forgiveness for taking her ex-boyfriend for granted. It's a swift, sharp jab to the heart. "Love Story" comes next, a sweet musical tale about ill-fated teen romance. It's a roundhouse to the head. The breezy, in-your-face-fun "Shake it Off" rounds out the mini Tay Tay Playlist. It's an empowering shot of adrenaline that lifts me up off the mats before the final bell rings.

We are up, jumping around my room, shaking our hands, and laughing until the very last jazzy trumpet note. We flop onto the couch, giggling like a couple of giddy, girly Beliebers.

"Are you ready to admit Tay Tay is the voice of a generation of pretty, popular, empowered nerd girls?" Poppy drops her iPhone in her bag. "She is an adorable woman coming into her own and yearning for a storybook love."

"I don't know if I am ready to bestow her with the title of Warbler of Wisdom, but I dig that she is a good girl in love with bad boys. I get that."

"So you can tolerate my membership in the Swifties?"

I laugh again. "I will permit it, as long as you don't tell me you have a Demi Lovato ringtone."

"As if," Poppy snorts. "Iggy Azalea's Fancy."

"Jesus, Mary, and Jessica Simpson!" I make the sign of the cross. "You might need to atone for your musical taste transgressions. Bubblegum Pop-py!"

"I like that name!"

"Very well." I dip my fingers in my glass of ice water and flick it onto Poppy's forehead. "I christen you Bubblegum Pop-py. Henceforth, you shall be referred by your Vivia-given moniker."

We laugh.

"You're a cool chick, Poppy Worthington."

"Thanks."

Iggy Azalea suddenly blasts from Poppy's iPhone. She grabs the phone and frowns when she looks at the screen. She jabs the button to mute Iggy. Thank God.

"Everything okay?"

"What?" Poppy looks up. "Oh, yes. It's just my mum. She must have realized she failed to meet her daily Poppy texts and is making up for it with a call."

"You have one of those, too?"

"Do I?" Poppy slides the phone back into her purse and affects a clipped, nasally British upper-crust tone. "*'What is this one heaaars about you spending the night drinking in a dodgy pub? A Worthington does not behave in such a common way. Poorly done, Poppy Whitney.'*"

I whistle. "I feel ya, sister. I got my own text-happy mum."

Poppy inhales and clasps her hands neatly in her lap. Bubblegum Poppy has left the building, ladies and gentlemen. Perfectly Pressed Poppy has returned.

"Have you heard from your editor yet?"

"Yes."

"No problems there, I hope."

"All good." I lean back and prop my feet on the table. "Except she's sending me to some sheep farm in Scotland."

"Really?"

I tell Poppy about the new rage in all girl getaways: working chick trips. I expect her eyes to glaze over and her lips press together to stifle a yawn, but she leans forward, listening with rapt attention.

"Big Boss Lady—" I have never publicly referred to Louanne by her nickname. I am not sure if Poppy will appreciate my chest-thumping, one-of-the-people joke since she is technically "The Man." "My boss wanted me to invite a few of my friends, but it is a big imposition to ask someone to cash in their vacation days to shovel sheep ca-ca."

"I'll go with you."

"You will?"

I play it off all cool, but I'd hoped Poppy would toss her hat into the ring. Stiff-Upper Lip Poppy is a bit off-putting, but beneath the pricey pants suits, she's a chair twerking, wise-cracking bubblegum girl just waiting to bust out.

"Sh-yeah!"

"Really?"

"Really."

"You would really come to Scotland with me? We are going to be living on a farm…shoveling sheep shit."

"I love sheep!"

"Shut up."

"I do."

Poppy tells me about her childhood summers spent at the Worthington's country estate—how she shadowed their gruff old Scottish groundskeeper, traipsing through the spongy fields and forests as he performed his duties.

"I would follow him to his cottage and help him tend the sheep." Poppy stares into space, lost in happy memories. "My happiest childhood memories include spending time with Liam. I even wanted to be a sheep farmer."

I try to conjure an image of Miss Boutique Hotels traipsing over mucky hills in search of a lost sheep, her Wellies smeared with sheep shit.

"Shut up."

"Serious." Poppy tips her head, looking at me shyly from behind her bangs. "So can I come with you?"

"Are you kidding? I would love you to be the Thelma to my Louise, the Samantha to my Carrie."

"I would prefer to be your Charlotte."

"Fair enough."

"So, you're in?"

"I'm abso-bloody-lutely in!"

"Sweet sauce!"

"What's the schedule?" She pronounces it the British way, with a beginning *sh* not *sk* sound. "I would like to send it to my assistant just in case she needs to contact me."

"We leave for Edinburgh day after tomorrow."

"Plane or automobile?"

"I am not sure yet, but I was thinking it might be fun to take the train, roll through the English countryside like Harry Potter on the Hogwarts Express."

"Ooooooor"—she draws the small word out far longer than I thought possible—"we could drive, like Thelma and Louise!"

"Maybe snag ourselves a Brad Pitt?"

"Pre-parenthood and unsightly facial hair."

"*Legends of the Fall* Brad Pitt."

"Now you're talking, my Colonial Friend."

"Colonial? We haven't been a colony for over two hundred and thirty-five years."

"Pishaw," Poppy says, waving her hand. "You'll always be our dear Colonials."

I laugh. I love that Poppy feels comfortable enough already to flip me some shit.

"Okay, let's do this thing."

"Road trip?"

"Road trip!" I squeal.

"We can take the backroads…"

"Maybe stop off in Chawton and retrace Jane Austen's footsteps…"

"Wrong direction."

"Then we can meander over the mist-shrouded moors of North Yorkshire in search of our own ill-fated, violent love."

Poppy stares at me with wide eyes and slack mouth, clearly perplexed by my literary reference.

"Emily Brontë."

Poppy doesn't blink.

"Heathcliff and Catherine, the ill-fated lovers in Brontë's *Wuthering Heights*?"

Poppy finally blinks. "I am British, Vivia. *Wuthering Heights* is included in our first school primer. I am trying to understand why you would want a lover as barking mad and downright bloody cruel as Heathcliff."

"Easy girlfriend." I pop a hand on my hip and wag my finger at her. "Don't diss my boy, H-Cliff."

"You're serious, aren't you?"

"As serious as Churchill on D-Day, as Victoria Beckham on a cleanse, as Queen Elizabeth at the opening ceremonies of the…"

"Okay, okay." Poppy holds her hands up and laughs. "I get it. Your affections for Heathcliff are quite serious. You really must learn to curb your proclivity for over-statements."

"Does that mean you're with me? We're going to meander around the moors in search of our very own Heathcliffs?"

"As appealing as that sounds, I am afraid a trip to the moors would be quite a detour. Our route takes us through the Lakes District, though. Perhaps the epic grandeur of Wordsworth's former stomping grounds will move you to poetry."

The Lakes District's verdant valleys and tumbling fells inspired Lord Tennyson, John Keats, Percy Bysshe Shelley—the world's most famous poets. Maybe a visit would inspire me to pen a sonnet stirring enough to recapture Luc's heart.

"That sounds epic, Poppy. As long as we are in Edinburgh by Thursday."

"What happens Thursday?"

"Fanny arrives."

"Fanny? Your best friend?"

"Yes!" I grin. "She is flying over to join us. I hope you don't mind."

"Are you daft?" Poppy beams. "I am excited to meet the infamous Fanny."

"This is gonna be fab!" I stop myself from giving Poppy another hug and settle for a hand squeeze instead. "I know you're going to be great friends."

Chapter 15

Ménage à Trois

Fanny and Poppy aren't ever going to be great friends. In the words of the immortal Taylor Swift, "Like ever." I must have reached into my old bag, pulled out my rose-colored glasses, and slipped them on my face when I envisioned the three of us bonding like some cheesy remake of *The Sisterhood of the Traveling Pants*. We are three wildly different women, and it will take more than a pair of magic skinny jeans to fuse us together at the hips.

Three days ago, Poppy picked me up in her zippy little BMW coupe and we followed the M1 from London to the M6 and the Lakes District, eventually making our way to Edinburgh. We spent the first night skulking down Old Town Edinburgh's narrow closes—or alleyways—listening to a tatted-up guide tell us titillating tales from the city's history. As cheesy as it sounds, we had a great time listening to stories of murder, adultery, deception, and debauchery. The guide, Aeden, was wicked cool and invited us to join him for drinks in this slightly seedy cellar bar called The Vault. Aeden is the lead singer for System Shattered, a Scottish rock band, which totally explains his muscular, tatted, cocky swagger. *Insert swoon sound effect here, please.* When Aeden told us his band was one of the opening acts for Palaye Royale, an up-and-coming fashion-art rock band out of Las Vegas, and asked if we wanted to "come oot and get ratarsed" I thought Poppy would beg off. Poppy might be cool, but I taxed my vivid imagination trying to envision Miss President of the Swifties getting ratarsed—drunk—at an indie rock concert. Poppy not only went to the concert, but flirted with the guitarist of the appropriately named London-based band, Dirty Thrills.

Dirty Thrills has a crazy cool blues-rock sound with wailing guitar riffs and melt-your-panties vocals. The guitarist looks like Colin Farrell, with sad, love-me-till-it-hurts brown eyes, pouty lips, and a mustache that could tickle a girl in all the right places. Poppy disappears after their set and reappears later, her lipstick slightly smeared, her shirt untucked and rumpled, a broad grin stretched across her pretty face. I'm not saying she hooked up with the guitarist, but she definitely looks like she got a few dirty thrills.

To use an Americanism, Palaye Royale was awesome. The indie rock band has a psychedelic sound and 80's theatrical look—like they're the love children of Culture Club and the Doors.

Aeden's band, System Shattered, was like the perfect bridge between Dirty Thrills's solid, wailing sound and Palaye Royale's liquid smooth harmonizing. It was an orgasmic musical trifecta.

Not to overstate, if God said He would create Vivia's Perfect Night, it would probably look something like that night—only with more chocolate.

Still glowing with the after-effects of our night of music and alleged moustache-love, we met Fanny at the Edinburgh Airport. Maybe I am naïve, but I fully anticipated Fanny would join in and we would have a happy little marriage à trois. Ha! What a rude awakening. Like a morning after let-down, when you roll over and realize the hot dude you brought home from the club the night before is really a finger-sniffing dud, I took one look at Fanny's tight expression and thought, "This is *so* not happening."

Following Big Boss Lady's dictate to write about offbeat places in Edinburgh—I found Arkangel and Felon, an eclectic clothing boutique, the Voodoo Rooms, a chic fringe bar with a burlesque show, and Angels with Bagpipes, a bijou wine bar on the Royal Mile. Next, we hit a spa where brawny kilt-wearing male therapists rubbed lavender scented lanolin into our sore muscles, a thirties combo Laundromat/swing dance class called Zoot Suits, the Museum of Pathology with jars of pickled human remains, and a neo-pagan fire festival where we sat around a huge bonfire and watched interpretive dancers and acrobats pay tribute to the May Queen.

Through it all, Fanny and Poppy verbally circled around each other like a pair of eighteenth century swordsmen preparing for a duel, assessing and testing reflexes with a stunning battery of thrusts, parries, and ripostes.

I keep waiting for the coup de grâce, the clean, brutal death blow that will bring one of my friends to her designer-clad knees, but they are determined to prolong their battle—death by a thousand small, thinly-veiled cuts.

You know that song that goes "you say po-tay-to, I say puh-tot-o, let's call the whole thing off"? Well, whoever penned that inane ditty must have spent time with a Frenchman and a Brit. If Fanny says po-tay-to, you better believe Poppy politely chimes in with her corrective, "Pardon me, but I believe it is po-tot-o." To which Fanny invariable argues the etymology of the word—how it most certainly comes from a French word because everyone knows the French are the masterminds behind civilization's most tangible and tangential achievements.

Now, Lord Jesus knows I love me some Fanny Moreau, but my best friend really can be a...snob. It's not her fault. She's French. If you have spent time in France, you understand arrogance is as much a part of their genetic makeup as bone marrow or superb fashion sense.

Fanny explained it to me once. She said, "Several hundred years ago, the French believed Paris was the center of the Universe. The farther one traveled from Paris, the more uncivilized the world became. It's a belief that has metastasized throughout the body of France. We genuinely believe France brought civilization to the Universe, and this belief gives us a sense of deep, unshakable superiority."

"So you believe you're better than the rest of the world?"

"Believe?" Fanny frowned. "We don't believe we are better, we just know we are."

Poppy might be British, but nature has endowed her with an equally healthy dose of arrogance. She is holding her own against anything Fanny is throwing down.

They have bickered about food, romance, literature, art, tea.

Yes, they had a spirited discussion this morning about the merits of consuming tea instead of coffee. Just when Fanny seemed on the brink of conceding her coffee to Poppy's tea, she volleyed back with her great "red wine" argument.

For Fanny, red wine is the elixir of life. One of my first memories of my best friend is of her taking long, dramatic drags of a cigarette while expostulating on her theory of the medicinal benefits of consuming at least one glass of red wine a day.

"A day without zee wine, *cherié,* ees sheet."

Fanny was a few glasses over her daily quota when she made that proclamation, which explains the heavy French accent. She speaks nearly flawless English except when she is very angry or very tipsy.

After the Great Tea Debate, they bickered about eggs. Eggs, for Humpty's sake! The hotel restaurant served our eggs slightly on the runny side—way undercooked by American standards. Poppy sent her plate back to the kitchen with detailed instructions on how to prepare the perfect poached egg.

Poppy was only being polite when she asked us if we wanted our runny-side up eggs recooked.

"I do not understand the British and their obsession with pasteurization and sanitization," Fanny said, waving the waitress away. "It's an egg, not a medical utensil."

And they were off...again...circling and thrusting, parrying and riposting. I managed to intervene and establish a wary truce by redirecting their focus to our impending journey to the sheep farm and my dire need for appropriate sheep shearing attire.

"I want a pair of Hunter Wellies. Tall, shiny, pink rain boots perfect for bog stomping." I tossed my napkin on the table beside my runny eggs and stood. "I saw a pair at that boutique on Victoria Street that had the cute pink cashmere fingerless gloves and scarf. I am going to get them. Who's with me?"

Two hours later, we are cruising over a bridge spanning the Loch Ness and I am sporting the fiercest pair of shiny pink Wellies and itching to stomp a bog. I can't stop clicking my heels together and staring at the glassine pink toes. I feel like a kid on Christmas morning, mesmerized by all of the pretty, shiny things.

"This is awesome!"

"Awesome," Fanny mumbles.

Fanny is crammed in Poppy's backseat, wedged between her two Louis Vuitton suitcases, her carry-on perched on her lap. Poppy's tiny trunk couldn't accommodate Fanny's travel accoutrement.

Fanny is the Rose DeWitt Bukater of our group. You remember Rose, the heroine in the movie *Titanic*? Remember the opening scene with Rose standing on the dock, dispassionately staring at the ship of dreams while her two car loads of steamer trunks and suitcases are unloaded? Yeah, that's Fanny.

"Are you sure you don't want me to hold your carryon for you?" I tear my gaze from my rain boots and look at my miserable best friend crammed in the backseat. "I don't mind."

"It's fine."

The flat tone and averted gaze tell me all I need to know about Fanny's attitude. She's pissed. The best way to deal with a pissed-off French woman is to pretend you don't know she's pissed off.

"I can't believe I am driving over Loch Ness," I say, staring out the window at a purple-painted ferryboat loaded with tourists. "It's spectacular, isn't it Fanny?"

"Eh." Fanny's tone is blasé and I imagine her shrugging her shoulders. "It's too touristy."

"Sometimes touristy things are fun. Remember when we rented electric bikes and rode them over the Golden Gate to Sausalito? That was fun."

"If you say so."

"Lighten up, Fanny. Your negative 'tude is harshing my mellow."

"Sorry."

She emphasizes the first syllable, drawing it out in an unnatural falsetto voice that tells me she's not really sorry.

I take a deep breath—drawing in light and positivity—and then exhale slowly—pushing the negative vibes away. "What a beautiful day."

"Look at those clouds." Fanny taps the window with her finger. "It's going to rain."

"Good! I like rain."

"You do?"

"Yes."

"That must be a new development because you hated rain when you lived in San Francisco."

"Only because I didn't own a super cool pair of Wellies."

Poppy glances over at me.

I smile apologetically. "The world looks different when you're wearing Wellies. You should have bought a pair, Fanny."

"Why?"

"They're fun."

"They're *rubber* boots."

"Rubber boots that come in cool colors."

"They're overpriced."

"Can you put a price tag on happiness?" Poppy chimes in. "I don't think so."

"Pfft."

Uh-oh. Fanny's pfft-ing. We're losing her. Someone grab a crash cart filled with bottles of French wine and tubes of Dior lip gloss, STAT.

"I can't wait to climb gorse-covered hills and stomp through a bog." I click my shiny heels together again, smiling at the rubbery thud sound. "Doesn't that sound like fun?"

"Fabulous fun," Poppy says.

"No." Fanny shifts her carryon, banging it into the back of my seat. "It doesn't sound like fun. People die in bogs, Vivian. Do you want to drown in a bog and then a hundred years from now have some Scottish farmer pull your leathery body out by one of your stupid pink rain boots?"

Black-cloud Fanny and her sunshine-stealing bad mood are really bumming me out. I want to pull out my happy umbrella and shield myself from her negativity deluge, but her unprovoked attack on my Wellies has stunned me. Complain about the weather, the tourists, the runny eggs, but leave my innocent overpriced rubber boots alone.

"That's quite enough!" Poppy engages the directional signal with unnecessary force. "Just because you have an abundance of negativity doesn't mean you need to share it."

"Sorry," Fanny says in an unnaturally high voice. "I'm French. I haven't learned how to do that fake stiff-upper lip routine. What you see is what you get."

"What I see is a foul-tempered woman with a Napoleon Complex. You're a small person with a large ego!" Poppy slaps the directional signal again to turn it off. "The world doesn't revolve around you, Fanny Bonaparte. Just because you're mood is in the gutter doesn't mean you have to pull everyone down with you."

Jesus, Mary, and Josephine! Poppy did not just call Fanny a midget-sized megalomaniac, did she?

"Hold up!" I raise a hand. "Let's pause this before someone says something she will regret."

Fanny and Poppy respond in unison. "Too late."

"Can't we just get along?"

"*Putain*! What did you expect Vivian?" Fanny spits. "England and France have been rivals for hundreds of years. The British have an inborn distaste for my country."

"Bollocks!" Poppy declares. "I love France. I simply dislike the French."

Fanny's response in her native tongue is too rapid for me to follow, but Poppy has no problem translating.

"I can answer that," Poppy says, glancing at Fanny in the rearview mirror. "I don't like the French because you're pseudo-intellectuals and insufferable snobs."

"You confuse sophistication with snobbery."

"Puhleez," Poppy laughs. "You're snobs about food, wine, art, fashion... About the only thing you're not snobbish about is your battlefield tenacity. Understandable, since you needed the British and Americans to rescue you from Hitler's clutches."

"*C'est des conneries!*" Fanny's this is bullshit ricochets around the BMW's quiet interior. "It's been over sixty years. How much longer do you British plan on cashing in your World War Two chits?"

"Probably about the time you French stop being pretentious snobs."

I purse my lips and let out a low, long whistle. This is getting ugly.

"The French are not snobby." Fanny pokes my shoulder. "Are we, Vivian?"

"Don't drag me into this." I hold up my hands. "I am Switzerland."

"You're American."

"I am neutral."

"So you do think I'm a snob?"

A dozen memories flicker in my brain—Fanny rebuking me for buying a knock-off Prada bag, Fanny clucking her tongue at an overweight woman sitting on a park bench eating a donut, Fanny wrinkling her nose at my grilled cheese and saying, "Processed American cheese? Really, Vivian? In France, we only use perfectly aged Gruyère."

I swivel around and look my best friend in the eye so she doesn't read more into what I am about to say.

"Well, at times, you can be"—I lift my hand and make a pinching gesture, leaving barely an inch of space between my thumb and index finger—"just a teensy, weensy snobby."

"Nice, Vivian," Fanny fumes. "Nice! Way to have my back."

"That is not fair!" I let my hand fall to my lap and swivel back around to stare out the front window. "I always have your back, Fanny."

"Not this time."

"*C'est des conneries!*" I swivel back around and stare into her flashing brown eyes. She looks surprised by my correct usage and pronunciation of the French oath. "That's right, sister. I can *parle* a few curse words, too."

We stare at each other—engaging in a classic game of "who will look away first." To keep the peace, I am usually the one who submits, yields, gracefully concedes victory of minor skirmishes. For this reason, Fanny thinks I am a pushover. She thinks I fear confrontation. She is *très, très* wrong. I choose to avoid minor skirmishes, preferring to save my firepower for the big battles. Fanny questioning my loyalty is escalating this into a big battle.

Fanny glances out the window and back at me. The confrontation-loving French girl just bowed her head and handed me her sword. A rare occurrence, indeed. Something is definitely up with my best friend. Bowing her head and yielding her sword is not in her nature. Also, although she's never been a "glass half full" kinda girl, her negativity this trip has reached new heights. It's like she is determined to make this trip a miserable experience.

If I didn't know better, I would think Fanny is jealous...of me. But that's ridiculous, isn't it? Fanny is beautiful, sophisticated, confident, and rich. Why would she be jealous of me? The notion is too ridiculous to entertain.

"One of the best things about our friendship is that we tell each other the truth." I reach out and give her knee a quick squeeze. "Has that changed?"

"No." She exhales and her shoulders slump. "And the truth is you think I am a snob?"

I am proceeding gently because I have never seen my battle-ready friend look so defeated.

"Sometimes."

"Why didn't you ever say it before? Why tell me now——" She darts a glance at Poppy and I know what she is thinking: Why tell me now, *in front of a stranger*?

"Because you asked."

I don't tell her that she's been particularly snobbish this trip, or that she becomes extremely combative when someone offers her constructive criticism. I also wonder if my reluctance to call Fanny on her bullshit stems from my pathological tendency to varnish the unpleasant things in my life in a rosy hue. This possibility frustrates me, because it would mean I am still struggling with issues I struggled with when I lied to my ex-fiancé about being a virgin. *Keep it real, Vivia.*

"What else do you think, Vivian? Really think?"

"I think you're a caring, generous, supportive human being, but you're not perfect. Everyone has flaws, even the French." I pause to let my compliment sink in. "You can be snobby sometimes. I never told you that before because I have just accepted it as part of who you are—a small part of who you are—just as I know you accept that I am a verbose, scattered, frizzy-haired redhead."

Fanny glances at Poppy again and presses her lips together. I know what Fanny is thinking. It's like she wrote her thoughts in a bubble suspended over her head. She wants to apologize for stealing my sunshine, but doesn't want to appear weak in front of her foe.

I squeeze her knee in encouragement before turning back around in my seat. Several minutes pass with only the BMW's softly purring engine breaking the silence.

"I am sorry if I have been negative—"

I don't know if she intended her apology just for me or as a white flag to end the Great British-French War. So, I wait.

"And I am sorry I called your boots stupid. They're not stupid. They're actually really cute, and you work them, girl."

"Yes, I do!"

Poppy chuckles. "Yes, you do."

We slip into a slightly more comfortable silence because there's still a big, fat elephant in the car.

One of my friends needs to apologize. If forced to bet, I don't know if I would place my money on France or England. I never understood how the two countries could have engaged in a war that lasted one hundred years. I get it now.

In retrospect, I should have considered the possibility that bringing two stubborn, slightly-controlling Type A's together would result in an end of the armistice. Bonjour, Mademoiselle Immovable Object, meet Lady Irresistible Force.

The tension in the BMW is still thick enough to cut with one of Fanny's Swarovski crystal-encrusted nail files. I want to say something to lighten the mood, but what? I wish I could text Jean-Luc. He's a born diplomat, adept at smoothing ruffled feathers.

Just thinking of my handsome, sweet French *lovah* makes my heart ache in places I've never ached in before.

I pull out my iPhone and check it for messages. No new voicemail messages, even though the little tower symbol in the right hand corner tells me I am getting a signal. I open my e-mail, hoping—praying—for an e-mail from Luc. Nothing.

The silence is killing me. Kill. Ing. Me. So I play the pathetic anti-feminist woman Gloria Steinem has written volumes about: the clingy, submissive, overly-dependent female.

Text to Jean-Luc de Caumont:
I have never missed you more than I do right now. Tell me what I can do to win your forgiveness and I swear I will do it. Je t'aime.

Do you hear that hissing? It's the sound of me tossing water on a bonfire of burning bras. Soon, I will be quitting my job to bake cookies for Luc's colleagues, mend the holes in his socks, and cook him hearty meals in my new crock pot.

Does committing to spend your life with one person mean you have to give up your soul?

I press a hand to the place between my breasts where Jean-Luc's engagement ring hangs from a chain. The morning I left London, before Poppy picked me up at the Rubens, I took a taxi to a jewelry store near Waterloo Station and purchased a thick white gold box chain. Wearing Luc's engagement ring on my hand didn't feel right—wouldn't feel right unless he was the one to slip it on my finger—but I still wanted it near me as a tangible symbol of my commitment to him.

I screwed up—big time—but I will do whatever it takes, for as long as it takes, to prove my love and devotion to Luc.

I just hope "whatever it takes" doesn't mean spending an eternity sending unrequited, groveling texts.

I am beginning to think it's going to take a miracle to earn Luc's forgiveness. With all of the wars, tsunamis, school shootings, and Hollywood sex scandals, Jesus is working overtime in the Miracle Dispensing Department. I doubt he has time for my silly prayers.

Chapter 16

Jonesing for a Geezer

Praise Jesus! Miracles do happen.

Poppy is deftly navigating the BMW around a traffic circle on the outskirts of Inverness when she breaks her silent standoff with Fanny with an apology.

"I am sorry for calling you Napoleon," she says, looking in the rearview mirror at Fanny. "It was brutally unfair of me."

"It was," Fanny agrees.

I spin around in my seat and shoot her a give-the-girl-a-break look, but she ignores me and focuses on Poppy's rearview mirror.

"Though, I probably would have done the same thing if I were trapped in a car with a boorish, hostile little person." Fanny smiles one of her genuinely dazzling smiles.

I exhale.

Huzzah! Field Marshall Lord Wellington has subdued *Le Petit Empereur*! Ascend the belfries. Sound the bells. We have a truce!

"Shall we begin again, then?"

"*Oui!*"

Poppy switches lanes and the BMW races past a sign marking the entrance to the Inverness Coast Guard Helicopter Search and Rescue Station.

"Did you see that?" I lean forward and watch the coast guard sign become a small black dot in the passenger side mirror. "Do you know what we just passed?"

"No," Fanny says. "What?"

Poppy looks in her rearview mirror and taps her brakes.

"We just passed a coast guard base."

"So?" Poppy frowns at me, pushing the gas again.

"So"—I look at Poppy and waggle my eyebrows—"I wonder if the coasties are as cute as Ashton Kutcher in *The Guardian*?"

"What is a coastie?" Fanny asks.

"Guardsmen," Poppy corrects. "They're called guardsmen, not coasties."

"What is a coastie?" Fanny repeats.

I flip my visor down and look at Fanny in the lighted mirror. "A member of the Coast Guard. Haven't you seen *The Guardian* with Ashton Kutcher?"

"*Non.*"

"What?"

Poppy and I look at each other with horrified expressions. Though we haven't been friends for long, we somehow manage to tune into the same frequency and begin sending each other a flurry of telepathic messages.

Is she serious?

You tell me, she's your best friend.

She hasn't seen The Guardian?

Is that even possible?

Hasn't every post-pubescent woman in the free world ogled—er, watched—Ashton Kutcher play a brash young recruit in the action-adventure drama about a small band of highly skilled Coast Guard rescue swimmers selflessly risking life and limb to save souls adrift on a ferocious sea?

We can't allow one of our own to stumble around, alone in the dark. We have to show her the light.

"Oh, this situation *tragique* must be remedied as soon as possible, *ma cher amie*." I flip the visor back up, pull out my iPhone, and check to see if *The Guardian* is available online. "Voila! *The Guardian* is available for download on iTunes and instant streaming on Amazon. We are watching it tonight."

"You're serious?"

"Completely!" Poppy says.

"It's that good?"

"Fuck to the yeah!" I slip my iPhone back into my pocket. "Let's put it this way. I would leap naked into the frigid black waters of the North Sea if I thought one of those guardsmen at the Inverness Station was half as sexy as Ashton Kutcher in *The Guardian*."

We all laugh.

I am so happy I can't stop from clicking my Wellies together. This is the way girl trips are supposed to roll. Laughing. Bonding. Talking about hot men. Traveling Pants moments.

Poppy and Fanny have dropped their swords, and, while they're not exactly bosom buddies, they are making an effort to get along. Do you hear that *wahhhhhhhhh*? That would be a celestial choir singing.

My phone blings, and I wonder if Jesus is sprinkling a little more miracle dust over my life. If He can soften one French heart, He can soften two, right?

I hold my breath and mentally cross all of my fingers and toes as I pull my iPhone out of my pocket again and open my e-mail application. I have a new e-mail, but it's not from Luc. It's from Big Boss Lady. I feel like someone plunged a dagger in my heart and is twisting and pushing it slowly, deeper. The air leaks from my lips in one long, defeated exhalation. I push past the pain and read the e-mail.

TO: Vivia Perpetua Grant
FROM: Louanne Collins-London
SUBJ: Assignment
Vivia,
Your Bishop Raine piece was hilarious. That was quite a get! Well done.

I know you will deliver an equally splendid piece about your visit to MacFarlane Sheep Farm. Mr. MacFarlane provided us with a wonderful press packet of his farm, but please be sure to take some photographs of the women in your group learning how to shear sheep. Naturally, you will need to have them sign the standard photo consent release forms.

Next week, you head to Glasgow to interview the principal actors in A Strange Case, a cinematic adaptation of Robert Louis Stevenson's Dr. Jekyll and Mr. Hyde. The director has forced everyone connected with the picture to sign a confidentiality agreement. He's keeping his casting choices hush-hush.

Your POC at Film City Studios in Glasgow is Tiernan Dawson. Check in with him at nine o'clock on the morning of the first at their press office, 401 Govan Road (T: 0141 445 7244).

All the best,
Louanne Collins-London
Managing Editor
GoGirl! Magazine

Fanny reaches forward and squeezes my shoulder.

"*Est-il de Jean-Luc?*"

"No."

I hand my phone to Fanny to let her read Big Boss Lady's e-mail because I can't speak. Disappointment has clogged my throat. Fanny has had my phone for only seconds before she lets out an eardrum piercing squeal.

"Oh. My. God!"

"What?" Poppy hits the brakes. "What's wrong?"

"Sorry!" Fanny's voice is girlishly high. She giggles and squeals again before reading the e-mail to Poppy.

"So?"

"So," Fanny says. "Everyone has been talking about *A Strange Case.* I don't even follow pop culture – not like Vivia, anyway – and I've heard the rumors about the gigantic budget, the Oscar-winning director, and the battalion of actors vying for the lead role."

"Oooo!" Poppy turns to look at me. "Maybe you'll get to interview David Tennant."

"Or Zac Efron," Fanny pipes in. "Zac freaking Efron!"

"Zac Schmack." Poppy takes her hand off the steering wheel and flicks her wrist as if shooing an annoying fly. "Did you miss the part about David Tennant?"

"David who?"

"Doctor Who."

"Who is Doctor Who?"

"Who is Doctor Who?" Poppy looks at me with her mouth hanging open. "Cor! Are you sure your best friend is from France and not some antediluvian island? How can she not know about David Tennant?"

I shrug. "I don't know who David Tennant is, either."

"I am gobsmacked." Poppy slaps a hand to her forehead. "You must know about Doctor Who. Your mum is British."

Poppy's mention of my mum unearths the wispiest ghost of a memory of visiting my grandparents at their home outside Manchester and watching strange television shows on their old Zenith while eating butter cookies with raspberry jam filling.

"Wait! Wasn't *Doctor Who* a silly science fiction show? If David Tenant was on that show, he must be ancient."

"Silly science fiction sh-show?" Poppy sputters. "What are you on about? You must be off your trolley! *Doctor Who* has been on the telly since the sixties. It is a significant part of British pop culture."

"Ooo-kay, but it's a science fiction show, right?"

Poppy puts both hands back on the wheel, inhales through her nose, and exhales through her mouth several times. Who knew a science fiction show could transform the unflappable Poppy Worthington into a hyperventilating Lamaze student? I have seriously taken the starch out of her stiff upper lip and it's kinda funny.

"*Doctor Who* is a science fiction program about a Time Lord."

"Time Lord?" Fanny repeats.

"Yes, the Doctor—or Time Lord—is a time traveling humanoid who explores the Universe in his TARDIS."

"Tar-dis?"

I have to bite my lip to keep from laughing.

"A time-traveling space ship."

"Okay, then," I say, opening my eyes wide. "It sounds…"

"I know, it sounds bonkers, but it is really quite brilliant…and funny. You should watch it some time."

"I suppose I will have to since I might be interviewing Doctor Time Lord."

"The Doctor." Poppy corrects me. "The Doctor is a Time Lord."

"Wait a minute!" I frown as the wispy memory materializes more fully. "I think I remember watching an episode with my Gran set on a planet of caves run by warlords who were, like, intergalactic arms dealers, or something."

"Season twenty-three. 'The Trial of the Time Lord!'"

"If you say so," I shrug. "I just remember my Gran kept feeding me stale butter and jam cookies so I would—"

"Jammie Dodgers!"

"What?"

"The biscuits. They're called Jammie Dodgers and they're the Doctor's favorite."

"Dude! You're totally fangirling over the Doctor."

"She is, isn't she?" Fanny chuckles.

"I am British." Poppy sniffs. "I don't do fangirl."

"Bullshit!" I poke Poppy in the arm. "You're a David Tennant fangirl. It's cool. I used to get that way over Ronnie Radke, the singer from Falling in Reverse."

"Used to?" Fanny cries.

"Yeah, I think I am outgrowing him."

"The end of an era."

"I know, right?" I switch my focus back to Poppy. "So, tell me, have you always jonesed for the geezers or is it just this old Doctor dude that gets your juices flowing?"

"Vivian!" Fanny slaps my shoulder. "That is disgusting."

"It's all good. I'm not an ageist."

"Ha! Ha!" Poppy laughs. "David is not a geezer."

"Leave her alone, Vivian."

Look at me, bringing foes together under a common banner. Too bad I couldn't pop into Doctor Who's space ship and travel back to the early nineteenth century; I'll bet a few hours with me and old Nappy and Wellington would be slapping each other on the backs and swapping war stories like a couple of old cronies. "Waterloo? Where's that?"

Poppy looks in her rearview mirror at Fanny. "You really like Zac Efron?"

I pull down the visor and look at my best friend.

"Well," Fanny confesses, blushing. "I wouldn't kick him out of bed for singing *High School Musical* ditties."

"I hear you," Poppy says. "And I wouldn't kick David out of bed for eating Jammie Dodgers."

While my two friends engage in girl talk, I send Bishop Raine a text.

Text to 44 20 7834 6600:
Thanks for the interview. You scored me huge points with Big Boss Lady.

Text from 44 20 7834 6600:
Who is this?

Text 44 20 7834 6600:
Vivia.

When he doesn't respond I send another text.

Text to 44 20 7834 6600:
Vivia Grant. We met at Boujis.

Text from 44 20 7834 6600:
Right. Are you the brunette with the flag pasties?

Text to 44 20 7834 6600:
No. I am the GoGirl! reporter in the sequined mini-dress you tongue raped.

Text from 44 20 7834 6600:
LOL. Right. I remember. Glad my musings put you in right with the man..or the wo-Man. If praise from authority is what motivates you, California Girl, I am glad I could give you a boost up the corporate ladder.

"That's odd."

"What's odd?" Poppy asks.

"I just sent Bishop a text thanking him for the interview, and he responded as if he barely remembered meeting me."

Poppy chuckles. "That's Bishop. Don't take it personally. You know the Hollywood types—they suffer from attachment ADD. They're only faithful to whoever is fawning on them at the moment. What have you done for me lately mentality and all."

"Wow. I thought you were friends."

"I am friends with Bishop—as much as anyone can be friends with a celebrity."

"I thought he was different."

"He is definitely different."

Poppy and Fanny laugh, but I stare bleakly at my girlish pink rain boots and curse my flirtation with Bishop "I fink my Mockney accent makes me sound urbane" Raine. What a fool I was jeopardizing my relationship with a truly urbane man for a night of hollow ego-stroking.

Then again, it's not like I had an affair. It was one stupid, meaningless, unsolicited kiss. How was I supposed to know Bishop Raine would stick his tongue down my throat or that the bobblehead bitches would snap a picture of us kissing and send it to Steven Schpiel? I love Luc, but he's being totally unfair about this one.

"Bishop Raine. Zac Efron. David Tennant. Steven Schpiel. Luc de Caumont." I cross my arms over my chest. "I am fed up with men. If a fleet of female aliens landed on this planet and enslaved every last one of them, I wouldn't care."

"Well then," Fanny says, "it's a good thing we are spending the week on a farm with only women for company."

Chapter 17

Make it Rain

Vivia Perpetua Grant @PerpetuallyViv
In 2009, a Scottish sheep farmer paid over $380,000 for an
8-month-old breeding ram. #BaaadInvestment

When we arrive at MacFarlane Sheep Farm, a cluster of charming cottages surrounded by rolling green pastures, the sun has settled low in the cleavage of two paps.

I read in my DK Eyewitness Travel Guide the Scottish refer to mountains as paps. I also learned: Drambuie, an aged malt whisky infused with honey and spices, is Scotland's most popular potent potable; "*sláinte,*" which means to your health, is the preferred drinking toast; Ecclefechan Tart is a fruit pastry served with ice cream; and women outnumber men by five percent. Sophisticated alcoholic beverages, desserts served à la mode, and female domination. Something tells me I am gonna love this place.

Poppy follows the winding dirt drive to the end and parks the BMW beside a stone barn. Thick gray clouds have rolled across the sky like an old down blanket, just waiting to fall and shroud the world in darkness. A few determined rays of light punctured holes through the clouds and are streaming from the heavens to the hills, spotlighting herds of trembling sheep huddled together against the dying light.

"Have you ever seen anything more beautifully ominous?" I whisper, holding my iPhone up to snap a shot of the landscape. "I can almost see Rob Roy MacGregor reiving cattle from the hills."

"It looks like a scene from *Outlander*," Fanny murmurs.

A tall, barrel-chested, broad-shouldered man wearing jeans tucked into Wellies and a thin T-shirt walks out of the barn and stares at our car, a scowl marring his handsome face.

"I do believe we just found your Jamie, Sassenach." I whisper to Fanny. "Sweet Shortbread! He's one delicious-looking man."

The scowl fades from the Scot's face, replaced by a roguish grin. We open our doors and get out.

"Fàilte lassies! Fàilte tae MacFarlane croft." He strides across the barnyard, closing the distance between us in three long-legged strides. "I didnea ken ye'd be arrivin' so early."

"My name is Vivia Grant," I say, holding out my hand. "I am the columnist with *GoGirl!* I believe my editor contacted you."

He takes my hand and shakes it.

"My name is Angus MacFarlane." He says, switching from his thick Scottish brogue to slightly accented English. "Welcome to MacFarlane Farm, lassie."

"Thank you."

Angus quirks a brow. "Nice Wellies."

I look down at my rain boots, the weak sunlight reflected off the glassine pink toes, and grin.

"Thanks!"

I am introducing the strapping Scot to my friends when several more strapping Scots emerge from the barn and form a semi-circle around Angus, muscular arms crossed over muscular chests.

I am vaguely aware that Angus is speaking. His lips are definitely moving, but my eyes are doing this crazy pendulum thing—as I swing my gaze from Angus to the hot Scots, Angus to the hot Scots.

Seriously? Some potent mystical substance must be in the water in the Highlands because the men are freaking huge—and gorgeous. I look around for a stripper pole and Matthew McConaughey in black leather chaps and cowboy hat because we must have stumbled onto the set of *Magic Mike III*. That's the only explanation I can think of for this freak testosterone explosion.

I am envisioning Angus kicking off his Wellies and dry humping the ground while I make it rain with a fistful of twenties, when Fanny elbows me in the ribs, pulling me abruptly and painfully from my dirty daydream.

"Ow!"

One of the Scots, a tall strawberry-blond hottie with a military crew cut and chiseled cheekbones, notices the rib jab and grins. I flush from the tips of my pink rubber clad toes to the tips of my ears.

"Vivia!" Fanny nudges me again. "Did you hear what Angus just said? He offered to take our luggage to our cottage while Fiona leads us on a quick tour of the farm."

I narrow the focus of my gaze on Angus, only Angus. "You don't grind, er, mind, I mean?"

"Och, ye're havering," Angus says, waving a hand at me. "Of course I don't mind. Dinnea ye fash yerself."

While Poppy opens the trunk to remove our luggage and Fanny wrestles half of the entire Louis Vuitton travel collection from the backseat, I pretend to send a text to avoid making eye contact with any of the Scots—but particularly the grinning strawberry-blond hottie. His piercing blue-eyed gaze has completely discombobulated me. It's like he used laser vision to peek inside my brain and read my dirty little thoughts.

My phone blings and vibrates. I open my e-mail box and the find the message I have been waiting to receive ever since Luc walked out of our hotel room five days ago. My stomach flips.

TO: Vivia Perpetua Grant
FROM: Jean-Luc de Caumont
SUBJ: I love you
I haven't called because I need some time to think. I've also been having problems with my mobile. I can't access my voicemail or text messages, so if you need to reach me, please send an e-mail or call the chateau.

The term ended last week, which means I am free for the summer. My brother asked me to lead a bike tour for Aventures Caumont. I leave for the Côte d'Azur in a few days, but will call you when I return.

Please be safe.
Luc

Luc sent me an e-mail! So why don't I feel relieved or reassured?

I start at the top and read the e-mail again, analyzing the text and the meta-text, what Luc wrote, and what he did not write. The message is neither loving nor dismissive. Other than the opening hook—the "I love you" subject line—he didn't give me a lot to grab onto.

He says he needs time. How much time? A week? A year? And what happens after he takes time to think? Will we resume our intense long-distance love affair—sending each other sexties, talking through the night, sharing our secrets and dreams, scheduling weekends of crazy-hot monkey sex and room service in Prague, Paris, Pisa?

I don't think so.

Something shifted after Luc discovered the linguistically adept Bishop Raine stuck his tongue down my throat—a subtle rearranging and redefining of our relationship. My urbane, sophisticated, sexually-liberated French lover traveled back in time, entered a prehistoric cave, and walked out missing a few relationship chromosomes. I recognized the primal flash in his eyes when he saw the photograph of Bishop kissing me, that primal desire to lay claim, to make me his woman.

Then again, maybe I am reading it all wrong.

I look at his unaffectionate, unromantic last line.

"Please be safe."

It's not exactly the closing salutation of someone staking a claim.

I slide my iPhone into my pocket and walk to the back of the BMW. Poppy has removed her suitcase and cosmetic trunk and is about to lift my pink bag from the trunk when I stop her.

"No, please," I say, reaching for the handle. "It's crazy heavy. I'll get it."

"Pishaw." Poppy lifts the bag from the trunk. "I don't mind."

"Thanks."

I walk around the car, grab my MacBook case from the passenger footwell, and help Fanny remove her elephant-sized bag from Poppy's peanut-sized backseat.

Magic Mike III's bit players returned to their work in the barn, but Angus and the grinning hottie are still standing with their arms crossed over their barrel chests. They look a lot alike, actually, except grinning hottie is younger, blonder, and a wee more handsome.

Grinning hottie notices me staring at him and winks.

"A'll see ye Monday next, then," grinning hottie says, giving Angus one of those Macho Man half hugs with the bruising back slap. "Lang may yer lum reek."

Angus laughs, slaps grinning hottie on the back, and repeats the salutation. He says it so fast, though, that it almost sounds like, "Long may your bum reek."

Since the Scots are distracted with back-slapping and bum reeking, I turn my back on them and whisper, "Who is Fiona?"

Poppy and Fanny look at me with matching "What the hell, Vivia?" expressions.

"Sorry, I kinda zoned out. It was hard to focus with Rub Roy and his brawny band staring at me."

Poppy snorts. "You are a cheeky monkey."

"Rub Roy?" Fanny frowns. "Who is Rub Roy?"

"She's making a pun on the movie, *Rob Roy,* starring Liam Neeson." Poppy explains. "I think our friend has a wee crush on the Scot."

"Really?" Fanny giggles. "Which one?"

I shrug. "Take your pick."

"Remember that thing you said earlier about the fleet of men-hating female aliens coming from outer space to gather up all of our menfolk to use as slaves?"

"Yeah, forget I said that," I grin.

Poppy and Fanny laugh.

"So," I say, kicking a stone with the toe of my Wellies. "Who is Fiona?"

"I am Fiona."

I spin around and discover a tall super-slender brunette with large, twinkling eyes and a mischievous grin standing behind me. Her jaunty ponytail, pixie bangs swept to one side, black denim pants tucked into high Wellies, and crisp white blouse rolled to the elbows remind me of Audrey Hepburn in *Roman Holiday*—or what Audrey Hepburn would have looked like if she'd made *Scottish Holiday* instead of *Roman Holiday*.

"Hello, Fiona. I'm Vivia." I look over her shoulder. "Where are your friends? Haven't they arrived yet?"

"Um—" Fiona's cheeks turn pink.

Too late, I realize my *faux pas*. I assumed all of the women taking part in this sheep-shitty excuse for a vacation would be traveling with their besties. Maybe Fiona doesn't have a bestie.

Fanny nudges me in the side, but I ignore her.

"What happened, Fee?" I playfully punch her arm. "Did you do an old bait-and-switch? Tell them they were going to spend a week at some chi-chi spa in the Highlands getting rubdowns by brawny lads in kilts, and then bring them here and say, 'Surprise! We're really getting up at the crack o' to shovel sheep poo!'"

Fiona's cheeks turn a deeper, more violent shade of pink. Poppy clears her throat. Fanny nudges me harder.

"It's all good, girl." I nudge the other woman. "You can work on our chain gang. I'll share a shackle with you. We'll be—"

"Vivian!" Fanny grabs my forearm and squeezes it. "This is Fiona MacFarlane. She owns MacFarlane Farm."

"What?" A quick glance at Fanny tells me I have, indeed, stepped in the proverbial sheep shit. "Fudgebuckets. Sorry. I thought you were…"

I let my thought trail off because I can't think of a word to finish the sentence without insulting my hostess. I thought you were…sad? Lonely? Rejected? Friendless? Why not just grab a cattle brand and burn a big fat L on her forehead?

Sheepballs! I'm the loser with chronic diarrhea of the mouth.

"Och." Fiona dismisses my apology with a wave of her slender hand. "I am just glad I can count on you to be my shackle buddy—should we ever find ourselves incarcerated. I didn't have a shackle mate the last time I was in the pokey and I spent all my time in solitary just to avoid becoming someone's biatch."

She delivers her declaration with such a deadpan expression, I wonder if she is serious. Finally, her lips begin to twitch, pulling up at the corners.

"Nicely played, Fiona." I grin.

"I had you going for a minute, didn't I?"

"I was sweating bullets."

"Worried you'd stepped into a scene from *Sheepshank Redemption*?"

"Ha!" I laugh. "I see what you did there. Nice."

Poppy groans.

"That bad?" Fiona asks.

Fanny wrinkles her nose and nods her head.

When we finish laughing, we take turns introducing ourselves.

It turns out; my shackle mate is married to Hottie MacScottie, also known as Angus. Fiona MacFarlane was born and raised in Toledo, Ohio, which explains her flat Midwestern patois and dry sense of humor.

"How did a girl from Toledo end up in the Highlands?" I ask a similar question each time I meet an American living abroad. More often than not, the answers fascinate me. "Was it love?"

"No." Fiona chuckles and shakes her head. "I came to Scotland because I was burnt out—of my job, my relationships, my life—and on the verge of a Chernobyl-sized meltdown. A colleague suggested I take time off and invited me to stay with her parents, who happened to own a sheep farm in the Highlands."

"This farm?"

"No," Fiona shakes her head. "That farm is nearby, though."

"If you don't mind my asking, what did you do before you became a shepherdess?"

"I was a psychiatrist at a substance abuse hospital for wealthy women."

I keep an it's-all-good smile plastered on my face, but inwardly I am cringing. I always feel awkward around psychiatrists, like they've got x-ray vision and can look through my skull at all of the anxieties and neuroses swirling around in my brain. I can almost hear her tsk-tsking, *"What a shame. An unhealthy need for approval, employs sarcasm when nervous, and addicted to chocolate. She appeared sane."*

I glance at Poppy and Fanny. They're twin deer caught in the headlights, anxious smiles frozen on their faces, eyes wide and unblinking. It's like they're afraid Fiona might turn her x-ray vision on them and discover a hidden personality disorder.

"Relax, ladies," Fiona laughs. "You will remain free from any psychological assessment as long as you don't lie down on my couch. Be warned, though. Enter my living room at your own peril."

Fiona says the last two sentences in a spot-on impersonation of Vincent Price delivering the "Thriller" monologue. I half expect her to end with a diabolical "Muwahahaha."

The sun quietly slipped behind the mountain while we were talking, casting us in muted shades of gray.

"Fiona MacFarlane, you are one twisted puppy." I grin. "I think we are going to be good friends."

She smiles. "I hope so."

In the distance, a dog barks and sheep bleat, until a rumbling drum roll of thunder drowns them out.

"So you left Ohio on a mental health break and just never went back?" Poppy asks. "Just like that?"

"Something like that."

"Go, girl!" Fanny says, pumping her fist.

"I felt a soul connection with Scotland and the Scots, as if I had been wandering my whole life and had finally found my home." Fiona begins walking and we follow, making our way down a brick path leading to six identical stone cottages. "I enjoyed helping my friend's parents tend their sheep, so I bought this farm and a herd of sheep from Collum MacFarlane, Angus's dad."

"Did he throw his son in as a bonus?" Fanny asks.

"No." Fiona makes a sharp right toward the third cottage. "Angus thought I was a silly American woman with more romantic notions than common sense. He was an ass, always scowling and muttering in Gaelic under his breath. He even started a betting pool at the pub in town. Most of the village placed bets as to how long it would be before I killed my herd or packed up and moved back to the States."

"Don't you miss the life you gave up?"

"I've never thought of it as giving up one life for another. That implies loss. I've lost nothing. I still have my friends, my family, my skills, my memories." Fiona pulls a ring of keys from her pocket and slides one of them into the lock on the cottage's front door. "In Scotland, I have made new friends, acquired new skills, and every day I am making new memories."

"What about your career?"

"What about my career?"

"Don't you miss being a psychiatrist?"

Fiona pushes the door open before turning to look at me, tilting her head and narrowing her gaze. It's an x-ray vision pose if I ever saw one.

"As a psychiatrist, I helped women on their journey towards empowerment. I believe I am doing the same thing with this sheep farm, giving women the opportunity to learn a new skill, challenge themselves, become more empowered by stretching their boundaries."

Fanny gives me her are-you-paying-attention look, and I know she is thinking about my fear of losing my identity through matrimony.

Fiona opens the door to our temporary home.

I think of Luc while Fiona shows us around the surprisingly posh little cottage. and while she answers questions about the work we will be doing on the sheep farm. After Fiona leaves, I think of Luc while I am unpacking, showering, moisturizing, and putting on my flannel sheep pajamas (Oh, yes I did!). I even think of Luc while composing tweets about my new Wellies (it's raining fabulous), journey over Loch Ness (no sighting), and first impression of the MacFarlanes (as charming as their cottages).

I fall back onto my bed, hug my iPhone to my chest, and stare at the ceiling, as if the answers to my problems are etched on the wooden beams.

What is wrong with me?

I changed my hairstyle, wardrobe, hobbies, and sexual history to be with Nathan, the man I thought I loved, but I won't change my mailing address to be with Luc, the man I know I love?

That's a rhetorical question. I know the answer. I am unwilling to bend because bending for Nathan nearly broke me; just as bending and scraping to please my father nearly broke my mum.

I am afraid if I give up my career, surname, and homeland to marry Luc, I will become a boring nonentity. I will become one of those sad, slightly-manic women you meet at the grocery store who initiate needless discussions with strangers about floor cleaner because they are lonely and desperate to connect.

I am imagining a future where I wear purple velour track suits to run errands in my minivan and spend hours torturing my Facebook friends with updates about my trip to the dentist.

Vivia Perpetua Grant-de Caumont

26 mins

Just got back from the dentist. The hygienist was a little rough and now my gums are sore. No root canal needed, though. So, yay me!

Maybe this is another case of my over-dramatic imagination running buck-stinking-wild.

If Fiona has been able to fashion a new life in Scotland, why can't I do the same in France? She struck a good balance between career and love. She's interesting and funny. She works on a sheep farm surrounded by brawny, belching, butt-scratching men, but can still hang with the girls and rock a pair of black skinny jeans.

Maybe I have it all wrong. Maybe Luc wants me to continue working as a travel columnist after we are married. Maybe he would be totally cool with me keeping my surname, blowing off his stuffy faculty functions, and wearing leather leggings and vintage band T's to the grocery store. After all, I had pink hair and a painful freshly-inked ass tat on our first date, and he was more than totally cool about it.

Since we've never actually had a serious conversation about getting married, I don't know what his expectations are for the future Madame de Caumont, mistress of his ancestral chateau.

Hope surges through my veins like a sixty-four-ounce can of Monster Energy Drink, making me feel amped up, jittery with unspent energy, and ready to take on the world.

I suddenly sit up. I know what I am going to do.

I'm calling Luc! I am going to call Luc right now.

Invigorated by my newfound confidence, I practically leap out of bed and begin pacing the length of my room, trusty iPhone clutched in my hand at the ready.

I will simply phone Luc and tell him to forget about the Bishop Raine BS, because that is precisely what it is: bullshit. I will tell him I love him and want to be with only him. Then, I will question him about his expectations for a wife, let him know my expectations and boundaries, and negotiate a marital contract.

Yes! I pump my fist in the air. Let's do this thing!

I dial his number. It rings once, twice, and then—

"Bonjour. C'est Jean-Luc. Veuillez me laisser un message et je vous téléphonerai aussitôt que possible. Merci."

My call goes to voicemail after only two rings. I know what that means. Luc looked at the caller ID, saw my number on the screen, and declined the call. It's the only explanation since every other time I called it rang five times before going to voicemail.

The adrenaline coursing through my veins screeches to a halt and I drop back onto the bed, like some dramatic post-energy drink crash. *Dude! I am, like, totally drained.* Someone give me twenty cc's of hope stat.

I toss my phone on my bed, grab my MacBook, and pad into the cozy living room. Fanny has made hot chocolate spiked with Amaretto—she grabbed a bottle when we hit the Tesco in town while I grabbed four boxes of Borders Strawberries and Cream Shortbread. Poppy has a small fire crackling in the fireplace.

Fanny looks up and frowns. She mouths, "Are you all right?"

"Chocolate, artery-clogging butter cookies, and friends." I force a smile and put the box of Borders Shortbread on the tray beside the chocolate. "What more could a girl want?"

"David Tennant," Poppy says.

"Zac Efron," Fanny counters.

"Luc de Caumont." I avoid their gazes as I place the cookies on the tray beside Fanny's steaming chocolate. "But I guess a girl can't get everything she wants."

"Boo." Fanny crumples a napkin and throws it at me. "You were supposed to say Ashton Kutcher."

"Ah, yes! Ashton." I hold my MacBook up. "Thanks to the wonder of online streaming, Ashton is always just one click away, always faithful and ready to charm."

We are in our wooly socks and flannel jammies, huddled together by the fire, watching the downloaded version of *The Guardian* on my MacBook, when it begins to rain.

When I fall into bed later, howling winds rattle the shutters and heavy raindrops plink against the windows like pebbles. I leave the curtains open and stare out at the forbidding inky darkness, thinking how perfectly the bleak, gloomy landscape matches my mood.

A bolt of lightning suddenly appears from the heavens, dividing the sky into two purplish-black jagged pieces—like the jagged pieces of my broken heart.

Chapter 18

Heavy Petting

Steven Schpiel @TheWholeSchpiel
Bishop Raine tells @PerpetuallyViv to just go, girl. Now dating New Age guru & founder of Hippie Chick Clothing, @SummerCane

Vivia Perpetua Grant @PerpetuallyViv
Did you know sheep spend 1/3 of their lives ruminating? #ZeninThePen #WiseWoolyBoogers Too bad some humans don't mimic sheep: #ThinkMore #BleatLess @StevenSchpiel

The day dawns insultingly bright, and I wake with golden sunshine bitch-slapping me in the face. It's Mother Nature's way of taunting me. "Get up you sad, sorry girl. Stop dreaming about romance and face loveless reality."

I rub the sleep from my eyes with my closed fists and stretch my legs, thrusting my feet out from the end of the flannel duvet cover. The frigid air instantly nips at my bare toes, so I pull them back into the warm flannel cocoon.

I don't want to, but I crack open one eye to confirm what I already know: Yep, it's a blooming, bleeding, brilliantly sunny day, which means I am going to have to get up, get dressed, and slap on my social face. No hiding out in the cabin, getting toasted on Amaretto-laced hot chocolate and watching sad sack rom-coms.

Poppy is humming in the shower down the hall, and Fanny is crashing around the kitchen, opening cabinets, slamming drawers, no doubt in search of coffee. Even though Fanny is not a morning person, I know my competitive, hyper-driven, let's go-go-go friend is suited up and ready to shear some sheep. It was Fanny's drill instructor-like cadence that pushed/shamed/goaded me to complete that skazillion mile Provence to Tuscany bike ride. She's a city girl, but just watch, she will shear more sheep, climb more paps, muck out more stalls than anyone else in our group—and in her spare time, she'll build Angus a new barn.

I grit my teeth. Sometimes I wish my super-charged compadre would just kick back with me. What's wrong with coasting every now and then?

I sit up, pull the duvet around my shoulders, and stare out at the obscenely beautiful landscape beyond my window frame.

Fanny knocks on my door.

"Come in, Fanny."

The door creaks open and Fanny pokes her head in. "How did you know it was me?"

"Puh-leez." I roll my eyes. "Do you hear her in the shower? Humming and singing like Cinderella? I knew it couldn't be you."

"Funny." Fanny steps into my room and rubs her arms. "*Merde*! It's cold."

"I know, right? And it's nearly summer."

I hold the quilt up, and Fanny bounds into my bed. We huddle together under the fluffy duvet and listen to Poppy singing Taylor Swift's "Shake it Off."

Fanny and I laugh out loud when *veddy* proper Poppy melodically declares she "has nothing in her brain."

"What song she is singing?"

"'Shake it Off' by Taylor Swift."

Fanny chuckles. "You're kidding, right?"

"Nope." I pull my knees to my chest and wrap my arms around them for warmth. "She's a Swiftie."

"Wow! Television shows about time lords and Taylor Swift. She's not what you expect when you first meet her."

"Right? I really dig her."

Fanny doesn't say anything.

"She'll never replace you, though." I grab her hand and squeeze it. "You're my BFF."

"Best French Friend?"

"Forever."

We let go of each other's hands and sit quietly, staring out at the paps covered in a patchwork of yellow and purplish-pink, flowers.

"When did Cinderella sing?"

"What?" I glance at my friend. "What are you talking about?"

"Before, you said Poppy sounds like Cinderella. I've read Charles Perrault's tale about the orphan girl forced to live in the attic, but I don't remember anything about her singing."

I forgot that my best friend has never watched an animated Disney film. Once, I tried to get her to sit down and watch *Beauty and the Beast*. I even belted out Belle's opening song about her little town full of little people waking up to say, "*Bonjour, Bonjour!*" She looked at me with that uniquely Gallic expression of haughty disdain.

"Disney's Cinderella."

"Ah."

"In the movie, she sings to her posse of mice and birds."

"Posse of mice?" Fanny slaps her forehead. "*Mon dieu!*"

Poppy pads down the hall fully dressed, a towel around her head. "Bathroom's all yours."

"Well"—Fanny tosses the duvet off her shoulders and bounds out of bed—"we better get a move on!"

I groan. "Do we have to?"

"*On se bouge!*" She claps her hands three times. "*On se bouge!*"

"*On se bouge! On se bouge!*" I reluctantly roll out of bed. "*Mon dieu, je déteste ces mots!*"

Fanny laughs as she leaves my room, closing the door behind her with a decisive click. She learned long ago the danger of feeding into my grumbling. Normally, I am like Gizmo, the soft, sweet, furry creature in the movie *Gremlins*, but feed my bad mood and I transform into a truly frightening monster.

On se bouge. I really do hate those words. Literally translated *on se bouge* means "we are moving." I became overly-acquainted with the words during my now infamous bike tour of France and Italy. While I was gasping for breath/resting on the side of the road/lagging behind the group/sprawled out in bed, Fanny or Luc would clap their hands like a pair of heartless cheerleaders and cheer, "*On se bouge*, Vivia!"

I look at the fluffy duvet cover and consider climbing back into bed, pulling the covers over my head, and spending the day dreaming about sheep, when my BFF—Ball-busting Fitness Freak—opens my door and pops her head in.

"Do you want an energy bar?" She grins as she waves a candy bar-shaped object wrapped in plain brown paper. "They're Açai berry and soy!"

* * * *

"Oooo! I love your Wellies!"

I look down at my feet and back at the perky, pretty blonde seated next to me on a wooden bench. We have gathered around a stone fire pit to sip orange spiced chai, nibble cinnamon muffins, and become acquainted with the members of our group.

"Thanks!" She's wearing pretty pink Burberry pashmina. "Love your scarf."

"Gee, thanks!"

The pretty blonde says her name is Devon. She's a school teacher from South Carolina traveling with her mother, Kathy, a fifty-something blonde with sparkling blue eyes and an infectious laugh, and her sister, Paige, a quiet college student attending the University of Virginia.

I have already met Lori Lee, Megan, and Mari, wives of U.S. Air Force pilots deployed somewhere in the Middle East, and Cindy, Lily, Victoria, and Kieran, romance writers looking for inspiration for their next novels.

The last two Chick Trippers to arrive at the breakfast bonfire are Tava and Lisa, two young mothers from Michigan who have joined our group of sixteen soul-searching, sheep-shearing sistahs to celebrate surviving breast cancer.

Wise-cracking Tava is laugh out loud hilarious, with a dangerous, devil-may-care, "I've survived worse than this; so bring it, *muthafuckas*" attitude. If there were a thought bubble floating over her head, it would read, *"I had Cancer for breakfast, now whatcha got?"* She is exactly the sort of colorful character I instinctually gravitate to at parties.

But it's Lisa's thoughtful demeanor that draws me in this morning. The willowy redhead sits with her long, slender fingers wrapped around a mug of chai and a quiet smile curving her lips. While the rest of the Chicks chirp away, Lisa sits alone, participating without interacting.

I don't know what I could possibly have in common with a young mother and cancer survivor, since I couldn't nurture a houseplant, let alone an infant, and barely survive my monthly menstrual cycle, but Lisa rouses my inborn desire to protect the underdog, to include the excluded.

"Mind if I join you?"

"Of course not." She moves over, making room for me on the bench beside her. "Love your rain boots, by the way."

What is it with these Wellies? They've been on my feet less than twenty-four hours and already a dozen people have complimented them! Who knew a pair of pink rubber rain boots would make such a crazy big fashion splash?

"Thanks." I sit on the bench and stretch my legs out in front of me, crossing my ankles. "I know it is ridiculous, but these boots make me silly happy."

"It's not ridiculous." She takes a sip of tea. "Life is too short not to be silly happy. Wear your rain boots and stomp in puddles with the giddy abandon of a child, if that's what makes you truly, silly happy."

"You know what?"

"What?"

"I just might go puddle-stomping later." I look into her wise-beyond-her-years blue-gray eyes. "Wanna come with me?"

"Thanks"—she stretches one of her legs out in front of her and lifts her foot—"but I don't know if these old things could take much stomping."

She's the only one in the group not wearing tall, rubber rain boots. Black utilitarian rain boots are the footgear of choice with the Chick Trippers, but Lisa is sporting a battered pair of Columbia hiking boots. I look from her nondescript worn hikers to my "Here I Am World, Notice Me" fuchsia Wellies and feel a stab of shame for prattling on about something as frivolous as overpriced rain boots to a woman who is probably just happy to have her feet still above ground.

"Looks like we are the odd women out, doesn't it?"

Lisa chuckles, but she tucks her feet under the bench, out of view. "It would appear so."

My friend Grace lost her mother to ovarian cancer our senior year in college. Poor Grace, a broke, recently graduated college student with a stack of hospital bills and student loans couldn't even afford a new suit to wear to job interviews.

I suddenly feel shallow.

"Listen to me"—I tuck my feet under the bench—"going on about a pair of stupid boots. You'd think I discovered the—"

I stop speaking and stare at the orange flames dancing toward the cobalt sky, too embarrassed to look at Lisa. My cheeks feel as hot as the flames.

"—cure for cancer?"

I mentally slap myself upside the head. I am such an assjack. What kind of person makes a joke about cancer to a cancer survivor? An assjack. I am mentally flagellating myself when Lisa rests her hand briefly on my knee. I look at her, notice the flames reflected in her pretty gray eyes, and realize this wallflower is not lilting.

"It's okay," she says, smiling. "Cancer took my breasts, not my sense of humor."

"Thank God, because if you plan on spending a week around me, you will need a healthy sense of humor."

Lisa chuckles.

The Chick Trippers continue to chatter about their lives back home and their hopes for the week ahead, but Lisa and I sit quietly, sipping our tea and staring at the bonfire. It's not an awkward or uncomfortable silence. It's easy and soothing. I don't have many friendships that offer the peace that comes from just being—and I like it.

Fiona catches my eye from across the bonfire and a slow I-am-so-proud-of-you smile curves her lips. It reminds me of my mum. Fiona and her spooky x-ray mind-shrinking vision. What else does she see when she looks at me? I look away before she peers deep into the dark, twisted attic of my psyche and discovers my obsessive-compulsive inability to consume milk if it is within two days of the sell-by date.

"Don't do that."

"Do what?" I flinch, practically shouting the words. "What did I do? I didn't do anything."

"Don't minimize your joy because you are worried what others might think. If boots make you happy, buy them, wear them, puddle stomp the heck out of them."

"It is silly to get so happy over such a little thing."

"I don't know." Lisa lifts her cup of tea and slowly inhales. "Big pleasures—trips to Scotland, new cars—they're great, but I've found it is the small pleasures—a good cup of tea, shiny new rain boots—that really matter in life. It's the little things that get us through each day, that sustain us through trials."

I raise my nearly-empty cup of tea to my lips, but instead of slamming back the last few drops, I inhale the spicy scent.

"You're a wise chick."

"Eh"—she shrugs—"I don't know how wise I am, but cancer has definitely given me a different perspective on life. Things that used to mean so much to me—my career, my bank account, my appearance—don't matter as much as they did before cancer. Now, the important things, big and small, truly matter."

* * * *

Fiona and Angus officially welcome our group of Chick Trippers to the MacFarlane Farm and promise us "an unforgettable week of recreation and relaxation."

"Today will be a long, busy, but hopefully memorable, day." Fiona says, walking in a circle around the bonfire. "We will begin by touring the farm and acquainting you with the flock. After we break for lunch, Angus will demonstrate the proper way to round up a flock of sheep. Later, you will be broken into pairs. Each pair will be responsible for the care and feeding of a mini-flock."

Holy Shit! She can't be serious. How am I supposed to take care of a flock of sheep? Maybe now would be a good time to tell Fiona the tragic outcome of my houseplant purchase. Excuse me, Fiona, I would like to be excused from this activity on the grounds I drowned a cactus.

I am about to raise my hand when Fiona stops walking, turns in my direction, and fixes her freaky mind-meld gaze on me.

"Now," she says, smiling. "I know some of you are worrying you lack the skills needed to take care of undomesticated animals, right?"

I nod my head and look around the circle at the other Chick Trippers. I am the only one nodding my head.

"Well, don't!" Fiona continues walking around the circle. "This week is about two things: nature and nurture. In the mornings, we will care for the flock, but the afternoons will be about caring for ourselves through Yoga, hiking, horseback riding, sightseeing, and therapeutic services like facials and massages."

Yes, now we're talking!

Fiona shares her philosophy on the therapeutic benefits of caring for animals and her vision for the McFarlane Sheep Farm as a destination vacation for women seeking balance, empowerment, and broadening experiences.

Fiona, Angus explains, is too much of a bleeding heart to raise sheep for slaughter—so she breeds her animals for the wool and milk.

"We keep a mini-flock, comprised of carefully selected rams and ewes, in a separate barn for breeding purposes," Angus says. "A few of our breeding beasts cost more than an automobile."

Devon, the pretty South Carolinian school teacher, raises her hand, and asks, "Are there different breeds of sheep?"

"Aye." Angus crosses his thickly-corded arms over his chest and leans back, evidently pleased with the more scholarly focus on his livestock. "We raise Scottish Blackface, Black Welsh, and Rambouillet for the wool and Friesian and Lacaune for dairy."

"Lacaune?" Fanny perks up. "That's a French breed. My grandmother had Lacaune sheep on her farm in Normandy."

"Aye." Angus nods. "The Lacaune produces milk with a higher milk solid ratio, which is why it is the breed of choice with French cheese makers, particularly those who make Roquefort."

"However," Fiona interjects, "we value each animal for the intrinsic and intangible value it brings to our lives."

Angus grimaces and rolls his eyes, reminding me of an animated character. When I catch his exaggerated expression, the reporter in me can't resist asking the slightly impertinent question.

"Are we to interpret from your expression that you don't share your wife's more holistic approach to sheep rearing?"

"Och, no!" He snorts and waves his hand. "I was raised to view the mangy beasts as commodities, not wee fluffy cuddlies." He looks down at his wife and grins. "But I love and respect Fiona, so…"

"…so he compromised for me."

"I dinnea ken what yer saying, woman!" His fierce scowl has me wondering how the Scottish could have possibly lost at Culloden. "You don't see me naming and petting the wee beasts like family pets."

"Ach! You protest too much, Angus Alexander Kinloch MacFarlane, but deep down in that rough, calloused Scottish heart of yours, I know you're aching to grab Goldiflocks and give her a good squeeze."

"Och!" Angus waves. "Away with you woman."

Watching Fiona and Angus together is creating an ache in the pit of my stomach, the same ache I got that summer when my mum made me spend three weeks at Camp Walahanka. I miss Luc the same way I missed my home, bed, mum, and dad. I miss the easy familiar. I miss the warm, all-consuming contentment of knowing I belong somewhere, to someone.

Knock it off, Vivia! You do belong somewhere, to someone. You are Vivia Perpetua Grant, GoGirl! columnist, and eager world traveler. You don't need a man to define you—do you?

We follow Angus and Fiona into a large, airy, well-lit barn, A brawny Scot wrangles several black sheep into a round observation pen.

"These are Black Welsh Sheep." Fiona steps into the pen, drops to her knees, and wraps her arm around the neck of one of the great black, wooly beasts. "And this is Baasheba, Daughter of the Oats. She is my most treasured Black Welsh because she is beautiful, gentle, and produces the healthiest lambs."

Fiona reaches into her pocket, pulls out a handful of oats, and offers them to Baasheba.

"Black Welsh Sheep are hearty, self-sufficient, and extremely maternal," Angus explains, his brogue becoming thicker the longer he speaks. "They produce lovely wool."

A large black demonic-looking ram with heavy curved horns ambles over to Fiona and nudges Baasheba out of the way so he can feast on the remaining oats.

"Awwww," several of the Chick Trippers croon.

Whatever. I'm not feeling the love. That massive lint ball from Hell could do some serious damage with his devil horns. Just sayin'.

I am about to pull out my iPhone to check how much longer until Braveheart rings the bell signaling our lunch break when a tall, muscular strawberry-blonde with a crew-cut strolls into the barn, a cock-eared Border Collie trotting by his side.

Cue the bow-chicka-wow-wow music, Magic Mike, Grinning Hottie has stepped back on the stage.

Angus's handsomer, blonder doppelganger leans against a wooden post and crosses his arms over his broad chest. He's totally casual, even though every Chick Tripper stopped watching Fiona frolic with her flock the moment he stepped into the barn.

Look at him! Standing there, grinning like the Grinch after he stole the last can of Who Hash. He knows the effect he's having on this estrogen-heavy crowd, and he's loving it.

I stubbornly return my gaze to the observation pen. I will not look at Grinning Hottie. I will not look at Grinning Hottie.

I look at Grinning Hottie.

An intense, prickly heat ignites in my cheeks and spreads down my body like California wildfire.

Grinning Hottie must be able to see my pink cheeks from across the barn because he grins even more, until two deep dimples appear in this tanned cheeks.

"Calder!" Angus strides over to his friend and slaps him on the back. His brogue becomes as thick as his forearms. "Whin did ye git 'ere, ye rogue? Ah thought ye said ye wouldn't be back 'til Monday next."

Calder? Okay, so that's kind of a badass name. *My name is Calder, Calder McCloud, from the Clan McCloud.*

"My flight was scrubbed, so I thought I would see if I could lend a hand." Calder stands up straight so he's eye-to-steely-eye with Angus. "Besides, since when dae I need an excuse tae spend time with my auld brother?"

"Vivia and Lisa," Fiona says, ignoring her husband and brother in law. "How would you like to be the first to bond with Baasheba?"

Lisa hops up. "I would love to!"

I dart a nervous glance at massive horned lint ball from Hell ramming his head into the side of the observation pen.

"Oh, that's okay," I say, "I'm not really the touchy-feely kinda gal."

"Yes, you are!" Poppy cries.

"Yes, she is!" Fanny chimes in.

Calder MacFarlane has walked over to the edge of the observation pen and is watching me closely, an I-Stole-The-Who-Hash grin twisting his lips.

"No, I'm not."

"Yes, you are!"

Damn Fanny!

"She's the most touchy-feely person you will ever meet!" Fanny vehemently declares. "She hugs her mail lady, her dentist, the man who makes her favorite spicy chicken…"

I consider offering the solid argument that Mister Foo never tried to ram me, but Fanny is full steam ahead in her defense of my touchy-feeliness.

"She once hugged a homeless woman we found wandering around Golden Gate Park in search of her lost cat."

"The cat died," I explain to Fiona. "Years before."

"She hugged me," Poppy pipes up, "within the first twenty-four hours of meeting me!"

"You see!" Fanny proudly declares. "She hugged a British woman, a strange British woman, which means she will hug just about anyone."

"Thanks." Poppy sniffs.

"Come on, Vivia," Fiona encourages. "Baasheba loves to be cuddled."

Fanny is beaming. Poppy is beaming. Fiona is gesturing for me to join her in the pen. The Chick Trippers are murmuring their encouragement.

Calder strides over.

"How about it, Vivia?" He holds out his hand. "Are you ready for some heavy petting?"

Chapter 19

Ewe Need a Good Ram Every Now and Then

Text from Camille Grant:
Dear Vivia, Have you considered writing an article about grown daughters who abandon and neglect their elderly mothers? I believe you would do a bang-up job. Let me know if you need a source. I might be able to help. Your faithful reader, Camille Grant.

"How about it, Vivia?" Poppy purrs.

"Arrre ye rrr-ready for some heavy petting?" Fanny butchers Calder's brogue. "Rrr-really, rrr-really rrr-ready?"

We are sharing a pot of Earl Grey and a carton of Borders Shortbread in the kitchen before rejoining the group for the afternoon's activities.

"What was that?"

"What?"

"That accent?"

"'Tis my brogue, ye wee lassie."

"Make it stop!" I press my hands to my ears. "It is literally painful to listen to you attempt a brogue, Fanny. You're worse than that actress in those awful whisky commercials."

"I dinna ken which commercials yer on aboot."

"I know those commercials!" Poppy sits up. "They were wretched. The actress looked like she totally lost the plot. What was it she said at the end of each commercial?"

"'Are ye thirsty, Angus?'"

"Yes! That was it. Barking mad."

"I dinna ken which commercials yer on aboot," Fanny repeats.

"YouTube it. You'll be ashamed."

"If ye're rrr-really rrr-ready"—Fanny whips the plaid dishtowel off the counter, wraps it around her waist, and grins—"I have a wee beast under my kilt you can pet, lassie."

"Eww!" I yank the towel off Fanny's waist, give it a twist, and snap her with it. "You're disgusting."

Poppy grabs a biscuit, pinches it between her thumb and forefinger, and gently dunks it in her Earl Grey, her pinky raised in the stereotypical blueblood way.

"Yeah, I'm out."

"Too far?" Fanny asks.

"Perhaps a smidgen." Poppy dabs her lips with her napkin. "Vivia has only just become acquainted with Mister MacFarlane. It is too soon to be making jokes about his genitalia."

"Thank you, Poppy."

"You're quite welcome, Vivia."

"Pardon me, Duchess." Fanny curtsies. "What is the customary waiting period one must observe before making a socially acceptable genitalia joke? A year?"

Poppy folds her napkin into a perfect square and places it neatly to the right of her cup and saucer, before fixing Fanny with an earnest look. "At least twenty-four hours."

Fanny bursts out laughing and Poppy joins her.

"Nice." I stand and toss my half-eaten cookie on my plate. "Really nice."

"You mean, rrr-really nice." Poppy gasps. "Don't you?"

* * * *

We spend an hour watching Angus, Calder, and one of the *Magic Mike III* bit players take turns shearing sheep "the old way," wrestling the poor animals to the ground and using a pair of traditional clippers. The newly sheared sheep huddle together in a corner of the pen, naked, pink, and trembling like pre-teen girls at a swim party. I feel sorry for them.

Then again, I wish a big brawny Scot would wrestle me to the ground and make half my body weight magically disappear. Or just wrestle me to the ground. That would be okay, too.

I glance around the circle of Chick Trippers surrounding the pen and my shame dissipates. I am not the only woman feeling the mojo vibes emanating from the virile men working inside the pen. Cindy, the romance writer, keeps fanning herself with her hand and muttering, "Oh, my Lawd. Sweet baby Jesus." Megan is snapping pictures with her iPhone. Devon and Paige are giggling like school girls. Even stiff upper-lip, raised-pinky Poppy looks completely discombobulated by the totally old-school masculine display.

I lean over and whisper in her ear, "What's wrong, Pop? You mean to say when you were dating Tristan Kent, he never whipped off his shirt and hogtied a ram for you?"

Poppy's only response is to flush red and sputter.

"Don't get me wrong, I love me some tall, dark, and brainy Frenchman, but there's something damned sexy about watching a broad-shouldered Scot roll around in the hay until he's sweaty and panting." I wink at Poppy and nudge her in the ribs. "You know what I'm saying? I've never wished for a good rammin' more than I do right now, but then, ewe need a good rammin' every now and then. Am I right?"

Poppy just stares at me, her eyes wide, her mouth hanging open. I am about to repeat my sordid little rant when I have that sudden prickly sense someone is behind me.

I turn around and find Calder standing on the other side of the pen, one sweaty, muscular arm resting casually on the top rail.

Maybe he didn't hear me. It is loud in here with all of the bleating and "Oh, my Lawd-ing" going on.

Calder pierces me with his blue-eyed gaze. It's one of those steely poker player stares meant to unnerve me into revealing my hand. He's bluffing! I knew it! He didn't hear a thing.

"Did ye have a question about the ram, Vivia?"

Oh Lawd! Sweet baby Jesus! He heard me! He heard me! Think, Vivia. Think. What did you say? What did you say?

"I-I don't know."

I can't remember exactly what I said to Poppy. I was just jacking around, flipping her some shit. Half of the time, I don't know what I am saying even as I am saying it. I mean, seriously, who could possibly keep up with my rushing stream of consciousness? My thoughts are like the Amazon—always flowing.

Ramming! I said something about ramming. I think I said I wanted him to ram me. Oh Lawd, Jesus, help me!

I begin fanning myself with my hand.

"If ye remember whit 'twas ye wanted tae ken aboot rams," he says, laying the brogue on thick. "I'd be happy tae help ye." Calder winks and walks away.

I turn to Poppy. "Did you hear that?"

"Yes."

"You know what that means, right?"

"Yes," Poppy whispers. "It means it is now safe to make jokes about his genitals."

Fanny snickers.

When Fiona calls an end to the sheep shearing demonstration and invites our group to follow her outside, I want to drop to my knees and give thanks to my Almighty for putting an end to my suffering. Seriously? How long can a woman worship at the altar of man before she loses her religion and starts thinking naughty things? Where wicked thoughts come, wicked deeds soon follow, my mum always said.

I am the first one out of the barn, bursting into the sunlight and gasping, like a drowning swimmer.

Lisa follows, links her arm through mine, and whispers, "I think you have an admirer."

"I have a fiancé," I whisper back. "At least, I think I have a fiancé."

Luc's vintage Tiffany ring hangs on a chain around my neck, the smooth three-carat diamond cold against my breast.

Lisa frowns up at me. "Sounds complicated."

"It is."

"True love usually is."

"Really"—I blink back tears—"because I thought true love was supposed to be easy. Boy and girl meet, fall in love, have a pesky little black moment, make up, and live happily ever after."

Lisa stops walking and unlinks her arm from mine. "Maybe in romance novels, but not in real life. If by 'Happily Ever After' you mean juggling work and home, raising colicky babies and tantrum-prone toddlers, losing a job, losing a parent, getting cancer…" Lisa shrugs. "If you mean that, then yes."

"Wow." I frown. "You make it sound so…bleak."

Tava, Fanny, and Poppy join us by a wooden fence separating two fields, two flocks of sheep.

"Life can be bleak, but the alternative is much bleaker."

"Amen, sistah!" Tava says, pumping her fist. "Preach!"

One by one, the rest of the group straggles over to the fence. The Chick Trippers are on a double-shot espresso buzz over the sheep shearing demonstration, practically vibrating with amped up adrenaline. It's like being at Starbucks at eight in the morning.

Fiona and Calder, his collie trotting at his side, exit the barn and begin making their way to us.

"Life can be bleak"—Lisa leans close and lowers her voice so only I can hear her words—"but it can also be a fourth of July fireworks explosion of color and light and joy, especially if you have someone special to hold your hand through the darkness and light."

"Now," Fiona says, drawing our attention. "We have one last demonstration for you before we set you free for the afternoon. Calder is going to show you how we use a dog to help us round up a flock."

"Good afternoon, lassies." Calder smiles a broad, Colgate smile.

Someone behind me sighs. Literally, sighs.

Calder. Of course, it has to be Calder. It couldn't be a fat, toothless, hairy, dimwitted man to lead the demonstrations, because toothless, ugly men don't exist in the Highlands.

"Now then, a weel trained herding dog watches over th' flock and can even prevent coyotes from attacking…"

Blah. Blah. Blah. He might as well be one of the adults on the Charlie Brown cartoons. His words make absolutely no sense. His good looks are distracting me, as is my annoyance with myself for even noticing his good looks.

He's taller than I realized, towering over Fiona and every lady in our group, and more muscular, too. The stubble outlining his chin appears red in the bright afternoon sunlight and his blue eyes sparkle like polished turquoise nuggets.

Polished turquoise nuggets? Did I really just think that? My humiliation is near complete. What happens next? Do I start having fantasies about Calder calling me Sassenach while ravaging me on a bed of heather?

"…a weel trained collie can bring even the orneriest ram to heel. Isn't that right, Shep?"

The collie sits obediently at Calder's feet, but his tail thumps wildly against the ground.

"How old is Shep?" Poppy asks. "Is he still a puppy?"

"Aye." Calder grins. "He's a little over a year old, but he's a clever boy."

Shep waits patiently at his master's feet, until a subtle flick of Calder's wrist sends him bounding over the fence and flying across the field toward a distant flock.

It's really quite riveting.

"Get a wee wee bye, Shep. Get a wee wee bye."

"What does that mean?" I ask.

"I am telling him to round up the flock"—Calder grins and pierces me with his sexy turquoise gaze—"starting with the wee ones."

He whistles, and Shep reverses directions, running counterclockwise around the sheep, until they clump together in one wooly mass.

"That is very impressive," I say to Fiona, who is standing beside me. "I've never seen such an obedient dog."

"Calder has a way with animals."

The Dog Whisperer/Sheep Wrangler whistles sharply twice, and Shep stops running, freezing in place with his head cocked to one side. Calder whistles twice again. This time, the precocious pup runs to a bush and hides behind it.

"Shep!"

The dog skulks from bush to bush like an African hunter stalking big game.

"Come to heel, you cheeky rogue," Calder says, rolling the r in rogue. "Come to heel!"

Shep pokes his head out from around the bush, as if making sure the coast is clear, before running across the field and leaping over the fence. The errant collie ignores the chorus of females crooning over him and trots right over to his master.

"You're a clever boy." Calder scratches the dog's head behind his ears. "A clever dog."

I don't want to like Calder, but even callous-hearted, puppy-skinning Cruella de Vil would find it difficult to resist his broad grins and easy manner. I am sucker for a man with a dog. Luc has two giant poodles. He found them when they were puppies, abandoned in a box on the side of the road near his chateau. Tall, dark, and extra shot of sexy Luc doesn't look like a poodle man, but there it is...

The other women circle around Fiona as she describes the many ways we might want to spend the rest of the afternoon—from hiking to an Iron Age hill fort to touring Strathpeffer, a charming Victorian spa town a short drive from the farm.

"If you do decide to visit Strathpeffer, be sure to visit the chocolate shop in town," she says, capturing my full attention. "The proprietors aren't very friendly, but the chocolate is the best you'll find outside Belgium."

Chocolate? Did someone say something about the eighth deadly sin? I am so in! Fanny will have to do the mini-triathlon to the Iron Age hill fort, and Poppy will have to engage in her heavy sheep petting session, *sans moi*! There's a cocoa-dusted truffle in Strathpeffer with my name written all over it.

"Vivia." Fiona cranes her neck looking over the top of Tava's head. "I figured you will want as much information about how the farm operates and the surrounding countryside, so I've asked Calder to allow you to ride with him as he does a survey of the flocks."

Fanny looks at me and waggles her eyebrows.

"Ride?"

Please, God, when she says ride, please let her mean in a truck, convertible, 110-foot yacht, or even a souped-up golf cart. Just not a horse.

"You can ride a horse, can't you?"

The last time I rode a horse was in Italy, and I very nearly died.

"You're not afraid of horses, are you?" Fiona asks.

I consider telling Fiona about the runaway Italian stallion and my near-death experience when I realize the entire group is staring at me—Lisa, Kathy, Cindy, the other romance writers, and Calder.

Owning it: I know I sound arrogant, but I decide not to confess my fear of becoming an equestrian homicide victim because I am worried it will get out in the Twitosphere and affect my rep as an intrepid columnist. #NoStreetCred #TimidTraveler

"I am totally cool with horses." I avoid making eye-contact with Fanny. "I ride all of the time."

"Good." Fiona gives one of her spooky I-know-more-than-you're-saying smiles. "Even if you didn't, Calder is an excellent horseman. You'll be safe in his hands."

"Mmm-hmm," Cindy mutters, fanning herself. "Sho 'nuff will."

The romance writers giggle as they turn to make their way back to their cabins. Poppy smirks and waves her hand in one of those stiff turning Queen of England waves. Fanny just gives me a thumbs up.

Why does Fate get off by sticking me in a saddle with a hot, foreign man riding my rear?

* * * *

Calder takes me on a sweaty, exhilarating, thoroughly-satisfying ride, through fields and black pine forests, over hills and past circles of ancient standing stones.

He's polite, attentive, witty, and one hundred percent professional. No grinning (darn), no winking (double darn), and no flirting (triple darn).

He gives me a lot of interesting background information for my column.

When I finally trudge through the field to return to my cottage, heavy clouds hang low in the sky like an indigo canopy, and I ache in places that haven't ached since I rode a bike from Provence to Tuscany. I fall into bed too tired to even think about Jean-Luc and his cryptic e-mail—much.

Chapter 20

Goin' Deep With My Hype Girl

Text to Camille Grant:
Dear Faithful Reader: Thank you for your confidence in my
ability to write an article about neglectful daughters. It is an
intriguing idea; however, I am far too busy writing The Guilt
Trip: Parents Who Use Emotional Manipulation. Love, VPG

We spend the morning performing the countless, thankless tasks associated with caring for a flock of sheep. I would like to tell you that feeding, watering, deworming—eww, don't even ask me to elaborate— and shearing sheep are deeply satisfying tasks, and that raising sheep is a great alternative career choice should this writing gig not work out for me, but I am not feeling Fiona's furry flock vibe.

Poppy is, though.

When Angus asked for volunteers to help deworm Snow White and Baashful, two parasite-riddled ewes, Poppy eagerly raised her manicured hand. She didn't even flinch when Angus pulled out a large curved wicked looking syringe/medieval torture device.

"I really don't mind the messy bits," she said, rolling up her sleeves.

If you had told me a week ago that Prada Poppy Worthington of the exclusive Worthington Boutique Hotels, the woman who shagged Tristan Kent and Britain's hot-hot-hot multimedia titan, would be up to her elbows in sheep excrement and intestinal worms, I would have thought you were Mad Cow Disease-crazy. As bloody wrong as it sounds, she is in her element.

In the afternoon, while the others are getting hot stone massages and lanolin wraps, I interview Fiona for my *GoGirl!* column. I have decided to write two sidebars to run alongside my column—one about how Fiona, an American woman with no experience in animal husbandry, is succeeding in a male-dominated business in macho Scotland. I want to focus on the practical side of moving to a foreign country—what it's like to be an expat, living and working abroad. I thought it would appeal to my career-minded readers.

The second sidebar is for my romance-minded readers. Filled with overblown language and poetic waxings about the rugged landscape, the sidebar will be about Fiona's big gamble, how she gave up a well-paying career to follow her heart to Scotland, and how it led her to the love of her life, Angus.

After my interview with Fiona, I return to the cottage eager to begin writing my column. I am typing my notes on my MacBook when Fanny knocks on my door.

"Wanna give your Wellies a little workout?"

"That depends," I say, frowning. "What were you thinking?"

For those of you who aren't yet proficient in Fanny-speak, "a little workout" could mean anything from a bucolic hike through the heather to a thirty-mile march wearing a sixty-pound rucksack, reminiscent of the Baatan Death March.

"*Juste une petite promenade*," she says, smiling innocently.

"Just a little stroll," I repeat in English, narrowing my gaze. "You don't fool me, Emperor Hirohito. I know all about your little strolls."

Fanny laughs.

Despite all of the good-natured teasing she's given me, my best friend hasn't been herself this trip. She's looked rawther glum, as Poppy might say. It's time I get out of my head and into Fanny's.

"Let's do this thing." I close my MacBook, shove my feet into my Wellies, and grab my iPhone. "It will give me some time to get the 4-1-1 on what's been happening in your life lately."

* * * *

We climb up a wooden A-frame ladder over the fence separating the grazing land from the cottages and begin a slow, steady hike toward a distant pap. My boots sink into the wet, spongy ground, with each step and make satisfying schloop-schlooping noises as I lift them out of the muck. I attempt to leap from one soggy patch of what passes as grass in the Highlands to another soggy patch, miss, and land in a boggy pool, the brackish water nearly spilling over the tops of my tall Wellies.

"Woo-hoo! This is way more fun than puddle stomping!"

Fanny chuckles. "Does that mean you want to climb to the top of that pap?" She points to a craggy mountain looming in the distance.

I stop leaping. I knew it! Didn't I tell you the little Emperor would try to turn this into a death march?

"Nope," I say, lifting my boot out of the primordial muck. "It most certainly does not mean I want to build you a railroad over the River Kwai."

"What?" Fanny laughs. "What does that even mean?"

I should be accustomed to my best friend's gross ignorance when it comes to movie trivia, but sometimes it still gobsmacks me. I stop walking and stare at Fanny.

"*Bridge on the River Kwai*?"

She shrugs.

"Sir Alex Guiness and William Holden?"

Fanny stares blankly. I might as well be speaking German or Spanish, except that Fanny speaks those languages, too.

"Academy Award-winning movie about World War II British prisoners of war at a Japanese prison camp who are forced to build a bridge through the jungle and over the River Kwai. Epic film."

I begin whistling the iconic "Whistle Song" from the movie and march with my arms swinging at my sides. Fanny marches beside me, but doesn't join in on the whistling.

"Wait a minute!" She stops marching. "Did you just compare me to a prison camp warden?"

I stop whistling and stare blankly.

"Nice, Vivian!"

"I was just kidding." I resume marching. "You are not a prison warden."

"I'm not!"

"You're not."

Fanny double steps until she catches up to me. "Am I really a warden?"

"You might be the teensiest, tiniest——"

"What?"

Bless her little French heart. She genuinely sounds bemused.

"——wardenish."

"Wardenish? Is that even a word?"

I shake my head.

"So what does that mean—wardenish?"

I look at her sideways. "Are you sure you want to know?"

"*Oui.*"

"Because you're not really good with negative feedback."

"Vivian! Just tell me."

"Sometimes, not always, but sometimes, you are—"

"Controlling? Exacting? Judgmental? Mean?"

"Wow!" I look at her full-on. "I was going to say exhaustingly competitive. Where's all this coming from?"

Fanny shrugs and looks away.

"Uh-uh! I don't think so. Out with it, Stéphanie Moreau. Who said you were controlling, exacting, and judgmental?"

"And mean. Don't forget mean."

Up ahead, there's an upcropping of flat-topped boulders covered in lichen. I walk over to one of the boulders, brush the fuzzy green top with my hand, have a seat, and motion for Fanny sit across from me.

"What's up, girl? Talk to me."

Fanny climbs up on the boulder. She's so short; her legs dangle like she's a toddler in a highchair. With her sad basset hound eyes and pouty lips, I've never seen her look more vulnerable than she does right now.

Fanny takes a jagged breath and begins filling me in on her situation— the real sitch, not the fake-upbeat-because-we-only-have-a-few-minutes-to-talk bullshit she's been giving me. She tells me the real deal about her new job as a Division Manager for Christian Dior Boutiques—how she had to fire a popular boutique manager for failing to uphold the company's exacting standards and put another manager on probation because she didn't "possess a strong enough knowledge of the luxury industry."

Fanny has been obsessed with Christian Dior—even repeating the couturier's quotes like mantras—since she was five years old, when her well-intentioned but hopelessly inept father gave her a diamond Dior flower brooch; so it is shocking to hear her dream job is turning out to be disillusioning.

"I spend a preponderance of my time assigning monthly sales goals, motivating my team to reach said goals, and disciplining boutique managers who fail to reach said goals." Fanny scratches the lichen with her fingernail. "My boutique managers hate me. They say I am too driven, that I am more concerned with sales goals than sales girls. One even told me I have a cash register where my heart should be."

"What an assjack!" I hop off down off my boulder and go to sit beside my best friend. "That's just bullshit. Don't let a couple of bitter burnt-out people steal your sunshine, girlfriend. You worked damned hard to get hired at Dior, and now you feel like you have to work doubly-hard to prove you're worthy of the shot. I get it."

"I guess."

She sniffs and quickly wipes her eyes before a tear falls.

"It's not true, Fanny." I wrap my arm around her shoulder and give her a good squeeze. "You don't have a cash register inside your chest; you have a big, generous, loving heart. You're the most generous person I know."

"Pfft."

"Don't you 'pfft' me!" I give her shoulders another squeeze. "Who called every single one of my wedding guests after Nathan ended our engagement? Who talked me into taking my honeymoon anyway? Who held my hair back when I was vomiting up a bad burrito and a pitcher of pineapple mango margaritas?"

"Me."

"And who just flew halfway around the world to help her best friend shovel sheep shit?"

"Me."

"Abso-bloody-lutely!"

"Okay, that word has to go"—Fanny laughs and wipes her cheek again—"along with boffing, freaking, and discombobulate."

"Oh, no, you didn't!" I snap my fingers and bob my head. "You can criticize my Prada knock-off; you can criticize my abysmal bike riding skills, but don't you dare diss my lingo. Freaking and discombobulate are sacrosanct, yo?"

"Yo? This new urban, street thug Vivia is freaking me out."

"Ah-ha!" I snap my fingers again and point. "You see? Keep it real, sistah. You know you like throwing down a freaking every now and then."

Fanny laughs but the shadows in her eyes remain.

"What else?"

Fanny inhales deeply, holds the breath for several seconds, and lets it go in a slow, measured exhalation. When she finally speaks again, it is in a soft paper-thin voice.

"I feel like I am lost at sea, adrift with no rudder or sail. I feel…like I have no purpose, no direction." She picks at the lichen with her fingernail again, avoiding eye contact. "You have this awesome job that lets you travel the world. You rub elbows with royalty and celebrities, make friends everywhere you go, have romantic trysts with your hopelessly devoted boyfriend. Meanwhile, I am selling over-priced handbags to blue-haired society matrons and then going home to my empty apartment to eat take-out sushi while standing over the sink."

I let my best friend drain her festering wound.

"I sound jealous, don't I?"

"Ach, aye." I try to mimic Angus's thick brogue in an attempt to lighten her mood. "Maybe a wee bit, woman."

Fanny just smiles at me, a sad smile that twists my heart into painful knots. I hate it when someone I love is in pain or struggling. I want to fix it, put a Band-Aid over it, make it better with a joke, but some pains go deep and require more to heal than a laugh.

I hug Fanny and tell her that she's not out on that ocean alone, that I am sailing right beside her.

"I won't let you drift too far for too long." I hop down off the boulder. "If you don't like the path you've charted, chart a new one. I'll help you."

"Thanks, Vivian."

"It ain't nothin' but a thang, girl. You know what I'm sayin'? I got your six, 'cuz you're my Hype Girl."

"Yeah, I have no idea what you just said, and it's not because English is my second language."

"Basically, I said I will always be here for you because you are my best friend."

"So Hype Girl means best friend?"

"It means you are the Ethel to my Lucy, the Woodstock to my Snoopy, the Tonto to my Lone Ranger."

"Okay," Fanny laughs. "I don't know who any of those people are, Vivian."

"It doesn't matter," I say, walking back in the direction of the cottage. "It just means I am glad you've decided to ride shotgun on this wild ride that is my life."

* * * *

We are on our way back down the hill to the cabin when we find an obese sheep lying on his back, skinny legs up in the air, tongue lolling out of its mouth.

"Ohmygod!" I stop walking and stare at the sheep writhing around. "I think that's one of Fiona's expensive black faced breeding sheep."

The sheep rolls to one side, jerks its legs, rolls back.

"Why is it doing that?"

"I don't know. Maybe it is having a seizure."

"Or maybe that's just the way sheep sleep." Fanny keeps walking. "Come on, let's just go."

"I don't think so…" I step closer to the poor beast. "His eyes are rolled back in his head and his tongue is purplish. I think he's dying."

"I don't think he is dying, Vivian."

"Yes!" I cry, jumping up and down and shaking my hands. "He's dying! Oh my God, Fanny, he's dying. We have to do something."

"What? Sheep CPR?"

"I can't just stand here and let this sheep die."

Before I even realize I've formed a plan, I am running down the side of the hill as fast as my Wellies will take me, arms waving like a demented person.

"Angus! Angus!"

I step on a squishy, boggy patch of grass, twist my ankle, and fall flat on my face. I hop right back up, ignoring the stabbing pain in my ankle, and continue racing down the hill.

"Ang-guuuuuus!"

Angus and the Magic Mike crew come out of the barn and stare up the hill at me.

"Angus," I cry, waving my arms again. "Help! Your sheep is dyyyyyyying."

The Scots don't move. They stand with their brawny arms crossed over their brawny chests.

What is the matter with them? There is a life-threatening emergency going on and they're just gawking like those people who slow down when they are passing an accident on the road.

When I finally reach the barnyard, I am covered in mud and sheep shit, dripping bog water, and wheezing like an accordion. I press my hand to my side and bend over.

"Breathe, woman!"

I stand up again, but continue to hold my aching side. By now, the entire group of Chick Trippers has assembled around us.

"Your sheep," I gasp and point wildly up the hill. "I think it's having a seizure."

The brawny Scots don't flinch. Their expressions remain as flat as lichen-covered standing stones...in fact, the hulking Scots look like a circle of standing stones.

"What sheep?" Angus asks.

"One of your big black-faced rams," I say, grabbing his arm and attempting to pull him up the hill. "He's on his back, writhing in agony. His tongue is out and his eyes have rolled back in his head. I think he's dying."

"Is he in a ditch by an auld shed?"

"Yes."

"Ach! That's just auld Torcach."

The Scots slap Angus on the back, the way men do when they mean to convey deep sympathy to one of their brethren, and walk back to the barn, chuckling and murmuring in Gaelic.

"What does that mean?" I remember what old Torcach looked like with his fat tongue hanging out of his mouth and I begin to cry. "He's old so you are just going to let him die up there?"

"That's just cruel," Lisa murmurs.

"Ageist," Kathy cries.

"Lassies, please." Angus raises his hands. "He's nae dying."

"Why is he on his back then?"

"The mangy beast falls, and he's so fat he cannae get up."

I suddenly see the old Life Alert commercial with the elderly woman sprawled out on the floor, calling out for help. "I've fallen and I can't get up."

"Maybe you need to get him a Life Alert bracelet."

"What?"

"Nothing."

Angus scowls before turning to go back into the barn.

"Wait." I grab his arm again. "Aren't you going to do something?"

"Like what?"

"I don't know." I shrug, looking helplessly at my female compatriots for support. "Something."

"Flip him back over," Lisa suggests.

"Or, I don't know," Tava cracks. "Maybe fill in the hole so he doesn't keep falling into it?"

"Or just let him die because he's old and no longer useful." Kathy mutters. "Ageist."

"Please, Angus." I tug on his arm again. "Please."

"Dinna fash yourself, Vivia, auld Torcach will put himself to rights, or he'll fall asleep."

"That's cruel!" I imagine the old ram being torn apart limb from twitching limb by a pack of rabid coyotes. "Please, Angus. Please don't leave him up there, alone and vulnerable. It's going to be dark soon. What if another animal comes along and attacks him?"

Angus scowls, but the twinkle in his eye tells me the bluster is for show, so he doesn't lose any of his gruff Scot street cred.

"Fine."

The Chick Trippers applaud as Angus stomps off to assist his old, half-blind, obese sheep. He passes Fanny on his way up the hill.

Ka-ching! You hear that? I just deposited another coin in my Karma Bank, and it's about time I get a little something-something back.

Chapter 21

Hitting It Hard

I return to our cottage as high as Wiz Khalifa, which, I assume, is a natural side-effect of flying down a mountain like a superhero to rescue a sheep in distress. I don't care what Angus said—*dinnea fash yourself, lassie*—poor, old Torcach would have died up on that mountain if not for my intervention.

"You saved that sheep," Fanny says.

"Boo-yah!" I punch the air over my head with my fist. "Yes, I did!"

"Easy, Wondergirl" Fanny laughs. "You're flinging mud all around the kitchen."

I plop down on the wooden bench by the kitchen door, shrug out of my wet rain slicker, and kick my Wellies off. Clumps of mud fall onto the slate floor.

"I am going to take a shower"—I stand and drop my pink wooly cap onto my rain slicker—"and when I am done, do you want to go into town and hit that chocolate store Fiona mentioned?"

"Chocolate? After our hike?"

"Shyeah! We've got to add a little weight on the calorie scale—just to keep things balanced."

"It doesn't work that way, Vivian." Fanny crosses her arms and tilts her head, looking at me from behind a thick veil of mahogany hair. "Do you know how many calories are in a Lindt chocolate truffle ball?"

"No, but I'll bet you do."

"Seventy-nine."

"Oh, the humanity!" I cover my eyes with my hands and rock back and forth. "Seventy-nine calories in a single truffle ball? Sweet baby Jesus, what evil is afoot in that factory?"

"You laugh, but that's thirty minutes of walking at three miles per hour to burn off the calories in a single chocolate truffle." Fanny uncrosses her arms. "But if you want to visit the chocolate shop, I'll go with you."

"Hit it."

"Excuse me?"

"Hit the chocolate shop. We are going to hit it. Hit. It. Hard."

I walk out of the kitchen and down the hall to the bathroom, knowing full-well that my best friend will be planking and squatting her little heart out while I am scrubbing off the evidence of my heroics. You've probably already figured this out, but Fanny has some pretty big issues about food. Sometimes, it crimps my style, but that doesn't bother me nearly as much as watching my beautiful best friend twist herself up over something that should be simple. If you're hungry, eat. If you have extra energy, exercise. Instead, she frets over every calorie consumed, mentally calculating the time she will need to spend on the treadmill or taking a Boot Camp class to work off a kale milkshake.

I take a hot shower, slather my body with L'Occitane Sweet Almond Oil, and slip on my fluffy pink robe. I am heading back to my room when my iPhone starts ringing. I make a mad dash for the kitchen, unzip the pocket on my rain slicker, and pull out my phone, but I am too late. The Caller ID reads UNKNOWN.

I hate missed calls from strange numbers because I obsess about them for hours. Who was it? What did they want? What if an anvil falls on UNKNOWN'S head, and they get amnesia and forget to call me back? Am I just supposed to spend the rest of my life in a state of suspense?

Was UNKNOWN a misdialer, a telemarketer named Dashika hoping to sell me a new Dell computer, or Luc? Maybe Luc was calling from a hotel. Maybe he has a new mobile number. Maybe that's why it registered UNKNOWN.

Maybe. Maybe. I don't do well with uncertainties.

Maybe I should just call Jean-Luc and ask him if he phoned me. Maybe he will say "no" and hang up on me. Maybe he will send my call to voicemail again. Too many damned maybes.

All right Bank of Karma, I've deposited some serious cash over the last few days and now I want to make a withdrawal. If I call Luc, you better show me some love.

I go back to my room, dial Luc's number, and hold my breath while the call connects.

One ring. My heart is beating like a drum. Boom dabaoom daboom. Two rings. I press my hand to my chest as if it will somehow slow my pulse.

"*Allo.*"

My heart stops beating when I hear the utterly unfamiliar, utterly female French hello.

"Hello?"

"*Oui, qui est-ce?*"

Who is this? Who the hell are you and why are you answering my boyfriend's phone?

"May I please speak with Luc?"

"*Désolé. Je ne parle pas Anglais.*"

Breathe, Vivia. There's probably a logical explanation for why a strange woman is answering Luc's phone—maybe he's gone deaf and she's his sign-language instructor.

"*Je veux parler à Luc, s'il vous plait?*"

"*Ah! Luc est dans la douche.*"

Wait! What? What does she mean Luc just stepped into the shower and why did she say it so casually, as if performing receptionist duties for a naked man—my naked man—is a regular occurrence?

"Who is this?"

I actually wanted to say, "Who the fuck are you?"

"*Quoi?*"

"*Qui est-ce?*"

"*Celine. Qui est-ce?*"

Who am I? I am the woman who is going to fly across the Channel, grab you by your scrawny neck, and shake you like a mother flipping ragdoll, that's who!

"*C'est Vivia, sa fiancée.*"

I tell her to let Luc know I phoned and jab my disconnect button repeatedly, half-crying, half-growling in fury.

Celine? Celine!

Celine is Luc's ex-girlfriend. She is a slutty little model who broke his heart by cheating on him with one of his best friends. Chantal, Luc's sister-in-law, told me Celine only dated Luc because he comes from an old distinguished French family and owns a chateau.

Really? Celine? Are you kidding me?

I grab my MacBook, sign into my Facebook account, go to Luc's wall, and—there it is—the horrible, awful, gut-wrenching, heart-shredding proof that Luc is over me.

So over me.

Celine Belangé added six new photos.

I click on the first photo, dated a year before I met Luc, and snapped at one of Celine's fashion shoots. She is wearing a dramatic crimson and orange ball gown made of wispy feathers, her ebony hair scraped back to highlight her sharp cheekbones and her pouty, crimson-lacquered lips. It is a candid shot, with a fog machine and light stand in the background, but could be an advert in a glossy fashion magazine. Luc is turned slightly away from Celine, as if preparing to leave. She is leaning away from him and clutching his tie like it is a leash restraining a high-strung poodle. There's almost something desperate about her pose—but her haughty expression, the lifted chin, the arched brow, the subtly smug smile, suggest something altogether different. The woman in the photograph exudes the quiet confidence of a puppet master, someone who knows they pull the strings, they make people dance.

The bile that began churning in my stomach when I heard Celine answer Luc's phone with her smooth *Allo* burbles up my throat.

I always hoped Celine was one of those ugly models—the ones with bleached eyebrows or flat-chested boy bodies—but no such luck. She projects the same detached sexiness as Angelina Jolie, but with Dita von Teese's sex-toy in stilettos beauty.

I study the next few photographs—also dated before Luc and I began dating—with the intensity of any self-flagellator, intent on inflicting as much damage as possible.

Luc and Celine paddleboarding in emerald waters. Jesus, Mary, and Thong-Wearing Joseph! Could she look any sexier in a swimsuit? I don't think so. Luc holding a pair of skis with Celine posing beside him in stylish snow bunny attire, hands on hips, elbows facing forward, back rounded. Luc in his Tour de France cycling gear, hair plastered to his sexy head, while Celine plants a kiss on his already red lipstick-stained cheeks.

Fuck. Fuck. Fuckedee Fuck.

So Angelina von Teese is a paddleboarding, skiing, cycling supermodel. Fantastic. She can probably make a sailboat out of popsicle sticks and bubble gum, finish the *New York Times* crossword puzzle while getting a pedicure, and bake pastries like Julia Child, but wearing only stilettos and crimson lipstick.

If the first four photos wounded me, the last two gut me like an eviscerated Thanksgiving turkey. Time stamped less than twenty-four hours ago, they show the glammed-up couple sipping champagne at some black-tie soiree. My heart flips when I make the picture bigger and look at Luc's handsome face, the smoldering gaze, the leisurely smile, the cleft in his chin I've kissed at least a thousand times.

"Vivian?" Fanny knocks on my door. "I thought we were going into town to hit the chocolate place? Are you okay?"

"No!" I let out a strangled cry. "I am definitely not okay."

Fanny opens the door and steps into my room.

"What's the matter?"

My strangled cry has become an otherworldly keening, a gut-level moaning usually only heard at funerals or movies set in insane asylums. Fanny rushes to my side. She takes one look at my MacBook screen and her eyes open wide.

"*Mon dieu!*" She says, grabbing my MacBook off my lap. "Is that Jean-Luc?"

"Yep."

"Who is the woman with him?"

"Celine."

"His ex? The supermodel?"

"Yep."

Fanny curses in French.

"Maybe they just ran into each other." She looks from me to the screen and back at me again, smiling brightly. "It's a plausible explanation."

"You run into your ex at the grocery store, when you're wearing baggy old sweats and in need of a shower, not dressed in formal attire and sipping champagne."

Fanny opens her mouth and closes it again. She doesn't need to admit her unexpected encounter explanation is as farfetched as an M. Night Shyamalan movie. We both know.

"Did you call him? What did he say?"

I hear Celine's *Allo* in my head and press my hands to my ears and rock back and forth, still keening like an Irish granny at a wake. Fanny wraps her arms around me. She hugs me until my granny wailing subsides to sad, jagged gasps.

"What did he say, Vivian?"

"N-Nothing." I sniffle. "Celine answered the phone."

"Shut up!"

I nod.

"What did she say?"

I shrug.

"Did you tell her who you were?"

"Of course I did!"

"What did she say then?"

"She said she didn't speak English and then she told me Luc was in the shower."

"What? Are you kidding me?"

I shake my head.

"Let me talk to her," Fanny says, holding out her hand. "Get her on the line."

I grab my iPhone up, hit redial, and hand it to her. She speaks in rapid, staccato French. I don't know what she's saying, but the longer she speaks the snippier she sounds. She hangs up suddenly.

"*Salope!*"

I don't need a translator to tell me what that word means. It's a colorful euphemism for a female canine.

"What? What did she say?"

"*Ce n'est pas important.*" Fanny frowns. "I don't like that woman and I don't even know her. She's sketchy."

"What did you say?"

"I told her to let Luc know his fiancée needed to speak with him as soon as possible."

He didn't actually ask me to marry him, so I'm not his fiancée. I look at the computer screen again. I might not even be his girlfriend anymore.

Fanny grabs my MacBook, shuts it, and shoves it in my top dresser drawer.

"Now, let's go!" She claps her hands. "Let's go into town, skip the chocolate shop, and head straight to that pub we saw when we first arrived here."

"I can't! What if Luc calls me back?"

"That's the beauty of an iPhone, Vivian, you can take it with you wherever you go, even to a pub in Strathpeffer, Scotland."

"I don't want to go to a pub." I grab one of my pillows and hug it tight. "I just want to curl up in the fetal position, pull the covers over my head, and listen to Adele songs."

"No!" Fanny grabs my arm and jerks me up. "You are absolutely forbidden from listening to your 'For When I Am Blue' playlist."

"But I *am* blue."

"Well holing up in this room listening to a singing barbiturate is not going to chase your blues away." Fanny tries to pull me to my feet, but it would take a lifetime of Boot Camp classes for the ant to become strong enough to move the rubber tree plant. "You know what you need?"

"A thong bikini and a supermodel's body?"

"Vivian!" She puts her hands on her hips and glares at me. "Do not let that *salope* get into your head. You are beautiful and you have a slamming body."

"Puh-leez," I snort. "I have a ginger 'fro and a muffin top. No wonder Luc ran back to Celine."

"Shut up!"

I am about to add pale alien-like legs to my list of hideous, anti-supermodel features when Fanny holds up her hand.

"I am serious, Vivian. I don't want to hear your whining. I've listened to you complain about your looks ever since we first met and I am sick of it." She feigns a truly laughable Valley Girl accent. "'Oh, poor me. I brush my teeth with salted caramel sauce, but I never gain a pound, and my legs are so long I don't need to wear high heels. It, like, totally sucks to be *me*.'"

"Whatever."

"Don't whatever me. It's true. You know I love Luc, but he is lucky to have you. Crazy lucky. If he doesn't call you back, then he was never worth the Dior." She snaps her fingers. "Now get your skinny ass out of bed. A few whiskys and a plate of fish and chips and you'll feel better."

I am hungry. "You know what goes with fish and chips, right?"

"No. What?"

"Chocolate."

Chapter 22

A New Man and A Manky Hole

Vivia Perpetua Grant @PerpetuallyViv
Did you know #whisky is uisge beatha in Scottish #Gaelic?
Try a few shots and see if you don't suddenly sound like you're
fluent in Gaelic.

"Nice Wellies."

"Thanks."

The barman slams two shot glasses on the bar, fills them with whisky, and returns to his regular customers clustered at the other end of the pub.

"Did you see that?" I whisper to Fanny. "Did you see the way he smirked when he said he liked my Wellies? What was that about?"

"I don't know, and I don't care." She lifts the shot glass to her lips and tips the contents into her mouth. "We've got whisky and a bar full of men in uniform. Who cares about a smirking old bartender?"

"Touché."

Several of the men at the end of the bar are dressed in green flight suits and throwing darts at a bull's-eye shaped board. One of them, a tall broad-shouldered blonde dressed in civvies, takes aim and sends a dart whizzing through the air. It lands dead-center and the pub erupts in raucous cheers.

I make a little salute with my shot glass before downing the whisky. The fiery liquid burns a path down my throat, igniting like a stick of dynamite in my belly. I shudder and cough.

"Good, right?"

I cough again. I am still coughing when the barman refills our glasses and Fanny downs her second shot.

"What were ye thinking, Dougal? Dinna ye ken ye cannae serve Dalwhinnie to a lass wearing pink Wellies, man?"

Jesus, Mary, and Scotch-drinking Joseph. I don't need to turn around to put a face to that voice, but I spin around anyway.

"Calder."

Just speaking his name reignites the fiery feeling in my throat, and I start coughing again. Coughing might not be the right word to describe my violent hacking and wheezing. It's embarrassing. The leather-throated whisky-swilling Scots have stopped talking and are staring at me with expressions that vary from amused to annoyed.

Calder reaches around to grab my second shot of whisky.

"Here—" he hands me the shot glass. "Drink this."

"Are you crazy?" I clutch my throat. "If drinking one shot of that liquid napalm can cause this kind of suffering, I'll stick to champagne cocktails and strawberry margaritas. Thank you."

Calder throws back his head and laughs. He has a seductive laugh, warm and rich like the amber liquid he's trying to get me to drink.

"You're in agony, lass, because ye dinnae ken th' proper way tae drink whisky."

Fanny giggles, and I shoot her a "Thanks Judas" look.

"Oh, is that why it feels like someone tossed a Molotov cocktail down my throat, because I dinnae ken the proper way to drink whisky?" I take the glass from him and slam it back down, causing a small amber wave to splash over the side and onto the bar.

"Aye." He crosses his arms and smiles. "Ye dinnae."

"And I suppose you know the proper way to drink whisky?"

"Ach, of course I dae." He stares into my eyes and the heat kindling in my throat spreads to my cheeks. "I'm a Scotsman; I was weaned on Dalwhinnie."

Calder's drinking buddies erupt in laughter. They are watching our exchange with keen interest. One of them says something in Gaelic.

"Please." I roll my hand. "Teach me the way, Most Exalted and Wise Jedi Master."

"Just Master."

"What?"

"Most Exalted and Wise Jedi Master is a mouthful. Just call me Master."

Fanny covers her mouth with her hand and pretends to cough, but I know she's just hiding her laughter. I think she likes this arrogant, grinning, sheep-wrangling Scot. I'm not impressed.

"Never."

Calder frowns.

"I will never call you Master."

"A challenge." Calder grins. "I accept."

Two of Calder's buddies join him. One of them, a fellow ginger with a mischievous glint in his green eyes, speaks in Gaelic while staring at Fanny.

"Allow me tae introduce my friends," Calder gestures to the men in uniform standing beside him. "Duncan and Connor."

The redhead holds his hand out to Fanny. "I'm Duncan. What's yer name, lass?"

"Stéphanie."

Fanny shakes his hand, but I can tell from her tight smile that she's not into him. She's not very comfortable making small talk with strangers. It's just not her thing.

"Hello." I hold my hand out to Connor. "I'm Vivia."

"I ken who ye are."

I frown because I don't recall meeting him before today. "Have we met?"

Calder flushes and adjusts his collar.

"Nae,. Connor smiles and shakes his head. "Calder was telling us aboot—"

Calder's arm shoots up so fast it reminds me of when I drive with my mom and she makes an abrupt stop. The swift forearm to the chest instantly silences Connor.

It's one of those supremely uncomfortable moments when a girl knows a boy has been talking about her to his friends because he likes her. Poor Calder. He possesses a certain brand of charm, but he's wasting it on me because I am still hopelessly in love with Luc.

Luc. Celine. My stream of consciousness carries me from peaceful emotions to a churning whirlpool of longing, grief, and blinding anger. I sneak a peek at my iPhone. It's been two hours since Fanny asked Celine to tell Luc to call me, and still no calls or texts.

"I believe you were about to show me the proper way to drink a whisky?" I look from my iPhone back to Calder. "Unless that was just you being blustery and braggadocious?"

Calder's friends whoop it up and slap him on the back. It's a, "Damn, Son, you just got called out" moment that brings me less satisfaction than I thought it would because Calder shrugs it off as if to say, "Ain't nothing but a thang." I think Fanny is right. My language and attitude have gone a little urban.

Calder gestures for a shot. Dougal slams a glass down on the counter—not a wee lassie-sized shot glass, but a brawny Scot-sized glass—and pours a generous amount of whisky.

Calder stares at me as he gently swirls the liquid around in his glass, then brings it to his lips, inhales, and takes a small sip. He holds the whisky in his mouth for several seconds before swallowing. His whisky-wet lips curve seductively, and I wonder how many times he's pulled this routine in pubs. How many women has he seduced with his deep stare and sex-you-up grin? It's good. He's good. I'll give him that much.

Calder tips the rest of the whisky into his mouth and swallows it.

I tear my gaze from his and look at Fanny.

"Is it hot in here?"

"No." She smirks. "Not at all. Are you hot?"

Calder sits on the stool next to me, his back to the bar, his long legs stretched in front of him, and grins.

I look into his eyes and say, "Nope. I am definitely not hot. In fact, I'm actually a little cold."

Even though my skin is flushed with the heat caused by the whisky and the Scot, I remove my jacket from the back of the stool and slip my arms in the sleeves.

"Let's go." He nudges my shot glass closer. "Show me what you've learned, Young Jedi."

I push the shot glass away and gesture for the bartender.

"Excuse me, Mister Dougal, but please give me a glass like that." I point to Calder's empty glass. "Thank you."

Calder's smile falters.

"Vivia." He leans closer and lowers his voice. "What are you doing, lass? Ye dinnae hae tae prove anythin' tae me. I was joking."

I fix him with one of my own naughty grins and lift the glass in a jaunty little salute. Check yourself, Highlander, because I am not some lilting British flower. I am an American, and in case you missed it, we don't know the meaning of the word retreat.

"*Merde!*" Fanny mutters. "Here we go."

I keep eye contact with Calder while I mimic each step in his whisky ritual, the swirl, sniff, sip, savor, and swallow. I finish by slamming the glass on the counter with the swagger of a skilled Scotch swiller. It's mostly bravado. The whisky is still burning my throat.

I cross my arms in my best badass Bring-It-Bitch pose, even though keeping eye contact is becoming more difficult with each second. The alcohol appears to have affected my facial muscles because my eyes want to cross and my lips feel cold and tingly, like they do after an injection of Novocaine.

I shouldn't be consuming alcohol with sexy-hot strange men—especially after what happened at Boujis—but the Novocaine numbness is spreading from my lips to my broken heart.

Connor pats me on the back.

"Weel done, Bùtais!"

I don't know what or who Bùtais is, but I mumble my thanks and take a quick swipe at my lips with my hand to make sure I am not drooling.

"She's nae what I expected," Duncan says to Calder, as if I am not sitting four feet from him. "Ye dinnae do her justice."

Dude! I picked up on his flirty vibe thing, but I didn't realize Calder was *that* into me. I wonder what he's been telling his pub pals about me.

I don't have to wonder for long.

"Calder told us about the ram." Duncan laughs and shakes his head. "I wish I could have been there for it."

What the…? I can't believe he told his buddies I said I wanted him to ram me. I glare at Calder.

"Duncan is talking aboot auld Torcach," Calder explains.

"How does he know about what happened with that poor old sheep?"

"I told him."

"How do you know about it?"

"Angus told me."

"Angus told you?" I am gobsmacked. "It just happened a few hours ago."

Calder shrugs. "'Tis a wee village."

As if on cue, another of Calder's friends joins our group.

"Is this the American lass who thought auld Torcach was having a seizure?" He slaps Calder on the back, and then looks down at my Wellies. "Ah, I see it is!"

"What did Angus say happened?"

The story Calder tells is far more humorous than my memory of the events. My heroic effort to save the life of an animal in distress has become a scene from a screwball comedy, complete with pratfalls and laughable cultural misunderstandings.

"That's not exactly the way I remember it"—I sniff and look away—"but if your brother needs to cast me in the role of village idiot to ease his guilty conscience for nearly abandoning a defenseless animal, so be it."

The men laugh uproariously, cackling like a pack of hyenas.

"*Whatever*."

Fanny reaches over and gives me a hug. "You were heroic, Vivian."

"Thank you, Fanny."

"Aye." Calder's tone is serious, even if his eyes still sparkle. "I believe ye were heroic. Is it true, then? Did ye force my brother to climb up the hill and flip auld Torcach back onto his feet?"

"Did Angus tell you that?"

Calder shakes his head. "Fiona did. Ye've become her hero. She has a soft spot in her heart for the foolish beast."

"Fiona's being generous."

"Fee is an excellent judge of character." He looks at me as if we are the only two people in the pub. "If she says ye're worthy of praise, ye're definitely worthy of praise."

His unexpected compliment embarrasses me. It must embarrass the others, too, because Duncan abruptly changes the subject by asking Fanny a question about her job. The men gather closer to her, as if it is perfectly natural for three, macho military men to be enthralled listening to a strange woman talk about selling designer handbags and lip gloss.

"Will you excuse me, please?" I slip my iPhone in my pocket and stand up. "I just need to…"

To what? Forcibly eject the contents of my stomach? Check my voicemail for a message from my almost-fiancé, who has apparently rebounded faster than Shaquille O'Neal back into the arms of his skanky ex-girlfriend? Get away from you because I am raw and lonely and your flirting is making me feel both happy and guilty?

I don't know how to finish the sentence, so I just walk away and leave him sitting at the bar with his disconcerting gaze and charming grin.

Since it is my first time in The Plastered House, I have to ask an elderly man wearing a plaid newsboy cap and nursing a pint of thick, foamy ale for directions to the ladies room.

He looks down at my feet.

"Nice Wellies," he says, pronouncing it as wheelies. His cap wearing companions chuckle as he jerks his thumb in the direction of the rear of the pub. "Second door from the left, lassie."

"Thanks."

The small unisex bathroom, located at the end of a narrow hall, is precisely the kind of facility one would expect to find in an obscure Scottish pub, poorly lit and without a single square of toilet paper to be found. It's the perfect place for me to reflect on my relationship with Jean-Luc. In fact, it looks like a setting out of a French film *d'amour*, shabby and steeped in ennui, the kind of place the heroine *tragique* would go to end her life.

I twist the rusty faucet until water spurts from the spout, then run my hands under the cold stream and press them to the back of my neck.

Snap out of it, Old Girl, you're being way too maudlin. Things might not be as bad as you think. Maybe Luc is getting ready to call you back right now.

After I dry my hands on my jeans, I pull out my phone to check for messages. I have no new voicemail messages and the only text I have received is from my friend G, inviting me to Cannes for the Régates Royale. G is a bazillionairess with loads of connections—she is the one who introduced me to Jett Jericho and persuaded me to get an ass tat. Every year in September, she hosts chi-chi parties on her yacht to celebrate the Cannes regatta.

Thinking about sailing makes me think about my first official date with Luc, when he took me sailing off the coast of Cannes, and made love to me beneath the turquoise Mediterranean sky.

The pain that stabs my heart nearly knocks me to my knees and I have to hold onto the sink to keep from crumpling over. I send my iPhone clattering to the floor.

This is it. I am alone, again, naturally. I have lost Luc, the only man I will ever love, the only man who ever loved me completely. My spontaneous cry echoes in the single stall bathroom and startles me with its raw force.

"Vivia?"

I press my hand to my mouth to stifle my sob.

No! Not Calder! Not now!

The door creaks open an inch.

"Vivia?"

He sticks his head in, sees me clutching the sink, a hand pressed to my mouth, and pushes the door open with such force it slams against the back wall.

"What is it, lass?" He grabs my arms and looks deep into my eyes. "Are you hurt? Has someone harmed you?"

He looks around the bathroom—at the stall, the closed window, the shadowy corner behind the trash bin—and then back at me.

This small act of compassion, this protective posturing, is more than my battered heart can take and fresh tears spill down my cheeks.

Calder wraps his arms around me. I know I should pull away from him, but it feels as if I was floating alone on a dark, angry sea and someone tossed me a life preserver. All I can do is hold on until the waves of emotion washing over me subside and thank God I am not alone.

The melodrama of the moment is not lost on me; the heroine *tragique* found weeping in a dingy bathroom by a strange man. It's so bad French cinema. If I weren't heartbroken, I would crack a sarcastic comment.

The door starts to open, but Calder puts his foot up and stops it. He does this without letting go of me. It's another compassionate, protective gesture that feels like aloe on my burnt heart.

The person on the other side of the door tries to push it open again.

"Away, ye bloody eejit!"

Calder's voice rumbles in the small room. The would-be intruder stops pushing on the door and footsteps fade down the hallway. Calder lets me go and I lean against the sink to put some space between us.

"Damn, woman, but ye're bonny!" He shakes his head. "Even when ye cry."

I do a half-cry, half-laugh thing.

"Thanks, but I'm not sure how bonny I am with mascara running down my face. I look awful without makeup."

"Ach, ye dinnae need makeup. Some lasses might, but not you." He reaches around me and pulls a paper town from the dispenser. "Now, dry yer tears and tell me what has you crying in this manky hole."

I take the towel, but I don't tell him why I was crying. I don't want to be that girl. You know, the ones who use their heartbreak as bait to reel in a new fish? Nothing makes a man more interested in a woman than the challenge of making her forget her love for another man.

I turn around to assess the damage in the mirror.

"It's not important." I wipe the mascara from my face and avoid making eye contact with Calder. "Just one of those silly, over-emotional female moments."

Calder crosses his arms. "You don't strike me as a silly, over-emotional female. Well, maybe a wee bit over-emotional when it comes to auld Torcach, but something tells me this wasn't about a ram."

I look at him in the mirror. "Okay then, Jedi Master, if you don't think I was crying over that old sheep, use the Force and tell me what I was crying about."

I meant it as a joke, to lighten the mood, and divert him, but he doesn't fall for it. He narrows his eyes as if peering into my soul, and says, "Only a man can make a woman cry like you were crying, like someone reached into your chest and ripped out your heart."

I turn around and stare at him. Just stare. What can I say? He didn't just hit the nail on the head; he drove it all the way through with a single blow.

"I don't want to say anything bad about the man who made you cry, because he must have some worth or you wouldn't care for him the way you do, but—"

"But?"

"Never mind." He shakes his head. "I dinnae want to be that man."

"What man? The man worthy of my affections and tears?"

"Nay, lass." He steps closer and wipes some mascara from under my eye. "I most definitely would like to be that man, but I dinnae want to be the man who steps into your heart by pushing another man out."

"You can't push someone who has already left."

The bathroom door opens and the elderly man in the plaid cap is about to stagger in when he notices me standing at the sink.

"Ach, lad! 'Tis a queer place to court a lass."

"Wheesht, ye auld bleating ram."

Plaid cap laughs.

Calder bends over and picks up my iPhone, grabs my hand, and leads me out into the hallway. Instead of turning left to go back to the pub, he turns right, opens another door, and leads me out into the gloaming. We walk through the parking lot to a sexy, shiny blue sports car that looks like it took a wrong turn off the Le Mans circuit and ended up in the Highlands.

Calder must notice my wide-eyed, open-mouthed expression because he laughs.

"You like it?"

"This isn't yours?"

"Really?" He holds up a remote and clicks it. The engine starts. "Then how did I get these keys?"

"How does a sheep farmer afford a"—I look for logos on the car to help me identify the model—"what is this, an Aston Martin?"

He shrugs. "I have a second job."

"If you say you're a brain surgeon as well as being a sheep-wrangling, dog-whispering, dart-playing hottie, I'm gonna—"

"So ye think I'm a hottie?"

"Puh-leez," I roll my eyes. "With all of your grinning and winking, you know damned well the effect you have on women."

He just grins and opens the door for me.

"Where are we going?"

"Trust me."

Strangely, I do.

"Wait!" I start to turn back toward the pub. "I can't leave Fanny."

"Text her and tell her you are with me." He hands me my phone and pulls his out of his back jeans pocket. "I will text Connor and ask him to make sure she gets back to the farm safely. Dinnae worry. I would trust Connor with my life."

I don't respond well to men bossing me about, but Calder does it with confident authority, as if he is accustomed to giving orders and having them obeyed.

> *Text to Stéphanie Moreau:*
> *Hey, babe! Calder is going to take me—*

"Where are we going, exactly?"

He stops typing and looks up from his phone, and the broad, dimpled grin is back. "Somewhere special. A place I like to go when I need a wee bit of clarity."

"Okay."

I finish typing and wait for Fanny's reply.

> *Text to Vivia Perpetua Grant:*
> *Tell that cocky cowboy if he does anything to harm my girl, I will wrestle him to the ground and use those big old rusty sheep shears on his... And please be careful, V. Luc hasn't said he doesn't want to be with you (not in words, anyway) and you don't want to do anything you'll regret.*

"Fanny says if you aren't a gentleman, she will castrate you with your brother's sheep shears."

Calder chuckles and keeps typing.

I slide my phone into my jacket pocket. He finishes sending his text.

"Are ye ready, Bùtais?" he says, holding out his hand to help me into the low-slung sports car.

"I'm ready," I say, trying to ignore the way Calder's hand feels wrapped around mine and the longing in my heart for Luc. "Lead the way, Master."

"Ha! I knew it wouldn't take long before ye were calling me Master."

"I meant to say Jedi Master."

He grins. "But ye dinnae say it, did ye, Bùtais?"

He closes the door before I can answer.

The inside of the car reminds me of a fighter jet cockpit, with glowing dials, molded leather seats, and a sloped windshield. If someone had told me sheep farming could be such a lucrative business, I would have skipped journalism classes and joined Future Farmers of America instead. I could rock a pair of overalls.

Calder opens his door, slides into the driver's seat, and secures his seatbelt. He revs the engine and we are off, looping around a dizzying series of traffic circles until we leave Strathpeffer behind. I would be a lousy liar if I said watching Calder operate the powerful machinery with crazy skill isn't a bit of a turn-on.

"What does Bùtais mean?"

Calder chuckles. "Boots."

"Why would your friends call me Boots?"

Calder glances over at me and grins. "'Tis my fault. I've been calling you Boots because of your Wellies."

Calder has been talking about me to his friends? My pulse does a strange little fluttery thing.

A few minutes later, he pulls his sleek sex machine off the side of the road at the edge of a dark forest, pushes the button to kill the engine, and looks at me.

"Ready?"

He grins one of his irresistible, make-the-girls-sigh grins and I wonder what I've gotten myself into. *Relax, just because he's driven you to some romantic secluded spot deep in the heart of the Highlands doesn't mean anything more than a brisk hike is going to happen. Does it?*

Chapter 23

Kissing Season

When a tall, sexy Scot calls you bonny and drives you to a romantic secluded spot atop a hill in the Highlands, it's probably not going to be for a round of golf. Just sayin'.

Calder's special place is a pap with a breathtaking view of the Scottish countryside and the MacFarlane Sheep Farm. It doesn't get dark in the Highlands, not like it does back home, so we can see Loch Ness in the distance, glimmering deep purple in the dying light of the gloaming.

Like a scene from *Outlander*, we reached the top of the pap to find a rocky outcropping of ancient stones standing sentry over the valley below. Calder is a wonderful guide, telling me about the history of the area and the legends of the stones.

"I can understand why you chose this spot to be your special place." I lean against one of the stones and stare out over the valley below. "It's beautiful."

"Aye." He comes to stand near me.

"I'll bet you've gotten lucky up here more than once." I look at him and waggle my eyebrows. It's another stupid attempt to divert him, because he's making me crazy nervous. "Well played, sir."

He focuses his intense gaze on me and I know what he's about to say will melt my heart as much as his grin.

"I've never brought a lass up here."

"Never?"

"You're the first."

"But probably not the last," I tease, bending over and plucking a yellow bloom from a thorny clump of flowers. "What are these? They're all over the hills."

"It's gorse." A slow, easy smile spreads across his face. "Have you ne'er heard the auld Scottish saying about the gorse?"

I shake my head.

"Weel, I believe it goes something like"—he moves so close I can smell the piney scent of his cologne—"whin the gorse is in bloom, kissing's in season."

"Are you flirting with me, Calder MacFarlane."

"Would ye like me tae be, Vivia Grant?" he says, rolling the r in my last name.

Would I? That's a good question. Calder is so sexy, he could charm the knickers off a nun, but he's not Luc. I wish Luc could be here, kissing me in the golden gorse, but he's too busy slow-grinding his sketchy ex-girlfriend to even call me back.

I am lost in a sticky web of thoughts when Calder leans in, traps me against the stone with his solid body, and kisses me gently, sweetly. It's not a bow-chicka-wow-wow kiss, but it is pretty fantastic.

I am about to wrap my arms around his waist when I feel a moment of panic. I'm not ready for this! I still love Luc, even if he is slow-grinding Miss Thong, and I'm not ready to give my heart to another.

Calder must sense my hesitation because he stops kissing me and moves back just enough so I can look at him without craning my neck.

"Am I movin' tae fast for ye, lass?"

I hold up my thumb and forefinger, leaving an inch between them. "Maybe just a wee bit."

He brushes an errant lock of hair from my cheek and smiles a leisurely smile that would have sent my heart flipping before I met Luc.

"Is there someone else for ye then?"

I nod.

I tell him about Luc, the Bishop Raine mix-up, our break-up, and I even tell him about Angelina von Teese, Luc's paddleboarding, pastry-baking, perfect ex-girlfriend—I leave out the little bit about her wearing a thong.

"I don't know how long it will take for me to get over Luc—or if I will ever get over him—and I can't ask you to wait around."

"Ye'll find I am a verra patient man. I am not going anywhere, Vivia. When ye are ready, I will be here." He steps back and holds out his hand. "Come on, let's sit for a while. Unless you want me to take you back?"

I shake my head because I don't want him to take me back. Not yet. I don't want to return to the world below this pap, a world of unreturned calls, unrequited love.

Chapter 24

Getting Down and Dirty

The morning dawns with flat gray clouds and an icy-cold driving rain, so Fiona cancels the sheep demonstrations/lessons, leaving us to our own devices.

Poppy uses the reprieve from the chain gang to catch up on work, sitting at the kitchen table tapping away on her laptop, Bluetooth headset stuck in her ear.

Fanny stays in bed, nursing a wee bit of a whisky headache. She staggered into my room late last night, long after Calder dropped me off at the cottage door, giving me a tender, friends-only kiss on the cheek. Fanny was chatty—she's also chatty when she drinks too much. It's comical, really. Her mouth becomes this super-charged vehicle of destruction, careening from topic to topic without caution or care, switching between English and French the way a NASCAR driver shifts gears. She told me about Duncan trying to grab her ass, Connor teaching her how to play darts, and her *peu l'engouement*. I had to Google Translate the word after she left to go to her own room.

Un peu l'engouement means a little infatuation. This revelation stirs up the guilt that had settled in the pit of my stomach like sediment in a riverbed. My best friend is crushing on the man who is crushing on me, while I am crushing on a man who is so over me. It's a confusing, warped little ménage à trois we've got going on here. Now, this is a French film.

I couldn't sleep after Fanny's mini-bombshell, so I stayed up and worked on my column, turning it in just before dawn. It's amazing how much you can accomplish when fueled by shame and hope. Though, the fumes of my hope are evaporating as the hours pass without a call from Luc.

I try to divert my mind by doing jumping jacks, reading the comments in the cottage guest book, organizing my unmentionables according to color, watching the rain trickle down the window, and conduct research for my upcoming interview with David Tennant. My research raises more questions than answers, like: As a classically trained actor, did you cringe at your Dr. Who catchphrase, 'Timey Wimey is Wibbly Wobbly?'

Finally, I call my long-suffering mum.

"Hello, Mum!"

"Who is this?"

"Vivia!"

"Vivia?" She hums thoughtfully. "That names sounds vaguely familiar. Where did we meet?"

"Mum."

I'm not in the mood for inane banter and my intuitive Mum picks up on it instantly.

"What's wrong, luv?"

There's no fronting with my mum. She can detect a forced happy tone faster than anyone I have ever known, so I unload my whole sordid, sad story on her. She listens without interrupting, which is wholly unusual.

"So let me see if I understand you, luv," Mum says after I've run out of words. "You love Luc desperately, but you aren't sure you want to marry him because you are afraid you will end up like me, a pathetic, boring, middle-aged divorcée?"

It sounds so much harsher coming from her lips.

"I'm sorry, Mum. That's not what I meant to say at all." I take a shuddering breath and give it another go. "You gave up your career and moved to another country to marry Dad, and look where it got you."

"Yes, look where it got me: Nearly thirty years of marriage and a beautiful, talented, darling daughter."

"A neurotic, deceitful daughter, with the legs of an extraterrestrial, you mean."

"I mean a wounded young woman who is terrified of being abandoned again, with beautiful, long legs."

My throat clogs with emotion and it takes me a minute before I can speak again. "Don't you regret giving up your life in England, your art career?"

"Life is about choices, my girl." She goes quiet for a second and I know she's doing that thing where she presses her hand to her mouth to keep herself from speaking before really thinking about what she wants to say next. "Thirty years ago, I made the choice to give up my career and follow your father to America. I did it because I loved him and because I couldn't imagine spending a day without him. Now, I realize it was because I couldn't imagine what I would do if I had to spend a day without him keeping me centered and focused."

"What are you saying?"

"I am saying, luv, that you inherited your tendency to go off the trolley rails from me, your silly old mum."

"Silly old mum I love. I do love you, Mum."

"I know you do."

We both fall silent. The Italian dinner music she likes to play when she cooks dinner plays softly in the background and homesickness plucks at my heartstrings, sending echoing notes throughout my soul.

"Mum?"

"Yes?"

"Don't you regret marrying dad? Regret having me?"

"Absolutely not!" She switches the call from speakerphone. "I regret that I let one choice dictate a thousand other choices. I could have made the choice to go back to painting, to teach, to show in galleries around California, but I didn't. I let the fear that comes with possibility cripple me."

Wow. It's strange to hear my mum taking accountability for becoming the downtrodden, powerless June Cleaver to my father's stern Ward Cleaver. It never occurred to me that my mum was once young and as hopelessly in love with my dad as I am with Luc. It never occurred to me that she wanted to become his June Cleaver.

"I am actually glad we are having this conversation now"—she clicks the music off—"because I have something important I need to tell you."

"Oh my God! Please don't tell me you have cancer."

"No, I don't have the cancer." She laughs, letting my blasphemous reference to our Savior slide. "With you traveling the world, I have decided to move back to England."

"What? Just like that?"

"Just like that."

"Won't you miss California?"

"No."

"What about your friends?"

"I'll make new ones."

"Who is this confident, free-spirited woman and what have you done with my stay-at-home mum?"

"I'm still your mum; I'm just tired of staying at home." She says it plainly and without accusation. "Besides, I want to be closer to my grandbabies."

"What are you talking about? I don't even have a husband!"

"You will."

"Someday."

"Someday soon, if I know my girl. I know you will fight for Luc. You won't let your fear stop you from being wholly, spherically happy, will you Vivia?"

"I guess not."

"Pardon me, luv? What did you say?"

"No," I mumble. "I won't let fear stop me from being happy."

"That's right! Because you're who?"

"Vivia."

"Vivia Perpetua Ass-Kicker Grant."

"Mum!" I've never heard my mum curse before—not when she stubbed a toe, not when I flashed my Wonder Woman bathing suit to our congregation during a Nativity Play when I was supposed to be playing a robed Mary, not even when my father told us he was shacking up with the kooky vegan. "I can't believe you just said a curse word."

"Oh, I can curse!" She assures me. "I can curse like a Manchester ball player. Do you want me throw down the F-grenade?"

I laugh. "Bomb, Mum! F-bomb."

"Do you want me to throw down the F-bomb?"

"No."

"Then tell me who you are with passion and conviction."

"This is ridiculous."

"Fffff…"

"Okay, okay!" I am only just wrapping my head around ass. I don't think I am ready for fuck. "I am Vivia Perpetua Ass-Kicker Grant, breaker of hearts and wearer of Wonder Woman underwear."

"Damn straight you are! Now, get over to France and make up with Jean-Luc. If you're going to give me grandbabies, you need to get going on the make-up sex."

Ugh! I inwardly cringe.

"Um, yeah. I'm not sure I am ready for this new liberated, uncensored Mum."

"Too bad," Mum laughs. "I've burnt my bras and am heady on the fumes of my new-found freedom."

I imagine my mother tossing a match on a mound of brassieres, surrounded by her prizewinning roses, while nosy old Mrs. Johnston pokes her nose over the fence. From Bible studies to Zumba classes—if my mum isn't afraid to take a risk and shake up her life like a snow globe, shouldn't I be brave too?

* * * *

I usually love rainy days, curling up with a good book, sipping hot cocoa by the fire, but today I am restless and irritable. My conversation with my mum didn't help either.

"You have been pacing for the last hour." Poppy looks up from her laptop. "What's the matter, Vivia?"

"I don't know," I stop pacing and look at my friend. "Have you ever felt like you just need to do something, but you don't know what?"

Fanny pads into the kitchen, her mahogany hair a wild nest perched atop her head, her eyes two narrow slits on her face.

"What or who?"

"Funny."

"You never did tell me what happened between you and Calder." She pours herself a cup of coffee and plops on the chair beside Poppy. "Out with it."

"There is nothing to tell. Seriously, do you think we ripped our clothes off and did the down-and-dirty against the standing stones or what?"

"It's not out of the realm of possibility," Poppy says.

"That's one tall, sexy possibility I wouldn't mind getting down and dirty with." Fanny looks at me over the rim of her coffee cup. "Tell us, Vivia. We won't judge you."

"Do you really think I would have sex with some random man I met at a pub? I am not a slut, Fanny!"

"I never said you were a slut, Vivian!"

"Whoa!" Poppy hold her hands up. "This is getting too intense. Do I need to play a Taylor Swift song?"

"No!" I snap.

My anger isn't over Fanny teasing me about a boy—it's about what happened at Boujis and the shame I feel about having flirted with Bishop—and now Calder.

"Did someone turn the heat up?" I irritably yank my shirt collar and resume my pacing. "Why is it so stuffy in here?"

"Would you like me to turn the heat down?" Fanny clutches her coffee mug and stands up. "Or open a window?"

"Don't bother."

I grab my raincoat, slip my iPhone in the waterproof pocket, and shove my feet into my Wellies.

"Where are you going?" Fanny frowns.

"Out."

"Out where?"

"Just out." I twist my hair into a knot and pull my wooly cap over my head. "For a walk."

"But it's raining."

"It's Scotland. It rains every day."

"Okay." Fanny dumps her coffee in the sink and puts the mug on the counter. "Give me a minute to grab my coat and boots."

"Thanks, Fanny," I say, heading for the door. "But I really just want to be alone. I need to think."

"Is that wise, Vivia?" Poppy taps her laptop keys and turns the screen toward me. "The storm is building. It could get nasty out there."

"I won't be gone long." I flip up the hood on my raincoat. "Besides, I'm from San Francisco. I'm not afraid of a little rain."

"Wait, then!"

Poppy runs to her room and returns with a flashlight.

"Take my torch then."

"I have a light on my iPhone."

"Your iPhone isn't waterproof. Just take the torch"—she presses it into my hand—"for me."

I slip the flashlight in my side pocket and leave the cottage.

Since I don't have an agenda, I move on habit, following the path to the barnyard, over the fence, and up the hill to the back pasture where I saw Torcach having his pseudo-seizure.

I just walk, and the more I walk, the more empowered I feel. I don't care that I am already soaked down to my boots. It feels good to be out in the cold exerting myself. Sometimes, you reach a point where it no longer matters if you are wet—you're just wet and so you embrace it.

Calf-deep in a puddle and looking at the distant fog-ringed pap, my agenda forms. I am going to climb that pap—the pap Fanny tried to convince me to climb yesterday. Who needs eating shortbread in my sheep jammies and reading the latest Sophie St. Laurent historical novel—a thrilling tale set during the French Revolution, about a renegade priest who assassinates revolutionary leaders and rescues condemned souls from the guillotine—when I can climb a mountain?

It's probably going to sound crazy, but my mind is inextricably linking making it to the top of the pap with winning Luc back.

I can do this!

I am running up across the field, leaping over boggy puddles, stomping on soggy patches of grass. I cross a stream, the water swirling around my boots, and begin the long, arduous climb up the mountain. From a distance, it appeared deceptively manageable, but an hour into the climb, I question the soundness of this self-imposed fitness test. This isn't an agoge. I'm not a young Spartan warrior trying to prove my fitness for battle. So why am I doing this to myself?

You're doing it because it's the only way you'll know if you can do it! You're doing it because you don't want to end up one of those middle-aged women suffering an existential crisis wondering about the road less traveled.

Reaching the top of the mountain is a triumphal moment. If my legs weren't wibbly wobbly—to borrow a Dr. Who-ism—I would be doing the football-slam End Zone Dance. Instead, I cup my hands around my mouth and let out a Ricola cough drop commercial yodel, before whipping out my iPhone for a few high-altitude selfies.

I snap a classic crossed-feet shot with my Wellies in the foreground and an expansive gray sky in the background, green peaks far in the distance. There's nothing about the shot that screams Scotland, but it is my favorite memento of the trip because it has personal resonance. After I sign into my Twitter account and tweet the photo with the hashtags #SawThePap #ClimbedThePap #TheseBootsAreMadeForHiking #HighlandSelfie.

I move over to the other side of the mountain to get a shot of the verdant Scottish Highlands rolling endlessly toward the horizon. I take a few selfies with the camera held far above my head to capture the steep drop behind me and slide the phone back into my pocket.

The rain is picking up again, so I take a last look at the stunning landscape before I begin the interminable climb down, when my boot slips over the slick rocky top and I find myself tumbling backwards over the edge.

Chapter 25

Hands on the Stick

Oh, Lawd, Sweet Jesus! Plunging to my death has long been one of my biggest fears, and now it is happening. It is really happening—in sickening slow motion. I freefall for what feels like an hour before landing with bone-shattering force and rolling, banging my head, scraping my knee, and finally landing flat on my back on a narrow ledge.

I stare up at the Heavens and perform a mental scan of my battered, aching body. I can wiggle my toes, move my legs, and lift my head. Amazingly, I appear to have escaped a wheelchair-bound future. It's just the crushing pain in my head I have to worry about now—that, and plunging to my death.

I sit up slowly, gingerly, and scoot far from the edge, pressing my back against the side of the mountain. Screwing up my courage, I lean to the right and look over the slide of the mountain.

Sweet Baby Jesus! It is a straight drop down. I am not good with calculating distances, but I would say it is at least four, maybe five, thousand feet.

You've heard the saying, "My blood ran cold?" Well, mine hardens to resemble arctic rivers.

I am going to die on this stupid mountain—all because of some misguided self-challenge. I remember what Calder said about well-trained border collies fending off attacking coyotes. What if coyotes attack me in the night?

Wait! Coyotes only live in North America—aren't they just the weaker cousin of wolves?

Wolves! There must be wolves in Scotland. There are wolves in England—I saw *An American Werewolf in London.*

And hounds! Demonic blood-thirsty hounds. Sir Arthur Conan Doyle wrote about the Baskerville Hounds. I try to remember how Sherlock defeated the homicidal hounds, but can't think over the thump-thumping pain in my skull.

I wish Luc were here. He would know exactly what to do. He would whip out one of those thin metallic blankets he keeps in his pack when we go riding and camping and fashion us a parachute or a tent.

Luc.

I unzip my inside pocket, feel something sharp slice across my finger, and pull my iPhone out to discover the fall shattered the screen.

I push the power button and—miraculously—it turns on. I push the button again and say, "Siri, call Luc."

"Just to confirm—do you want me to call Luc de Caumont?"

"Yes!"

The line crackles, but it connects the call.

One ring.

And then silence. An all-engulfing silence. I don't need an operable screen to tell me what I already know: dropped call.

I try it again, but get no response.

"Damn you, Siri."

My head is pounding and it hurts to keep my eyes open. I wipe my hands on my wet jeans and run them over my skull, checking for bone shards or brain matter. Nothing sharp and nothing squishy. I look at my hands and a burble of bile rises in my throat. A salmon-pink color now stains them that I know didn't come from the dye in my pink woolly cap.

I am bleeding! I probably split my melon on my way down the mountain and the only thing keeping my brains from oozing out is my woolly cap.

Well, if that is the case, I will die with my boots and my hat on. Let the unfortunate hiker who stumbles upon my bloated corpse deal with that mess. I can't deal with the site of blood. Brain matter?

Uck! I shudder.

I bring my knees up to a sitting fetal sitting position and pull my hood down low. Someone will come for me soon. Fanny will realize I am lost, organize a search party, and lead the Chick Trippers on a rescue mission.

The wind shifts, driving the rain to fall at a sharp angle. I rest my head on my knees and wrap my arms around myself.

Of all of my mishaps, this is the most embarrassing. Certainly it is the most ignorant self-induced mishap. Hiking up a mountain in the rain. What am I, an idiot?

I can't even say I was doing something epic, like rescuing a lost sheep or taking part in an archeological exploration in search of Noah's Ark.

Damn Donna D'Errico! The former Baywatch actress fell off a mountain during an expedition to find Noah's Ark in Turkey. She totally jacked my excuse. Who's going to believe the old "I fell off a cliff looking for Noah's Ark" excuse now?

I shift and Poppy's cold, heavy flashlight bangs against my bruised side. I pull it out of my hip pocket, say a prayer it still works, and push the button. The warm golden glow comforts me, especially now that it's dark, but since I might need to use it to flag down rescuers, I click it off again.

The rain stops, but the pounding in my head does not. The dark moonless night and my heavy lids make keeping my eyes open difficult.

What was that?

I swear I just heard someone call my name, but when I click on the flashlight and aim it into the yawning abyss, there is nothing but empty, lonely blackness.

I want to close my eyes against the pounding in my head—the flashing pulse of light I keep seeing when I move my eyes too fast—but I think people with concussions are supposed to stay awake. And I am pretty sure I concussed my noggin.

The darkness isn't helping. It's like an indigo velvet curtain pulled before my eyes. It makes me sleepy just looking at it.

Hours pass before I finally click on Poppy's flashlight and put it on the ground between my booted feet, pointing the beam toward my face. Get me, I'm a prisoner in a gulag.

"We vill break you. You vill sleep. Sleep, damn you, sleep."

I am chuckling at my own perverse sense of humor when the distant whoosh, whoosh, whoosh of an approaching helicopter drowns out my laughter.

I should be jumping up and down, waving my arms in the air, like people who have been snatched from roaring rivers or lifted from burning building, but the bones in my legs have suddenly turned to jelly. Wibbly wobbly doesn't cover it.

And then the Coast Guard Search and Rescue helicopter is hovering over me and a disembodied voice is telling me not to move, that help is coming.

A man wearing a neon yellow hardhat takes a backward step out of the helicopter and descends on a cable to my ledge. He unhooks from the cable and comes to me.

"Can you stand?"

"I don't know."

He bends down, puts his hands under my arms, and helps me stand. I am trembling like a newborn colt, my legs shaking beneath me.

"It's okay. I've got you."

I look up into his face for the first time. He has a stern jaw and an intense gaze. He's wearing an earpiece.

"You don't look anything like Ashton Kutcher, but I still want to give you a big kiss. Thank you for rescuing me from this ledge and the pack of wolves waiting out there to gnaw on my bones."

His earpiece crackles.

"Ma'am, we don't have time to talk right now."

The crew lowers a basket. My rescuer grabs the cable to steady the basket and turns back to me.

"What is that for?"

"You need to get into the basket, ma'am."

I look at the basket attached to the slender cable. "Are you crazy? I am not getting into that basket. No way."

I don't tell the not-quite-Ashton-Kutcher-but-still-very-handsome-hero that if he makes me ride in that basket, I am afraid I might soil myself. I am not going down like that—flat as a pancake and covered in my own piss. No way. Uh-uh.

"Ma'am, I ken ye are a wee bit frightened, but you have to get into the basket."

"I am not a wee bit frightened; I am full-on freaking terrified. And stop calling me ma'am. You're making me feel old. I might feel like pissing myself right now, but I am hardly geriatric."

Great. And there it is. I just admitted I wanted to piss myself. To a man who rappels out of helicopters.

"My name is Collum," he says in a low, steady voice, keeping his hands on my waist and his gaze on my face. "Vivia, right?"

"Y-Yyes."

"Vivia, I need you to get into the basket so we can hoist you to safety. You've got a pretty bad bump on your head, and we need to get you to hospital."

"Please don't make me. I will wait until morning and walk back down the mountain."

"This is serious, Vivia. You can trust me. I won't let anything bad happen to you. Besides, there's someone in that helicopter who would probably throw me off this ledge if I let anything bad happen to you."

Luc! Maybe Fanny called Luc and told him I was missing. Maybe he caught a direct flight to the local airport, joined the rescue crew, and is up there with them now.

"Vivia, please get in the basket."

This man is risking his life to save me. The longer we stay on this ledge, the longer the pilot must fight to keep the helicopter steady, fighting against winds and rain, and the greater the chance something could go tragically wrong.

"Fine"—I say, inching closer to the basket—"but if I piss myself, you have to promise not to tell a soul. Ever."

"I promise."

I lie down in the basket, cross my arms over my chest, and take deep breaths while Collum secures the slender straps that will hopefully prevent me from rolling out of this flying coffin and plunging to my death.

Collum steps back, gives the thumbs up, and the basket lifts. I feel myself spinning and spinning, and then someone pulls me into the helicopter. I look around for Luc, but when I realize he is not one of the men strapped into the blue jump seats I want to ask them to put me back on the ledge.

They hoist Collum back into the helicopter and we are off, blades whooshing, flying blind into the stormy night.

Collum fusses over me, pointing a slender flashlight at my eyes, checking my pulse, securing blankets around my trembling limbs.

"Ye're safe now, Vivia. The best pilot in Her Majesty's Coast Guard is at the controls of this copter."

The pilot looks over his shoulder at me and...

...and it's Calder MacFarlane.

My vision narrows like the picture screen on an old-school television set, until the world appears to be a tiny dot and finally fades to black.

Chapter 26

Pack a Tight Chute

I wake up in a strange hospital room to the muted sounds of beeping machines and distant conversations. Poppy, Fiona, and Fanny are standing around my bed, all anxious expressions. They look fuzzy. If fact, the whole scene looks slightly out of focus, like an old-school soap opera.

I expect a plasticky-looking doctor to diagnose me with a brain tumor and tell me I only have three weeks left to live, unless I can track down my previously unknown twin and convince her to agree to a brain transplant.

Fiona's lips begin moving, but there's this five-second delay thing going on in my brain where the words don't match up with my comprehension. It takes me a few seconds to understand she's going to let the nurse know I am awake.

My eyelids feel heavy and my mouth full of cotton. I am wearing an ugly mint green gown and an IV is jammed into my right arm.

This is really happening.

Fanny gently sits on the side of my bed.

"How are you feeling, Vivian?"

"I am warm all over and totally chill." I close my eyes. "Am I stoned or something?"

"Non, *ma cherié*. You had an accident, remember?"

My skull feels tight, like my woolly cap shrank in the rain and is now too tight for my head. I reach up to pull off my cap and feel thick gauze.

"Why is my head bandaged?" I open my eyes and struggle to sit up. "Did they shave my head? Am I bald?"

Fanny half laughs, half cries.

"No, you daft cow." Poppy wipes a stray tear from her cheek. "Your hair is fine, it's your brain that needs some fixing. You really scared us."

Poppy's use of the word brain triggers a hazy flashback of being on the ledge and staring at my bloodstained hands.

"I was taking a selfie and I fell down the side of the mountain."

"Why were you on the mountain in the first place?"

"It had something to do with Luc and Spartan warrior training and—"
I shake my head and wince as a pain shoots from my temples to my toes.

Fanny darts a worried look at Poppy.

"It sounds crazy now, but it made sense at the time."

Fanny chuckles softly. "I'll bet it did."

"So when are they bringing the discharge paperwork? I want to get out of here."

Fiona returns with a plump grandmotherly nurse carrying a needle and small glass bottles.

"Ye're not going anywhere, lass." The nurse sticks the needle into one of the bottles and pulls the plunger. "Ye've suffered a traumatic head injury."

I throw the cover back and try to swing my legs out of bed. "I can't stay. I have to go."

I have to see Luc. I have to tell him about my near-death experience and the epiphany I had as I was clinging to the side of a mountain, to life. Without him in my life, the world is a monochromatic place, devoid of color and depth.

"I talked to your boss and told her what happened," Fanny says, misreading the cause of my anxiety. "She is very worried about you. She said to take all of the time you need to heal and not to worry about Glasgow. They'll be filming the movie for the next few months and the interviews can be rescheduled when you are well."

Glasgow? I don't care about going to Glasgow or interviewing a pampered over-preening actor about his role in some big-budget hack job of a classic. I don't care that I spent hours researching David Tennant and memorizing Dr. Who quotes just in case he turns out to be the lead actor in the movie. I care about getting to Luc.

"You don't understand." I try to sit up again. "I have to get out of here."

The nurse jabs the needle into my IV line and pushes the plunger. I suddenly feel flush all over.

"What is that you put in my IV?"

The nurse pushes me back against the pillow and adjusts my blankets. "The doctor ordered an antibiotic, an anticonvulsant, and pain medication. This is phenobarbital. It helps to reduce swelling of the brain, but it might make you sleepy."

"Now, lassies"—she turns to my friends and makes shooing motions with her hands—"visiting time is over."

"Wait!" I grab Fanny's arm. "Can I just have one minute to talk to my best friend, please?"

"One minute." The nurse holds her finger up. "I'll be back."

Okay, Arnold Schwarzenegger. Don't shoot!

Fiona and Poppy give me hugs and hurry out of the room before Nurse Terminator returns.

"I'm sorry, Fanny." I grab my best friend's hand and give it a squeeze. "I didn't mean to worry you."

"Well, you did worry me." Her voice cracks, and tears fill her eyes. "When you didn't come back to the cottage—and then when you posted that photo of the top of a mountain—I imagined all sorts of horrible things."

I've never seen Fanny cry. She's normally so self-contained and unflappable. I'm usually the over-emotional Henny Penny, dashing about and crying, "The sky is falling!"

The phenobarbital must be working its magic because it's becoming an effort to keep my eyes open.

"I love you, Fanny, and I know I've probably called in all of my chips with this latest stunt, but I need you to do me a favor."

"If you're going to ask me to make a ladder out of sheets and help you climb out the window so you can go interview David Who, you're crazy."

We don't have much time left. Nurse Terminator will be back any second, so I quickly tell Fanny about my mountaintop epiphany, my determination to win back my man, and my decision to travel to France to ask him to marry me.

"You want to propose to Luc?"

"Yes, but it has to be epic. I am talking violins and flowers and white doves and fireworks."

"Please tell me you don't want me to release the doves; you know birds freak me out."

As promised, Nurse Terminator returns. She stands in the doorway and repeatedly taps her wrist with her finger, even though she isn't wearing a watch.

"Ten more seconds," I say, slurring my words. "I prom*ish*."

"Ten...nine..."

"Fanny, I need a ticket to Montpellier, a new iPhone, and a new pair of pink Wellies. My credit card is in my wallet."

"Why—"

"...five..."

"I'll explain later." I squeeze her hand. "Will you help me?"

"…three…"

"Leave everything to me."

* * * *

Nurse Terminator adjusts my IV, closes the blinds, and turns down the lights. I am asleep before she even leaves the room.

I wake up sometime in the afternoon and sense I am not alone in the room.

Calder is sitting beside my bed, long arms resting on his knees, intense gaze focused on my face. He's wearing a flight suit, and his close-cropped hair is flat against his head from having worn a helmet. He looks impossibly handsome…and impossibly exhausted.

"Ye worried me something fierce, Boots."

"So it was you piloting the rescue helicopter. I thought I dreamt it."

"First ye call me Master and now ye admit ye dream aboot me." He laughs. "It wilnae be long before ye have me picking out China patterns."

I don't know how to say what I need to say to Calder, so I just smile. Is there an easy way to tell the man who just saved your life that you don't love him and never will? The thing is, I like Calder…a lot. He's just not the man for me. He's exhaustingly, ostentatiously flirty and charming. With his constant winking and grinning, he's like the attention-seeking middle child. Luc, on the other hand, possesses the easy, confident manner of a first child.

"How long have you been sitting there?"

"Not long." He fidgets.

I know he's lying.

He reaches down and lifts a wrapped box from the ground. "I brought you something."

"What is this?"

"A wee gift."

"A gift? For me? I should be giving you a gift."

"What for? I dinnae fall off a bloody pap."

"For saving my life."

"Ach." He shifts.

It's the first time I have seen Calder embarrassed.

"I was just doing my duty."

"Well, then, thank you for doing your duty and saving my life."

"You're welcome." He hands me the box. "Open your gift."

"I can't accept a gift from you. Not when…"

Not when I plan on begging another man to marry me.

Calder looks into my eyes, reads the words I did not speak, and smiles sadly.

"Just go ahead and open your gift, lass."

I open the box and pull out a small nylon triangle.

"What is it?"

"An emergency parachute—just in case you go for another hike."

"Very funny." I stick my tongue out at him. "Some men bring flowers when they visit people in the hospital."

"Aye." He smiles, and his dimples deepen. "And some lasses dinnae jump off cliffs to get a man's attention."

We laugh.

Nurse Terminator comes in to check my blood pressure. Calder stands.

"Well, I am going tae leave ye to rest." He bends down and gives me a quick kiss on the cheek. "In case I dinnae see ye again before ye leave, blue skies, happy travels, and pack a tight chute, Boots."

"Thank you, Calder...for everything."

He's halfway out the door when he stops.

"If things dinnae work out with..." He shrugs. "Remember what I said when I took you to see the stones and the gorse."

He leaves before I respond.

"The gorse," Nurse Terminator says, strapping a blood pressure cuff around my arm. "Ye ken what they say about the gorse, don't ye, lass?"

Chapter 27

Beating Around My Bush

"Do you have my flight itinerary?"

"Yes, you're flying into Montpellier. I called Chantal to let her know you would be arriving. Philippe will meet you at the airport." Fanny hands me my tickets and new iPhone. "I think I remembered to pack everything in your suitcase, but if I forgot anything I'll just send it to you."

"You? Forget something? I don't think so."

Perfectly Polished Poppy lifts my carryon out of her trunk and rolls it over to me. I rest my MacBook on top of my suitcase and open my arms to give her a big hug.

"What the bloody hell do you think you are doing?" She leans back on her high heels. "You've already exceeded your annual allotment of hugs."

"Yeah, I know," I say, laughing. "You don't do hugs. Now get over here and give me a little British love."

"Bloody brash American, breaking all the rules."

"Damn skippy!" I wrap my arms around her and give her a good squeeze. "Be good, Bubblegum Poppy, and thanks for everything."

Poppy sniffles.

"Are you crying?" I pull back and look at her face. "You are crying!"

"Rubbish! I am British, remember? We don't do weepy."

"Liar! You have tears in your eyes."

"It must be my damned bloody allergies again."

I open my purse and pretend to fumble around inside, looking for my Visine.

"Fine," Poppy confesses. "I might be the tiniest bit melancholy over your departure. I detest good-byes."

I give her another quick hug. "It's not forever. I'll be back…like Nurse Terminator, only without the scary needles and brogue."

The intercom makes a dinging noise, and a perky Scottish voice says, "Flight BE1322, Inverness to London City, ready for immediate boarding at gate…"

"Thank you for picking up the pieces of my life again, Fanny," I say, grabbing my best friend and hugging her until it hurts. "You're the best friend in the entire universe. I am sure you won't ever make such a mess of your life, but if you do, I will be there to pick up your pieces."

"Promise?" she sniffles.

"Double pinky promise."

We stop hugging. I grab my suitcase by the handle, put the strap to my MacBook case over my shoulder, and give them both a little wave.

"Wait!"

Poppy steps off the curb and reaches into her trunk. She pulls out a big black box embossed with the word "Hunter."

"You almost forgot your new Wellies." She tries to hand me the box. "Though, I can't imagine why you would need two pairs of shiny pink rain boots."

"They're not for me." I begin rolling my suitcase toward the automatic doors. "Give them to Lisa and tell her I said to go stomp in a puddle."

* * * *

At Gatwick, I make it to my connecting gate just as they are about to close the doors. The terminal attendant takes one look at my bandaged head and ushers me onto the plane, carrying my MacBook and stowing my carryon.

Trust Fund Fanny booked my seat in first class, which means I can sit in any of the available seats. There are two seats open—one beside a woman holding a squalling red faced infant, and another beside a tall, hollow-cheeked man who is making a valiant effort to avoid all eye-contact.

Hmm. Rosemary's Baby or Mister Asperger's? Since I have had a dull headache for three solid days—ever since I woke up in the hospital—I opt for the hollow-cheeked man. The eye-contact avoidance thing is a big tip-off that he's probably not going to want to tell me about his job as a bathroom fixtures salesman or pepper me with questions about what it's like being a reporter.

It's only as I am standing in the aisle beside his seat that I realize I have seen his face before—on IMDB.

"Excuse me, I am a columnist with *GoGirl!* Magazine and I was wondering if you had the timey wimey for an interview?"

* * * *

By the time I arrive in Montpellier, I have an interview in the bag and an engagement ring for Luc in my pocket.

I bought the ring during my second layover in the duty-free jewelry shop in Charles de Gaulle. It's a simple thin white gold band with an antique finish, reminiscent of a Tiffany's wedding band. I will have to drain my savings to pay off my credit card, but you know what they say, "Go big, or go home." Since, technically, I don't have a home, I went big.

I told the jewelry store clerk my story *tragique* and my plan to propose to Luc.

"Are you not afraid he has started seeing someone new?" she asked.

I imagined Jean-Luc having crazy-hot monkey sex with Angelina von Teese—aka Miss Thong, aka Celine—and a wave of nausea washed over me. I told the clerk about Celine answering his phone and asked her if she thought I should be worried.

"*Je ne sais pas,*" she said, raising her hands. "You know zee French men. They are notoriously irresolute."

Now, I am standing on the curb outside the *Aéroport Montpellier Méditerranée* as Philippe, Luc's brother, loads my bags into his van. I am still wearing the engagement ring Luc intended to give me on the chain around my neck. It's become my talisman, reminding me of Luc's love, warding off the doubts, urging me to have courage.

Philippe comes around to the passenger side, opens my door, and helps me into the van. He's been especially solicitous since meeting me at the gate, repeatedly asking me how I am feeling, whether I am dizzy, if I need anything to drink.

Luc's brother jumps in the driver's seat and looks at me anxiously. "Fanny told me about your accident, but I wasn't prepared to see you like dzees." He waves his hand at my head. "Dzee wound, ees eet bad?"

"No," I say, self-consciously touching my bandage. "It's just a little cut. I'll be fine."

Nurse Terminator removed my whole head bandage before she signed my discharge papers, replacing it with a smaller stick-on bandage, which looks less frightening but reveals more of violently bruised forehead.

"*Bon!*" He turns the key and reverses out of the parking spot. "Now we go 'ome, you will rest, and in a few days, Jean-Luc will be back."

"A few days?"

"*Oui,*" Philippe says, guiding the van out of the parking lot and onto a busy thoroughfare. "Jean-Luc ees still in Provence."

"Provence? Why is he still there? I thought he would be home by now."

Maybe it was the conk to my melon or my tendency to leap without looking, but I brain-spaced the possibility that Luc would not be home when I arrived.

"He ees with zee model."

My heart drops to my feet. "Celine?"

"*Oui*." He frowns and pronounces oui with such disdain it sounds more like whay. "He ees with Celine."

"So they are back together again?"

"What?" Phillipe takes his eyes off the congested road just long enough to fix me with an outraged expression. "Zee fall must 'ave wounded your common sense. Luc would never go back to Celine. Not after zee way she betrayed 'eem."

It's not exactly a "he loves you, Vivia," but I will take it. I can work with it.

Philippe explains that a French reality TV show about top models wanted to film a segment with the models on a bike tour in Provence.

"Celine is one of zee models." Philippe switches lanes. "In fact, she told her producer she would only go on zee trip if Luc was zee guide. Of course, Luc agreed because he realized eet would be great publicity for *Aventures de Caumont*."

Jesus, Mary, and Janice Dickinson! Angelina von Teese is also a reality television star? Fuck me. What can't the woman do?

Philippe glances at me again and frowns.

"What?" I say, forcing a bright smile. "What is it?"

"You know I do not beat around your bushes, right?"

"Beat around my..." I laugh. "Oh, you mean beat around the bush?"

"Yes, this is what I said."

I don't bother telling him the subtle but important distinction between the and your in that sentence.

"Go ahead. Hit me with it, Philippe."

"What?" Philippe frowns. "I do not hit zee women."

"No, it means tell me what you have to say."

"Ah." He makes another turn and we are on the A9, headed to *Chateau de Caumont*. "I saw zee photographs."

"Photographs? Of Bishop Raine kissing me?"

"*Oui*."

"It's not what you think, Philippe."

"I think he ees a very funny man. I love *Audition at the Apollo*." Philippe chuckles and shakes his head, but his humor fades a second later. "If you 'ad a leetle... How do you say *indiscrétion*?

"Indiscretion."

"If you 'ad a leetle indiscretion with zee comedian, I zink my brother will forgive you, but only if you are honest with 'eem. Luc is a tolerant man, but 'e does not tolerate zee lies."

Philippe stops at a traffic light and looks at me.

"Philippe, I swear on my mother's life I did not have an affair with Bishop Raine. I love your brother. I have many faults, and I am probably not worthy of Luc's love, but he is the only man I have slept with since we met on the bike tour a year ago. The Bishop Raine thing was a stupid misunderstanding. I didn't handle it well, but I am going to do whatever it takes to win Luc's trust and forgiveness."

"So you do not love Bishop Raine?"

"Oh my God! No!"

"I knew eet. I told Chantal you would not date zee man who smuggles zee heroin in his…you know what."

"Thank you, Philippe." His loyalty brings tears to my eyes and hope to my heart. "It's an odd endorsement, but I'll take it."

He pats my knee.

"Philippe?"

"*Oui?*"

"Would you please drive me to see Luc?"

"We are going 'ome and Luc will join us in a few days, yes?"

"No." My voice cracks. "I can't wait a few days. I need to see him now."

"But Luc ees in Roussillon."

"So?"

"So"—he pulls the van off the side of the road and turns to face me—"Roussillon ees at least one hundred and sixty kilometers away."

I don't speak because I don't think I could without blubbering like a baby. I'm an emotional wreck—on pain killers, no less.

Philippe clucks his tongue. "Okay, we go," He puts his blinker on and pulls back on to the A9. "*On se bouge!*"

"*On se bouge!*" I squeal and press a kiss to his whiskered cheek. "*Merci, Philippe. Merci beaucoup!*"

We are four miles out of Roussillon when Philippe's van starts belching noxious black smoke. Philippe curses.

"What's the matter? Why is it doing that?"

"*Bâtard!*" Philippe releases a torrent of French curses as he eases the dying van off the road and onto the shoulder. He turns off the engine and slams his fist onto the dashboard. "*Merde! Merde!*"

"Why are we stopping?"

"She is not going to make it, Vivia."

"She has to make it. We are almost there."

Philippe raises his hands and does one of those Gallic "Eh, what can you do?" gestures.

I try to quell my rising frustration. When Philippe stopped for gas at the turn off to Roussillon, I popped into the Lidl and purchased a dozen sunflowers wrapped with a broad silk bow, six *je t'aime* Mylar balloons, and a bottle of champagne. Unfortunately, Lidl doesn't sell fireworks or doves, so my epic proposal plan is turning out to be a little less than epic. After making my purchases, I ducked into the bathroom to freshen up and change into my beaded dress. There was nothing I could do about the bandage on my head or the post-flight bags under my eyes, but I spritzed myself with some of Luc's favorite perfume, reapplied my smoky eyes, and rubbed a little anti-frizz serum on my hair.

"But I put on my dress!"

"Eet won't be long, *cherié*. Just another hour or two."

"An hour? Or Two?" I fan my face with my hands and take quick, shallow breaths. "I can't wait another hour. My flowers will wilt. My hair will frizz. I can't ask Luc to marry me sporting a ginger 'fro."

Philippe shrugs again.

I open my door.

"Where are you going?"

"I can't just sit here. "I grab the bottle of champagne from the space between the seats. "I will walk to Roussillon if I have to."

"But Rousillon ees five kilometers away."

"I don't care."

"What about your head?"

"I have to do this, Philippe." I look at him. "I am walking to Roussillon whether it's five kilometers or fifty-five."

"Or you could ride."

"Ride? What do you mean ride? Hitchhike?

"No, that would be stupid." He pronounces stupid as two words—stoo-peed and uses his thumb to gesture to the back of the van.

I turn around. An *Aventures de Caumont*'s aluminum touring bike is in the back of the van.

"Ride to Roussillon?"

"You do not like zee riding."

I hate zee riding, but it is rather apropos since I met Luc on a bike tour. It's like I have come full circle.

"Let's do this thing, Philippe." I grab the flowers and balloons. "Hook me up!"

"You must change your clothes. You can't ride a bike in zat gown."

I look down at my beaded dress. It's the prettiest thing I have ever worn, and it makes me feel super sexy.

"Superman had his cape, Wonder Woman her lasso, and I have this slinky little dress." I give the beads a shake. "Besides, how could I compete with a bunch of super models if I show up wearing ripped jeans and an old Guns N' Roses T-shirt?"

"There ees no competition, cherié." Philippe shakes his head. "Luc fell in love with you when you were wearing a *reediculous* shirt with a cartoon marshmallow, remember?"

"Sushi roll. It was as sushi roll." The memory brings misty tears to my eyes. "Thank you, Philippe."

He lifts the bike out of the van and pushes it over to me.

"Won't you at least change your shoes?"

"No, absolutely not." I shake my head. "Luc loves these shoes."

"Okay."

I wrap the balloons around the handle bars and then reach into the van, take my MacBook out of my briefcase, and stick the champagne, flowers, and my iPhone inside. I drop Luc's ring in a pocket and zip it shut. I sling the case over my shoulder like a messenger bag and look at Philippe's brother.

"Which way to Roussillon?"

"Stay on zees road. It will take you to zee village." He reaches into the van and grabs a helmet. "If you don't find 'eem on zee road, go to zee Hôtel Sainte Honore."

He hands me the helmet, but I don't take it. I don't care if I just suffered a head injury.

"I am not wearing that thing. Do you know what it will do to my hair?"

Philippe fixes his brown gaze on me and smiles languidly, one eyebrow raised. I know the look. Luc has given me the same look dozens of times. It says, "Do you really want to throw down with me, because we both know I am going to win this one."

"Fine." I grab the helmet from his hands. "Give me the stupid helmet."

I put the helmet on my head, adjust the chin straps so they're loose, and I am off.

"*Bon chance*, Vivia!" Philippe calls after me. "*Allez trouver votre homme.*"

Allez trouver votre homme? Oh yeah, I am going to get my man.

Chapter 28

My Epic Failure: Love

There's a very good reason Monsieur Christian Louboutin doesn't offer athletic shoes in his line; because the pampered and privileged grand dames who can afford to clutter their closets with the pricey pumps don't ride bikes. They recline on chaise lounges while muscle-bound minions carry them from place to place.

It doesn't help that *Aventures de Caumont* bikes are proper touring cycles, with proper pedals designed for proper cycling shoes. The only way I can make it work is to wedge my toe under the front lip and let my spiked heel hang off the back. My toes are throbbing, but I refuse to stop even for a rest.

The champagne bottle is banging painfully against my hip, the Mylar balloons keep smacking me in the face, and my dress keeps riding up. Every hundred yards or so, I have to stand on my tiptoes and yank my skirt down. I haven't checked, but I am almost certain I have left a trail of beads and sunflower petals.

A truck full of road repairmen slows and the driver yells, "*Oolala, la vache!*"

Cars beep their horns as they zip by on the narrow road. A few of my balloons pop, my ass hangs out of the bottom of my dress, and my head pounds-pounds-pounds, but I don't stop until I reach the hill leading to Roussillon.

I have to get off the bike and push it up the final steep climb to the village. Perched atop magnificent rust-colored cliffs, Roussillon is a major must-see in the South of France. Visitors from all over the world come to marvel at the village carved into the cliffs, the view, the vast Provençal sky stretching for miles, like an enormous blue canopy. It's the perfect setting for a romantic rendezvous, even if you have to climb in shaky Louboutins to get there.

Though, I am not feeling all that romantic. My feet ache, my dress is shedding beads like a stripper shaking her moneymaker, and I don't need a mirror to tell me my ginger 'fro is plastered to my sweaty, bruised head.

And I have to pee. Sweet Jesus in Heaven, do I have to pee! It could be nerves or the bottle of Coke I downed in the van on the way here. At this point, I am running on masochistic adrenaline and caffeine.

On my discharge papers, Nurse Terminator wrote in big BLOCK letters, "Take pain medication as needed and no strenuous activity for ten days."

I chuckle a little maniacally. If the old Terminator could see me now, she would jab a hypodermic needle full of phenobarbital into my arm and push the plunger until I was out cold on the rusty road.

When I finally reach the village, I am gasping for breath and limping like a long-distance marathon runner crossing the finish line. I don't know what is propelling me forward—sheer determination or rampant insanity—but I am determined to make it to the hotel, find a bathroom, repair the damage to my appearance caused by the death march, and ask Luc to marry me.

My stomach aches at the thought of proposing, but I am determined to make it epic, even without the fireworks and fluttering doves. I will knock on his door, hand him the flowers and champagne, and lead him out unto the balcony with a panoramic view of the hills and valley. Then, while the setting sunbathes us liquid gold, I will get down on one bruised knee, declare my love for him, and beg him for his hand in marriage. It will be unexpected and quirky-cute. It will be the stuff of two-hankie rom-coms.

An orange-painted sign points me in the direction of the village square, so I follow it and unwittingly push my bike smack-dab into the middle of some kind of photo shoot. The spotlight is, quite literally, on me—and a dozen impossibly beautiful models posing seductively on or beside shiny touring bikes.

Fuck. Fuck. Fuckedee. Fuck. This is not happening. This is so not happening. I did not just hobble into Angelina von Teese's photo shoot.

I look for a quick escape route, but I am too late.

"Vivia?"

Maybe if I close my eyes real hard and click my heels together, my Karma Godmother will whisk me far away from this nightmare.

"Vivia? What are you doing here?"

When I open my eyes, Luc is standing about ten feet away from me and the models have peeled themselves from their bikes to inspect the 'orrid leetle creature brazen enough to interrupt their fifteen minutes of fame.

This is it. This is the way my epic proposal is going to go down, and there's nothing I can do to change it. I look a ratchet mess and Luc looks... oh, freak me...Luc looks more handsome than I remember him to be. He's still in his cycling gear, the tight-fitting spandex black shirt and riding shorts that accentuate every chiseled ripple of his Michelangelo worthy physique, and his aviator sunglasses. The Provençal sun has tanned his skin a rich brown.

"Luc."

Now that the moment is finally upon me, I don't know what to say. "Luc, will you marry me?" sounds lame. My bones suddenly feel as if they have turned to JELL-O—my legs wibbling and wobbling above my dusty heels.

"Who is zat?"

Angelina von Teese herself steps closer to Luc, hands on narrow hips, lips pursed like she's taking a duckie face selfie.

Luc ignores her and steps closer to me.

"Vivia? Why are you here? What happened to your head?"

"La!" Celine's red-lacquered lips curl on her fashionably pale face in a way that reminds me of Heath Ledger as the Joker. "So zhees ees Vivia?"

I drop my bike and shoot Miss Thong a look that says, "You better just back the hell up. I am hungry, tired, nervous, and my meds have worn off."

"Vivia? Did you ride here wearing those shoes?"

I look down at my feet, notice the blood staining the toes, and look back at Luc. "You said you liked them."

Celine rolls her eyes.

A cameraman moves closer. He is preserving this entire humiliating encounter digitally. It will probably end up on YouTube under the title *Sad American Girl Chasing Disinterested Frenchman.* Great! Just add video humiliation to my curriculum vitae of social media disgraces.

The models snarl at me as if I just said the dirtiest word in their lexicon: cellulite.

"Luc, I called you the other day because I wanted to tell you—"

"When? When did you call me? I didn't get a message."

I narrow my gaze on Celine and she takes a step back. She never gave Luc my message. I figure out her game in a model-skinny minute. The Facebook photographs, the super models bike tour, the phone call. She's making a play for Luc. She realized she had a good thing and she's trying to get him back. Well, sister, take a number and step on back. I'm the one with the bubbly and the ring, so I figure I got first crack at him.

Luc takes off his sunglasses and reveals his beautiful, soulful, smoldering eyes. The lights, the cameraman, the sneering models, even Celine, fade to the background and there is only Luc. I forget my pretty speeches, reach into my bag, and pull out the mangled sunflowers.

"This was supposed to be an epically romantic moment, one you would remember for the rest of your life, but I've bungled it." I take a deep breath and exhale. My breath sends several sunflower petals spinning to the ground. "I've bungled a lot of things, actually. First, I let Bishop Raine kiss me and then I tried to cover it up. That was a big bungle. The other day, I went hiking in the pouring rain and fell off a mountain. Another epic bungle. A pack of coyotes would be using my bones for toothpicks if a Coast Guard Search and Rescue crew hadn't found me."

Luc frowns. I don't know if he's angry or concerned.

"I was sitting on a ledge, thousands of feet above the ground, bleeding and in pain, and all I could think about was you." I pause to wipe the tears from my cheek. "Luc, I don't know how to paddleboard or ski or bake pastries. If you did put me on skis, I would probably veer hopelessly off course and end up causing an avalanche. I can't speak French fluently, deworm a ram, outdrink a Scot, or pose like a supermodel. I am only really good at one thing: loving you madly and deeply."

I hand the flowers to the cameraman and reach into my bag to pull out Luc's ring. I planned on getting down on one knee, but my legs are so shaky I would probably end up flat on my face, with my bead-less derriere up in the air. So I hold the ring on the palm of my hand and present it to Luc.

He doesn't take it. He stares at me as if I...as if I am wearing a mangled designer gown and cycling helmet.

The models snicker. Celine giggles. The cameraman pulls back to get a wide shot, presumably of the Sad, Stupid American Girl proposing to the Disinterested Frenchman. I just know any moment Luc is going to turn and walk away, leaving me with a ring I couldn't afford and a bundle of wilted flowers.

I am about to lose my grasp on the slender thread of hope I've been clutching all day, when Luc puts his hand around the back of my neck, pulls me close against him, and kisses me the way only a tall, dark, über-sexy Frenchman can kiss.

The villagers who gathered burst into applause.

"Does this mean you will marry me?"

"You never asked."

"Luc, will you—"

"*Oui, mon cœur.* I will marry you." He kisses me again. "And I promise, I won't ever ask you to deworm a sheep."

Text from Stéphanie Moreau:
Pls, Im begging u, pls do not pick cotton-candy pink as the color for yr bridesmaids dresses. Bisous.

Text from Poppy Worthington:
Congratulations! I've watched the video of your proposal on YouTube a dozen times. Your bravery inspired me: I am resigning from my position with Worthington Boutique Hotels and buying a sheep farm in Plockton, Scotland.

Text from Poppy Worthington:
Aye, lass, I am serious.

Text from Camille Grant:
Vivia, it's your mum. Guess what? Anna Johnson's daughter was arrested in Golden Gate Park for committing lewd acts... and she wasn't with her husband! Anna is beside herself. I've been praying all day that God would forgive me for feeling just the teensiest bit happy.

E-mail from Fiona MacFarlane:

Dear Vivia,

We read your articles about our farm and couldn't be more flattered. Thank you, Vivia. If you ever want to visit again, we would love to have you and Luc.

This from Angus: I filled in the hole by the old shed and Torcach hasn't had a "seizure" since.

Calder has accepted an assignment to a Coast Guard station in Alaska, but he asked me to relay the following message, "Tell Bùtais I am verra happy for her and to please avoid choosing mountainous destinations for her honeymoon."

All the best,

Fee

Leah Marie Brown

Meet the Author

http://www.kensingtonbooks.com/author.aspx/31669

Be sure not to miss Leah Marie Brown's first book of the *It Girls* series

Faking It

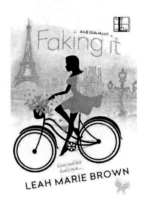

Haven't you ever told a little lie in the name of love?

Vivia Grant couldn't be happier. She has her dream job and is about to marry her dream man. Does it really matter that she's led him to believe she's a virgin? After all, being in love makes every experience feel like the first time anyway! But an unexpected encounter with an ex-lover is about to expose her embarrassing lie...

When Vivia's fiancé discovers the truth, he ends their engagement—via text—and uses his connections to get her fired. Unemployed and heartbroken, Vivia begins planning her new future—as a homeless spinster. But her best friend has a better idea. They'll skip the Ben & Jerry's binge and go on Vivia's honeymoon instead. Two weeks cycling through Provence and Tuscany, with Luc de Caumont, a sexy French bike guide. Too bad Vivia's not a big fan of biking. And she's abysmal at languages. Will she fib her way through the adventure, or finally learn to love herself—and Luc—flaws and all?

Faking It on sale now!

Learn more about Leah Marie http://www.kensingtonbooks.com/book. aspx/31338

Chapter 1

Saint or Sinner?

All right, I'll admit it; I have told more than one man he was my first lover. I don't know why I started lying about my sexual history, but I think it could have something to do with my name.

What's in a name? If you're looking for the poetic answer, check out Shakespeare. If you want a real-life example of the importance of a name, of how it helps shape the personality and sexuality of an individual, read on.

I'm Vivia Perpetua Grant. I know what you're thinking. What in the hell sort of name is Vivia Perpetua?

I'm a little shaky on the details, but apparently old Vivia Perpetua was a noblewoman who lived a thousand years ago and was imprisoned because of her faith. I'm not sure if she was known for her modesty *or* her virtues. Either way, my grandmother—*God rest her soul*—raised my mother to believe that Saint Vivia Perpetua had been the superlative woman, someone who knew that chastity and humility paved the road to Heaven, just as wantonness paved the road to Hell. Saint Vivia Perpetua spent her last few morally-correct moments on earth in a Roman amphitheater being torn limb from limb by a boar, bear, or leopard. I don't remember which wild animal mauled the martyr, but that's not really the point.

My mother named me Vivia Perpetua because she believed naming me after some long-dead, mostly forgotten saint would motivate me to spend my life collecting unused eyeglasses for the blind or doling out mosquito netting to malaria-plagued Africans. Not that there is anything wrong with those efforts, but *please*. Even more important than my mother's desire to raise a socially conscious do-gooder was her desire to raise a young woman who would guard her chastity until matrimony.

It didn't work.

I never dabbled in drugs—not even a puff on a joint, despite the fact one of my friends promised me smoking pot would make me popular and increase my breast size—but in high school I cranked Aerosmith and had sex. I've been out of high school for ten years now. I still like rock and roll and I still like sex.

In fact, I *love* sex.

My mother could have named me something more normal. I could've been one of a million Jennifers or Amys, and it wouldn't have made one bit of difference. But no. She had to saddle me with Vivia Perpetua and a load of baggage about sex. I have more baggage than the Louis Vuitton flagship store on 5th Avenue in New York City, which I visited once with my best friend Fanny Moreau who works as a Regional Merchandiser for LVMH. Fanny is gorgeous, smart, talented, and has sophistication oozing from her otherwise immaculate pores. She's French, so I'm pretty sure the sophistication gene is hardwired into her DNA. Fanny *never* lies about her sexual history. She is confident and blunt.

Like when I first met her. She told me her name was Stéphanie Elise Girard Moreau, and I told her mine was Vivia Perpetua.

"How *horrible*," she gasped, as if I had just confessed to having been born one half of a blind and deaf Siamese twin. "I cannot call you this name. To me, you shall be Vivian."

She pronounced the name in such a seductive way it made me wish my name was Vivian.

"Like Vivien Leigh?"

"*Exactement*." She smiled. "Only less *tragique*."

We were best friends from that moment on. We talk every day, and we share *all* of our secrets.

The first time I told her I'd lied to a lover about my sexual prowess, she said, "Honestly Vivian," pronouncing the end of my name with her charming nasal accent, "I do not understand why you lie about such things. If a man won't accept you for who you are, he is not worth the Dior Gloss."

Fanny and I are addicted to Dior's Addict Ultra Lip Gloss, but at $25.00 a tube, we're careful to use it on only the most delectable and Dior-worthy dates. It has become our code-phrase.

"Was he Dior-worthy?"

"I thought he would be, but he spent sixty-eight minutes talking about his ex, suggested I pay half of the bill, and then tried to use a Groupon to pay for his half."

"*Chérie*, I hope you saved the Dior."

Fanny is obsessed with Christian Dior. Not the conglomerate, but the couturier. She even quotes him.

"Remember Christian's mantra: 'The tones of gray, pale turquoise, and pink always prevail,'" she once quipped, in an effort to persuade me to wear an absurd fuchsia bubble skirt.

But I digress.

I was supposed to be telling you about my pathological need to portray myself as a virgin, why it is my mother's fault, and why I am now in the eye of the maelstrom that has destroyed everything I once cherished.

Maybe I should start at the beginning....

Chapter 2

Losing My Virginity

I lost my virginity when I was seventeen to Leo Crandall, a gangly cello player who lived down the street from us. My mom fell in love with Leo from the first time he rode his Little Fire Chief Big Wheel up our driveway and declared he was "on duty." She proclaimed his mop of blond hair, wide brown eyes, freckled nose, and slight lisp "blooming precious" and insisted we play together often, even though I complained he used his Transformer to crush my Strawberry Shortcake doll. As he grew, Leo became more studious, earnestly practicing his cello while other boys his age were perfecting rad tricks on their BMX dirt bikes.

In our junior year, we both worked at Sonic Burger. Sometimes he would give me a lift home. Leo was sweet and dependable, like a sad-eyed basset hound, but he didn't raise my pulse. If Steven Spielberg ever wanted to turn my life into a movie, Leo's part wouldn't be played by Ryan Gosling or Brad Pitt. Leo did not have leading man appeal. He was more of a supporting character, like Harry Connick, Jr. in *Independence Day*.

I had sex with Leo because I was angry that Jason Thomas asked Carrie Stemokowitz to the prom instead of me. Jason had been the subject of my preteen fantasies ever since he'd blocked a dodge ball from hitting me in the face during fourth grade PE. Carrie was my arch nemesis. Petite, popular, pretty, and the captain of the pom-pom squad, she was my polar opposite.

I was angry with my mother for insisting I go with Leo to the Prom and for making me wear one of her vintage store finds, a ruffled gown in a shade she called *delicate daffodil*. I disagreed, saying it was more of a junkie jaundice yellow, which prompted my mother to cross herself and my father to peer at me over the top of his tortoiseshell glasses. My dad, a professor of Religious Studies at UC Davis, could make a lecture hall full of self-impressed students tremble with a single disapproving glance.

I was angry at Leo, too. Why'd he have to ask me to the prom? Why not Carrie Stemokowitz? After all, Carrie was the one with the super-huge crush on Leo. Not the silently-suffering, worship-you-from-afar kind of crush I had on Jason, but a creepy stalker-like pseudo-obsession that reminded me of that Glenn Close movie—the one where she has an affair with Michael Douglas and then becomes unhinged when he won't leave his wife. I'm not saying Carrie would have killed someone over Leo Crandall, but if pushed, I think she could have been a bunny boiler.

The way she always stared at Leo was kind of disturbing. She twirled a lock of her wavy hair around a finger and batted her long, curly eyelashes at him. Once, in Chem class, Leo's Chap Stick dropped out of his pocket and rolled across the floor without him noticing. Carrie picked it up. Later, I saw her pop the lid off, sniff it, and then rub it over her lips. She had this weird look on her face, a bit like when Buffalo Bill tossed the bottle of Jergens down to his victim in *Silence of the Lambs*. I half expected her to moan, "It rubs the Chap Stick on its lips."

If Leo had asked Carrie to the prom, I think Jason would have asked me to be his date. So my first sexual encounter was the product of this bizarre love triangle fueled by molten teenage anger.

I liked Leo, but I didn't love him. And that's all I could think about when we fumbled around in the back of the rented limo. *Why aren't I doing this with someone I really love? I'll bet Jason Thomas wouldn't be so awkward.*

I didn't have sex again until my senior year in college. I was too busy trying to keep my GPA up and my waistline down. Freshman fifteen? Try freshman forty. The night I met Travis Trunnell, I was uncharacteristically hammered. My then-BFF, Grace Murphy, had lured me to a cheesy bar called the Tijuana Yacht Club.

"The servers wear tight speedos and dance on surf boards," she'd said.

"Speedos and surf board dancing? Are they straight?"

"Vivia, *seriously*! You can't study all of the time or you'll die an old maid, like Mary Shelley."

I was into Gothic literature at the time, and more than a little obsessed with Mary Shelley, so her comment was like a jugular shot.

"Mary Shelley experienced one of the greatest love affairs of all time. She did not die an old maid," I argued.

"Are you sure?" Grace squinted. "Because I am pretty sure Professor Atkins said she died a virgin."

"Mary Shelley did not die a virgin! She was Percy Bysshe Shelley's wife. When they were courting, they would meet at her mother's grave and Percy would recite poetry."

"Eww!" Grace grimaced. "Is that what you want, Vivia? To marry an effeminate necrophiliac who recites poetry as foreplay?"

Unable to argue with such logic, I slipped into my tightest jeans and followed Grace to the ramshackle bar with sand on the floor.

I had just slammed my sixth Hawaiian Punch Shooter and stumbled onto the dance floor when I noticed a tall, muscular beach boy staring at me from across the bar. My stomach flipped and I had a sickening vision of me hurling all over his feet. I thought I looked so cool, gyrating to 2 Live Crew's old school anthem, "Me So Horny," but when Travis Trunnell stared at me, I suddenly felt lame.

I was grinding away to the climactic moan backtrack when I caught my reflection in the club's mirror, hips rotating, booty shaking. Years later, Grace described my smooth moves as a sad epileptic white girl's imitation of a twerk. Harsh. Could anyone look sexy dancing to lyrics that include *"Sucky, sucky. Me sucky, sucky"*? I don't think so.

Travis waited for me until the song ended, a slow, easy smile stretched between his dimpled cheeks. I must have stopped breathing because he leaned down and whispered in my ear.

"Breathe, baby, breathe. You don't want to pass out here. You'll wake up with your pretty face buried in a sandbox."

I don't remember what I said. I just remember looking into his blue eyes and thinking I would die if I didn't have sex with him. I didn't know his name. Didn't know his story. But I had to have him. Grace, the psychology major, called it primal lust.

Travis ordered me another Hawaiian Punch Shooter, and beneath the glow of neon palms, we pretended to be interested in each other's lives when all we really wanted to do was drop and have dirty, sweaty sex.

Travis attended UC Berkeley on a full ride football scholarship. The more we talked, the more I liked Travis. His slow, sexy drawl and his hand on the small of my back made me feel fuzzy all over.

I still wanted to have nasty sex with him, but I also wanted something more than a bar hookup/bootie call connection. I didn't want him to think I was a slut. I summoned the last vestiges of my common sense and told him I would have to call it a night.

That's when I realized Grace had encouraged me to dance with Travis and then slipped out the back door. She even took my purse. Clever bitch.

No Grace meant no ride home.

Do you believe in serendipity?

I do.

I don't believe *everything* is preordained. I doubt our higher power involves Herself in every detail of our lives. If you had the universe at your disposal and an infinite amount of time stretching before you, would you fill your days deciding whether Nancy Jones should have Caesar Salad for lunch? Probably not.

I decided Fate had brought Travis to me. A higher power was telling me to abandon my no one-night stand rule and go home with the sexy Texan. After all, when the universe gives you a tall, handsome gift, you don't give it back.

We went back to his place, a third floor apartment with a frat house vibe. He offered me a warm Corona and put on a slow jazz CD. I hate jazz. All of those horns. It's like someone handed out musical instruments at an asylum and ordered the patients to play whatever came to mind. He had a fake mink blanket on his bed. That's about all I remember: jazz, warm beer, and a cheap blanket.

I woke the next morning with a case of bedhead and a tennis ball-sized rug burn on my tailbone. What would Saint Vivia have said if she looked down from her celestial perch to witness my walk of shame? I had to walk the five miles from Travis's house to the dorms, heels in hand, pride in shambles.

Travis and I hooked up a few more times, but I was never able to get over the way we had met. My shame was *that* huge. Little did I know, my naughty night with Travis would come back to haunt me like a Kardashian sex tape.

I vowed to abstain from sex, graduate college, and channel my energies into my Journalism career. I worked freelance until I landed a job at *San Francisco Magazine* writing fluff pieces for the Style Section—ironic, since the bulk of my wardrobe consisted of heavy metal band Ts and jeans. Fashion was not my forte. Once, I bought a fake Prada from a sketchy boutique near Chinatown. A burgundy satchel in buttery soft leather, with braided biker chain handles. Later, Fanny pointed out the shiny emblem read *Prado* instead of *Prada*.

The editor who interviewed me said she dug my "edgy youth on the verge vibe" and hired me on the spot. Since then, I've been assigned pieces titled *Out of the Recycle Bin and Into Your Closet* and *Fabulous & Faux: How to Rock a Fake Fur*.

It isn't hard-hitting, investigative journalism, but I like to think my work at *San Francisco Magazine* serves an educational purpose. Besides, if I hadn't gotten that job, I might not have met Nathan. Nathaniel Edwards, III.

Nathan's family owns Opulent Style Publications, the publisher that produces *San Francisco Magazine* and a slew of other upscale monthlies devoted to culture, art, and posh living. He is a junior partner in one of the largest law firms in the Bay Area, but also serves on Opulent Style's Board of Directors. He is smart, driven, stable, respectable, and honest. He would make any woman the perfect husband. In fact, in seventy two hours and thirty four minutes he is supposed to become *my* perfect husband.

CPSIA information can be obtained
at www.ICGtesting.com
Printed in the USA
FFOW04n0204150915
16873FF